Y0-DBY-948

TORAWARE

by

Robert W. Norris

The year is 1983. The place is the Kobe-Osaka area. A 33-year-old American drifter has just arrived in Japan seeking one more adventure and an escape from his past. A promiscuous, rebellious, 23-year-old Japanese woman has just returned from a two-year homestay in a Canadian missionary, where she was sent by her parents to cure her suicidal behavior. A snobbish, upper-class, 22-year-old Japanese woman who cannot distinguish between fantasy and reality is about to graduate from university and enter the frightening world of adulthood. The three are about to become inextricably involved in a relationship that will change each of their lives forever. Deeply moving and beautifully written throughout, *Toraware* is a story that captures all the obsessions, suspense, sadness, misunderstandings, difficulties, joys, and humor that are involved when people from very different cultures, backgrounds, and classes are brought together by fate to find the separate life paths they must follow.

Touka Shobo titles
by Robert W. Norris

LOOKING FOR THE SUMMER
TORAWARE

TORAWARE

by

Robert W. Norris

囚われ

Touka Shobo

First published in Japan in 1998 by Touka Shobo,
Hanahata 3-45-5,
Minami-ku, Fukuoka, 811-1356
Japan

Library of Congress Cataloging-in-Publication Data
ISBN4-924527-93-9 C0097

First Edition

Cover painting by Cao Ya-Gang
from his book Cao Ya-Gang Selected Paintings
(Touka Shobo, 1997)

Acknowledgments

I wish to thank my publisher Yasushi Azuma and the staff at Touka Shobo for the countless hours they worked to make this book a reality. For his critical reading and excellent editorial advice, I thank William Appel of Edit Ink. For their patience, guidance, and friendship during my early years in Japan, I thank "Ian" Inatsugi, Shigeya Kitamura, the Kamejima family, and all the members of the real Sasa Softball Club. For all their love, worry, and support during the times I was wandering the globe, I thank my mother, father, brothers, and sisters. And for putting up with all my idiosyncrasies and giving me a reason to stay put in one place, I thank my wife Shizuyo from the bottom of my heart.

This book is dedicated to
all the victims of the
Great Hanshin Earthquake of 1995

toraware [囚われ] *n.* captivity; slavery; imprisonment; confinement

torawareru [囚われる] *v.* 1. be caught; be seized; be taken; be captured; be arrested; be apprehended 2. be a slave to [stick to, adhere to] (a habit, a tradition); be a stickler for (formalities); be in thrall to; be shackled by (convention); be enmeshed in (obsolete thinking); be swayed by (pas-sion) 3. be seized with (panic); be ridden by (fears); be struck with (terror)

⎯*Kenkyusha's New Japanese-English Dictionary, Fourth Edition*

Concerning neurotic patients, the problem of mental pre-occupation with the symptoms caused by anxiety and tension in the manner of symptom aggravation is called *toraware* in Japanese. It is a form of obsessive behavior.

⎯*a Japanese neuropsychiatrist at an international conference*

Obsession.

⎯*a Japanese interpreter when asked about the meaning of* toraware

TORAWARE

1

There was an ear-piercing screech as the local train pulled into Hankyu Ashiya Station and came to a stop. Several passengers stepped out of the train and onto the platform. Those who had been waiting boarded. Sachiko Yasui waited for the others to board first before getting on the train and finding a seat separate from them. She knew it was a mistake to go to Harlan's apartment unannounced, but her desire to see him was too strong.

The train began to move. Sachiko settled back in her seat and looked out the train window at the passing scenery. Buildings of steel and concrete, serried rows of drab apartment buildings with their many-antennaed roofs, rushed by. Near Nishinomiya she saw the UCLA conversation school where she had first met Harlan. At Tsukaguchi Station Sachiko changed trains to the Itami line. A week had passed since the last time she visited him. She had gone to Itami to return his novel. They had talked about it and he seemed happy she understood it so well. There were many questions she wanted to ask, but her English had failed her.

He had touched her. She did not shrink away. His touch was gentle and reassuring. She massaged his back on the futon. Then she lay down and he massaged her back. She relaxed. He kissed her and took her blouse off. She did not have the courage to take her dress off. He did not force her.

Harlan took his pants off. She touched him and asked if she could hold him. He consented. She took him and tasted his tumescence. Later, in the darkness of his room, they huddled by his small electric heater. He said he liked her. He said he mistrusted the word "love." It had little meaning for him. She understood. She liked him very much. It was a relief he had come into her life.

She had written him a letter the next day telling him not to worry. She would not tie him down. She had learned from her experience with Tom, the American who had taught her Spanish before she went to Mexico three years ago. She knew what a vagabond's life was like. Tom had deceived her, had settled down with another woman. She was glad Harlan was honest. She liked to be with him. She knew he was not her possession. No one was her possession.

The train stopped at Hankyu Itami Station. From the elevated platform Sachiko could see the large apartment complex where Jose's coworkers had lived. It was a squalid, ugly building where common people lived.

2

Itami City itself was squalid and ugly because of the association. Jose had been her other unrequited love. He and his family had been her neighbors in Ashiya for a year when he had come to Japan on business. Sachiko later visited the family in Mexico. Jose had not read her the way she had hoped. She had been too young and naive and her disillusionment had been deep.

The walk to Harlan's apartment took about 15 minutes. The February morning was grey and cold. Sachiko pulled her muffler and jacket tightly around her. She walked quickly and kept her head down, avoiding any kind of eye contact. She passed the hat factory with its weather-worn boards and rusty pipes. She put her hand over her nose to ward off the foul smell that came from a nearby trash barrel.

Finally, she approached Harlan's apartment building. It, too, was old and dilapidated. An overweight, middle-aged woman peered suspiciously at Sachiko from inside one of the apartments on the ground level. Sachiko climbed the single flight of steps to the second floor. There were four apartments. Harlan's was the last one on the left. Sachiko felt her heart beating quickly. She held her hand out to knock on his door, hesitated, then pulled her hand back. She took a deep breath, exhaled slowly, and knocked softly two times.

Sachiko heard a rustling sound inside and the murmur

3

of two voices. An icy wetness broke out under her armpits. The door opened. Harlan came outside on the balcony and closed the door behind him. He was wearing only his jeans. His hair was ruffled. He rubbed his eyes as if to get the sleep out. Sachiko stared at his tall, lean figure and tried to force a smile.

"Sachiko, what are you doing here?" Harlan said. There was no anger in his voice, but his eyes revealed his surprise.

"I'm sorry. Did I wake you?"

"Not really." Harlan paused a few seconds. "Look. You can't come in. I've got company. Is it about my book?"

Sachiko nodded, knowing it was a half-lie, but no words came to her.

"Well, I'm sorry, but your timing is not so good today. I'll call you later in the week and we can talk about it then. Is that OK?"

Sachiko nodded again and said, "I understand."

"I'll talk to you later then."

Sachiko said good-bye, then descended the steps. The woman in the first-floor apartment was still staring out the window. Grief and powerlessness beat within her breast as she walked back to the station. It was her own fault, she told herself. She should have yielded herself to him before. She had known what she would find today.

For a brief moment she imagined the other woman making love to Harlan, ripping and tearing him with her fingernails, trying to suck the marrow out of his bones, riding him wildly. She stopped suddenly, somewhat taken aback by the impurity of her thoughts. A faintness came over her, then passed.

*   *   *

Harlan took his pants off and got back under the futon cover with Yoshiko. He snuggled close to get warm. Yoshiko shivered at his touch and giggled.

"Your feet are freezing, Harlan. So who was that?"

"Sachiko."

"Sachiko?"

"Yeah. You know, the one I told you about before. The one who read my manuscript and liked it and wants to help me get it published."

"The student at the conversation school?"

"Yes."

"What did she want?"

"I suppose she wanted to talk about the book. She and her friend quit the school over some price squabble and I haven't seen her in a while. The last time I saw her I made a joke about how she should be my agent because she seemed to understand the book so well and liked it so much. I think she took me seriously and has

5

been checking around about publishing possibilities in Japan. Anyway, I told her I had company and today was a bad time to come."

Harlan got up and put his clothes back on. He went into the kitchen and put a pot of water on the single-burner stove to boil. Yoshiko also got dressed, folded the futon bedding, and tidied up the six-mat room. It did not take long. The only things in the room were the futon, the electric heater, and the *kotatsu* table. Her parents had given her the furniture to give to Harlan a month before when Julie had brought him home from work because he had little money and no place to stay. She had found the apartment a few days later and talked the landlady into renting it to him.

Harlan returned with two cups of coffee. The two of them sat silently at the *kotatsu* sipping the coffee and thinking their separate thoughts. Harlan got up, went through the three-mat room, and bumped his head trying to squeeze into the narrow entrance to the squat toilet. He returned with a sheepish grin on his face.

"I don't think I'll ever get used to this apartment," he said. "It's too small. I keep forgetting about the low doors. So what are your plans for today?"

"Oh, I think I'll clean up my apartment, visit with Julie, and do some laundry. Maybe later Julie and I will do some shopping and cook a nice dinner. You can eat with us if you want."

"Not tonight. Thanks though. I want to do some studying and I have a few letters to write. Maybe I'll take you up on your offer tomorrow night after Julie and I get off work."

Yoshiko kissed Harlan lightly on the cheek, said good-bye, and took the back streets home to her own apartment. Julie was gone, but had left a note saying she would be back in the afternoon. Yoshiko looked around the modest apartment, the same apartment where she had grown up. Many strange and haunting memories were fixed in every corner. Her parents had moved to a nicer apartment in recent years after her father's construction equipment business began to prosper. They had kept this apartment for Yoshiko and her brother Masanori. Masanori had moved to the new apartment when Yoshiko returned from Canada with Julie four months ago. It seemed strange to her to think that after all the years of turmoil in her family there was now relative harmony. Julie had a lot to do with that.

Yoshiko ran a hot bath and cleaned the kitchen while the tub filled up. When the bath was ready, she rinsed herself, washed thoroughly, and eased herself into the steaming water to soak. As she relaxed in the warmth of the water she thought about her two years in Canada and how she and Julie had become best friends.

Yoshiko had been a problem in her teens. Her rebelliousness and suicidal behavior had become so acute by the time she was 19 that her parents desperately sought the advice of the local priest. There was an exchange program with a Catholic mission in Canada to which some of the younger members of the Itami Catholic Church were allowed to go every year. The priest recommended Yoshiko take part in the program. Her parents consented eagerly.

The first year had been difficult, working in the mission's kitchen, not understanding anything anyone said, smiling at everyone to be polite, being treated like a child because she could not speak English well, returning to her room alone every night, crying and drinking herself to sleep. She had a drinking problem, but the nuns showed great patience in leaving her alone. Although there were three other Japanese with whom she could speak, she avoided them.

A year passed. During that time she gradually became accustomed to her new life. Never before had she felt more a part of nature, more a love for nature, than in the wilderness of Canada. The evergreen stretches of forest, the leaden and ominous winter skies, the clouds that churned like whirlpools, and the snow that fell in a thick, silent veil softened her tough exterior and showed her the beautiful mysteries of God's work.

One day she was working in the kitchen with Ichiro, one of the other Japanese, when Julie entered. Julie looked like a lumberjack with her broad shoulders, big boots, and work clothes. "Where's Joe?" Julie asked in a gruff voice.

That first encounter had intimidated Yoshiko, but it also aroused her curiosity about who this Joe was. She later met him and, although she never slept with him, fell in love with him, a love that still consumed her. Her life took on a new dimension. Long-buried feelings found their way to the surface again. By falling in love with Joe, Yoshiko became at odds with Julie. In the beginning she and Julie had glared at each other, but when Joe left the mission a month later the two became best friends. Yoshiko took the first step by offering her friendship in the form of a visit to Julie's room. She picked some flowers in a nearby field and gave them to Julie.

When she apologized about Joe, Julie told her, "You can use anything you want in life, but never use people." Yoshiko had since reflected upon this a lot. She had suffered considerable grief from having hurt Julie's feelings. She expected a lifelong enemy after stealing Joe away, but instead of anger and abuse, which had always spurred her rebelliousness, she was greeted with kindness and love. It was her first experience with forgiveness.

They had talked about God. Julie was unlike any Christian Yoshiko had met. She radiated sincerity, belief, confidence in God. With Julie Yoshiko felt a presence of warmth and love, of giving without expecting anything in return. Julie did not put on affected airs. Julie had a jaded past herself about which she was not ashamed. This, too, was a new experience for Yoshiko: the belief that God loved all people, good or bad, and forgave all their sins. She had always had the impression God loved only those who were truly pious. She had understood God only as something abstract, something from which, because of her rebelliousness and promiscuous behavior, she was condemned to be forever excluded. Through Julie, however, God became something tangible, something she could believe in without guilt, something that could fill the void in her life.

Julie had told exciting stories of her experiences with men. Yoshiko played the role, more through the language barrier than affectedness, of an innocent young woman wanting to learn from the worldly experiences of an older sister. Julie made her feel as if her past, over which she had felt so much guilt and confusion, was really not so bad. She had not sinned as terribly as she had thought. Julie made her feel as if God loved her, too.

She was overjoyed when Julie decided to return with her to Japan. Readjusting to life in Japan would not be easy, had not been easy. Julie was her link to the West and to her own family. Yoshiko's parents had welcomed Julie as if she were one of their own. All the family were now attending mass regularly together. Yoshiko's parents seemed proud of Julie and Yoshiko for joining the weekly group the church sent to Nishinari, the section of Osaka where the homeless and destitute gathered, to hand out blankets, food, medicine, and a little love to those whose lives were nothing more than a scrap of food or a bottle of cheap sake where they could find one.

Yoshiko finished her bath. After she changed into a clean pair of jeans and a sweater, she checked the mailbox. There were three letters. One was from Joe. She started to open it, then decided against it. She would save it for later when she was in the right frame of mind. Right now was not a good time. She always felt a certain loneliness when she read his letters, a sense of something slipping away.

She remembered the time when Joe promised to meet her at the Toronto airport but did not show up. She wanted to know why he had not met her, but in all her letters to him she had never been able to summon the courage to ask. She had wanted him in the same way she now wanted Harlan. She tried to compare Joe to Harlan. Joe was shy, withdrawn, hated society. But he was also strong, independent, and gentle. He was a hermit-philosopher. He always wrote her beautiful letters about nature, animals, God — things he had never expressed to her in person. Perhaps he had found contentment. Perhaps he might still share his life with her. Harlan: He was a question mark. There was something cold about him. Perhaps it was because he was in a foreign country, like when she went to Canada. Perhaps deep inside he, too, was simply afraid.

Yoshiko put the letter in her purse and went to the refrigerator to see what vegetables were left. She decided to make some curried rice. It was one of Julie's favorite dishes.

* * *

Sachiko was seated at her desk in her bedroom. Her head was seething with images and ideas. She felt she would explode if she did not write them down or explain them to someone. She picked up her private phone and dialed Yumi's number. Yumi answered the phone.

"Yumi, this is Sachiko."

"Hi, Sachiko. How are you?"

"I'm sitting here going out of my mind. I had to talk

12

to someone."

"Is it about Harlan?"

"Yes."

"I thought so. What's wrong? What happened?"

"I don't know if anything is wrong, but I went to his place today and he was in bed with another woman."

"You're kidding! That's terrible. Did you actually see them in bed together?"

"No. I knocked on his door and he came outside with just his pants on and told me there was someone else there."

"What did you do?"

"Nothing. He said he would call me later, so I came home. I didn't know what to say. I can't seem to speak English well when I'm with him."

"Did he know you were going to his place?"

"No. I just went there today on an impulse. I wanted to see him. I felt bad because I hadn't slept with him before. I thought maybe I should have. I was too scared that last time. I wanted to make sure today that we were still friends."

"Sachiko, you're crazy! You should have told him you were coming. You always set yourself up for a fall. You have to learn to be more careful."

"I know, but I can't help myself. I'm too impulsive. Besides, it was not really that shocking to me. He's a writer, and artists and writers are usually passionate and need more experiences than other people. I know he likes me. He's very honest about everything with me. He wants me to help him get his book published. I'm his agent."

"I think you are hopelessly romantic."

Sachiko and Yumi talked for over an hour. By the time she hung up, Sachiko had calmed down. Yumi thought Sachiko was mistaken in wanting to get involved with Harlan, but she had also said that Harlan was a nice person and was glad Sachiko and Harlan were friends. Yumi had hated Tom. She was afraid Sachiko would eventually be abandoned by Harlan, too. She said she could not bear seeing Sachiko get hurt again.

Sachiko had met Yumi four years ago at Kobe Women's University. In another month they would graduate together. They had done everything together these past four years, confessed all. If everything went well, Yumi would be married in June. Yumi had met an American, Terry, who was married and had two children, at a summer Christian camp. He had returned to the U.S., divorced recently, and was now planning to come back to Japan.

When Sachiko had met Yumi, Yumi was under great pressure from her family to break off the relationship.

14

Yumi waited patiently for a reencounter for two years. Finally, she went to America to meet him. This caused a great uproar. Terry was the first man with whom Yumi had slept. She loved him as passionately now as she did the night she lost her virginity. The plan was for Terry to return and work as a teacher. Sachiko hoped all would work out for them.

It seemed to Sachiko human contact was such a fragile thing that the hope two people would want each other in the same way at the same time and with the possibility of doing something about it was remote. It was possible some people could encounter their soulmates in this lifetime, like Yumi and Terry, but she doubted the possibility for herself.

She felt as if she were destined to be a voyeur of life's passions, a vicarious participant in life's sensuality. Her role as helper in Yumi's affair was an example. When Yumi had gone to America, it was Sachiko who spoke to Yumi's family to calm them down. It was she who took a day to prepare a list of English schools in the Kansai area for Terry to apply to, this with the idea he would think it was Yumi who had done so. Whenever a letter for Yumi from Terry arrived, it was delivered to Sachiko's address.

Sachiko enjoyed the role of go-between. It was her nature to help people. But sometimes she wished she were the person involved. She sometimes thought she would die a virgin. It was her burden. She and Yumi often talked about this. One time Yumi had said, "After Terry and I are married, perhaps you should come to our house and watch us make love. It is beyond imagination!"

Yumi and Terry would live in Ashiya when they were married. Sachiko wondered where she and Tom would have lived if they had married. Sachiko preferred Ashiya because it was quiet and refined. Kobe was nice, too. It was a beautiful city with an international flavor, unlike Osaka. Either Kobe or Ashiya would have suited Tom. There were many foreigners in Kobe and Ashiya who seemed sociable and liked to gather together. There were few foreigners in Itami City. Sachiko supposed Harlan did not care for sociable types. She had taken him to a popular restaurant in Ashiya for their one dinner date. He had hunched his shoulders and peered suspiciously at the other foreigners.

Sachiko opened the top drawer of her desk and pulled out some stationary. She began to write. Only in her letters could she express her true self in English, her true feelings. She could confess everything in her letters to Harlan without being intimidated by his presence. The words flowed smoothly. She shut herself within the walls of her private world. In her thoughts she talked to

16

the letter as if it were a living person. She hummed a song as she wrote.

Dear Harlan,

How are you? I'm glad you are honest. My brain is always full of imagination, so I have imagined you and she will get much closer. Nothing was shocking to me. As I told you, my character is complicated. I myself even enjoy this situation, which is subtle and risky, or unbelievable to others. I think I am more tolerant than other women, and I prefer to like someone rather than to be liked. I like you very much. I was happy to hear that you liked me. I would not like to disturb your private life with her, but I would like to see you if you have time.

I wish I could speak English more fluently. I feel I had spoken English better before I went to Mexico than now. I don't know why I can't speak my third language well when I'm with you. Anyway, I'm your crazy pen pal. I can't express how much I'm glad you read my letters...

She continued to write for an hour. She wrote about Yumi and Terry, about the job she would take in Osaka after graduating. She hated the thought of working in such a vast and nightmarish city. It was a dirty, desecrated, scrounging metropolis where the buildings were touched with a rat-like grimace, the trees had a spiderish look about them, and the people were soot-stained and dead-looking. She wrote about one of the dreams she had had about Harlan. She had dreamed a man like a ghost was standing beside a bed where a young serviceman lay bound without liberty to move. It had appeared the ghost was going to throw something like acid over the serviceman's face. It was strange the serviceman had been equally she and Harlan. Two egos might have been attached to the man. She/Harlan had screamed and tried to move, but it was impossible. Then she had woken, her heart beating furiously.

...It was just like a scene out of a book or movie. Will you continue writing? I enjoyed your novel so much. I understood the characters so much. Will you write about Japan? I want to help you any way I can to get your book published. I like you a lot, but please don't worry. I like to be with you, but I know you are not my possession. I understand you. You are a nice person. In May or summer, if we have time and money, let's go to Tokyo.

I'll write you again tomorrow. Don't worry about today. I understand you and she will get closer. I don't want to bother you in your private life. Be a great writer. Eat vegetables.

Your agent,
Sachiko

She sealed the letter in an envelope and put it aside to mail the next day. She was tired and got ready for bed. It had been a long day. Writing the letter had further exhausted her. When she had pen and paper in hand, she could not control herself. Yumi always said writing letters was Sachiko's incurable disease.

It did not matter if he did not write back. He was probably too busy writing another novel. Sachiko had never known a writer before. The world of artists and writers had always seemed remote, but now she knew one, knew the magic of his words, his physical presence. She had felt his lips upon hers, upon her breasts, then taken him with her hands and mouth. That night was one of uncompromising clarity. He had appeared before her as a savior, but things were different now.

2

arlan and Julie were walking home from Hankyu Itami Station. It had been a busy day at the conversation school and they were both tired. The night was cold, the sky clear. There were few people on the streets. Julie was not her usual self. She seemed distant tonight, somber. She stopped suddenly and looked Harlan in the eyes.

"Harlan, tell me honestly what you think of Yoshiko."

"I don't know. She's become a good friend. She's well-read and speaks English very well. I like the conversations we have about books. She seems a bit pensive at times, as if she's pondering some great existential question. I suppose she doesn't fit the typical Japanese stereotype. I like her aloofness, her questioning mind. I think she's much more mature than most 22-year-olds."

"I don't mean that. I mean what do you really think about her? Do you have any strong feelings for her? Do you think you love her? I know you've been sleeping with her."

TORAWARE

Harlan paused for a moment. This was an unexpected line of questioning. He was more accustomed to Julie acting like a veteran of Japan teaching a new recruit the ropes when they walked the streets to the station and home together, rode the train, and taught the classes. She was always pointing out landmarks to remember so he would not get lost, interesting shops, ways to save money, how to use the train system, personality traits of the evening students that could be used in conversation when the lessons became slow and there was a lull. She was always remarking how polite the Japanese were, how she loved the way they bowed to one another, how she loved the children's smiles. She had never tried to probe his inner feelings.

"That's a difficult question," he said. "I know I like her a lot. Love? I have a hard time with the word 'love.' I think that takes a long time to develop."

"She's a very sensitive woman, you know."

"Yes, I get that feeling."

"I just don't want to see her hurt. She's tried to commit suicide before."

"I've noticed the scars on her wrists."

"Did you ask her about them?"

"No. I figure that's her business. If she wants to tell me, she probably will. Why are you bringing all this up now?"

21

"Because I've decided to return to Canada and go back to school to get a nursing degree. My visa extension is up soon and I can't get another visa unless I find a company to sponsor me. I've been looking around and haven't been able to find anything."

"Does Yoshiko know what you've decided?"

"We've talked about it, but I didn't make up my mind until today. When I get home, I'll tell her. That's why I wanted to know what you felt about her. I think after I'm gone she'll be lonely and vulnerable. She needs someone to talk to and to care for her. Please be careful with her, Harlan. Please don't take advantage of her. She really likes you a lot, maybe she's even falling in love with you. Will you promise me you won't hurt her?"

"I promise."

They arrived at Yoshiko's apartment.

"You go ahead," Harlan said. "It's a bit late and I want to take a bath. I know what you have to say to each other is private. I'll grab something to eat later."

"Are you sure? Yoshiko's probably made dinner for both of us."

"No, that's OK. I'll see you later."

Harlan went home, got his towel and some fresh underwear, then headed toward the *sento* public bath. He had been self-conscious the first time he went there a month before, but now he was a regular customer and the master and other customers treated him kindly.

He took off his shoes at the entrance, entered the locker room, greeted and paid the master. He stripped, put his clothes in a locker, and entered the steam-filled bathing room. In the middle of the room was a long trough of water. Along the walls were taps where several bathers were soaping and rinsing themselves. At the far end was a large tub in which more bathers were soaking contentedly. A forested mountain overlooking a calm lake was painted on the tiled wall behind the tub. Harlan squatted on a miniature stool next to the trough, rinsed himself with a plastic bucket, soaped, scrubbed, rinsed again, then immersed himself in the large tub. He had come to love this ritual. There was only the moment and the smiles of the other bathers.

He thought of his new job. He did not consider himself a teacher in the professional sense. He felt more a student. Already in his first month on the job he was finding out how little he really knew about his own language. And he had had the audacity to call himself a writer! He believed himself lucky to have found the job. Perhaps it was the start of a new apprenticeship. By being in daily contact with the language, reexamining the fundamentals of language structure, becoming conscious once again of the words he chose to express himself in order to be as clear as possible (instead of spewing forth a flood of words without regard to grammatical order or clarity as he had done in his first novel, which now seemed an amateurish attempt at a theme far beyond his capabilities), his future writing would benefit.

The students at the school came from all ages and walks of life. The conversations, particularly with the higher-level students, covered a wide range of topics. Harlan thought he could learn as much about Japan in his little teaching booth as he could travelling the entire country. He did not know how long the job would last as he was working illegally on a tourist visa, but for the time being his salary of ¥220,000 a month (for teaching eight hours a day, six days a week) would allow him eventually to pay off the key deposit on his apartment and put a little in his pocket. He could extend his travel visa for another three months in April. Beyond that he trusted in faith and good luck.

After his bath, Harlan decided to take a walk. He enjoyed walking the narrow, labyrinthian streets of the neighborhood, just as he had explored the many cities of his wanderings, always driven by hunger and thought. The architecture of the homes here was different from anything he had ever seen — the slated roofs, the ubiquitous gardens of trimmed shrubbery (each garden with its stone shrine and walls of stone or concrete), the narrow, wooden gates that looked as if they were made for dwarves.

He heard a strange sound like the blast of bagpipes. It had a mournful resonance. He heard it again. He ran through a dark alley and across a wider street to see where it was coming from. On the main street of the nearby shabby business district he saw a dim light moving. He caught up with the light. It was the soba noodle man blowing his horn and pulling his wooden cart.

A gruff-looking old man ordered a bowl of noodles. Harlan held up one finger as the old man had done. He stared in fascination as the soba man prepared the noodles. With swift, graceful movements, the soba man threw two portions of noodles into a pot of hot, steaming water; snapped two styrofoam bowls off a shelf; ladled broth out of another pot into the bowls; poured a shot of soy sauce into the bowls; scooped out the now-cooked noodles with a strainer; flipped them into equal-sized portions; slid them carefully into the bowls; grabbed a well-manicured assortment of vegetables and meat from some plastic containers; placed the assortment on top of the noodles; sprinkled some seasoning on top; and handed the bowls to the old man and Harlan. Clouds of steam rose into the night air. More customers gathered. Harlan and the old man slurped their noodles noisily. Harlan continued watching the soba man. It was as if he were witnessing the performance of a man who had found his niche in the world, accepted it, loved it, and made it his art.

Harlan finished his noodles and returned home. There was another letter from Sachiko in his mail slot. He had not noticed it earlier. He sat down at the *kotatsu*, pulled the blanket around his legs to keep warm, leaned back against the wall, and read the letter. She seemed not to have been shocked at finding Harlan in bed with Yoshiko a couple days before, but he could not be sure.

Sachiko was a mystery, but that intrigued Harlan. She was a dark, shy, good-looking woman whose reticence gave him an impression of condescension, but beneath that veil of silence lay a sensitive, brilliant mind. Although English was her third language, she possessed a greater vocabulary than any of the other students he taught. She was familiar with all the books and writers he talked about. Harlan had the impression hers was an artistic soul trying to break free from her tangled emotions, her confusion, and the restrictions placed on her by Japanese society.

After Sachiko and her friend quit the school, Harlan received a letter from her. In the letter she expressed a warmth in having met him and an interest in a book he had recommended. He bumped into her at the

TORAWARE

Nishinomiya train station a few days later while on his dinner break. They dined together, visited, and agreed to have dinner again that Sunday night. They met in Ashiya and she took him to a small restaurant she said was popular with foreigners. She had seemed at times aloof, lost in thought. Harlan did most of the talking. He gave her his manuscript to read and joked about her becoming his Japanese agent.

Since that time he had received letters from her almost on a daily basis. He was getting to know her more through her letters than from any of their conversations. He had been surprised to find out that their brief dinner date was her first with a man. He could not have foreseen that she would be the first person to understand what he had attempted to express in his novel. She truly wanted to help him publish it. When she showed up at his apartment to return the manuscript, they agreed on her representing him. Then, they lay down together and he kissed her breasts and she took him orally.

Something about her bothered him. He felt he had merely taken advantage of the opportunity. He did not feel any passion for her, but he was attracted to her calm intellect. He did not feel comfortable with the way she seemed in awe of him. She seemed unable to speak to him directly, yet her letters revealed a complicated depth of emotion. She had written about the self-destructiveness of her emotions and the hatred she directed at herself. She seemed aware of who and what she was, but, at the same time, she was filled with a plethora of confusion. The world to her was empty, alien, meaningless. Harlan understood this feeling well. She was, in a sense, the female counterpart to the main character of his novel.

An icy blast of wind penetrated the room and Harlan shivered. A peculiar loneliness came upon him. It was the same feeling that had dogged him since his experiences in both Vietnam and India when the realization of the impermanence of all things, all relationships, had struck him so hard. His life since those experiences had been that of a moving, anonymous shadow among men. The ghost of India in particular still dwelled within him. It called him to return, to be shocked again into witnessing and experiencing how alone man really was and how eternally and vastly distant people were from one another.

He remembered his return to the States, to Seattle, where he had worked for a while as a stevedore on the docks before finding a job as a mailman for a firm of corporate lawyers. He passed the weekdays of that winter collecting and distributing mail to the 150 lawyers and secretaries who worked in the top three floors of the First National Bank building. His evenings and weekends were spent either pacing the wet Seattle streets or locked up in his skid-row room drinking cheap beer and smoking dope, reliving the Asian experiences in his mind, dwelling too much on the disparities between Asia and the United States, despising once again the country that had sent him and his generation to Vietnam, thinking of the States as an adolescent nation in need of waking to the realities of his Asian death-visions, first experienced in the war and most recently in India. It was as if he had possessed a prophetic vision of the decline and demise of the States and could therefore condescend to preach about it to those who did not know the horror and darkness of life the way it existed in many parts of the world.

Winter passed and the urge to move on consumed him. He drifted back down to California and worked as a cook first in Garberville and then in Monterey before heading to Texas to work on the oil rigs. Everywhere he went a misanthropy gnawed at his insides with a potency that nearly drove him mad. Everywhere he saw numbers of poor and drifting people searching for work in a portent of a new Great Depression: ex-cons, Vietnam veterans, scam men on the run from the law, drifters whose wives had left them, rednecks from Texas, Cajun coonasses from Louisiana, the many from Michigan and Ohio migrating to the South in droves like a cancer out of control.

He put his vision down on paper. Through the therapy of writing the story of what he had been through, he tried to exorcise the demons that clutched him so tightly. He wanted desperately to make sense of the insanity and cruelty of life and turn all of it into something positive.

The writing of the book exhausted him. He had poured all his passions and frustrations and anger into it. He moved on to the bleak, snow-covered emptiness of Wyoming and worked in an oil camp 20 miles outside Evanston until receiving a letter from Jeremy Boston, a writer friend who was then living on the island of Maui. Jeremy invited Harlan to visit and stay as long as he wanted.

The few months in Maui were tonic for his weary soul. Then his money began to run out. There was the possibility of going back to work in a tourist restaurant, but he was tired of the cooking trade. A change was called for. He felt the need to be jolted into a different reality. Jeremy was called back to the mainland to promote a new book and with him gone there was no need for Harlan to stay on the island. Jeremy suggested Harlan go to Japan, where the possibility of finding a job teaching English was said to be good. Jeremy gave Harlan some names and addresses of places to stay until getting set up. Two weeks later Harlan took a plane to Osaka.

Now he was in a foreign country again for the first time since he had left India. He wondered how long he would be able to stay in Japan. He wanted to stay at least long enough to become proficient in the language and save some money to finance the next step. But to where? India loomed large in his thoughts.

Harlan got into his futon. There was a soft knock on the door. Yoshiko entered the apartment, silently took her clothes off, and slipped into the futon beside him. Harlan put his arms around her, grateful for the warmth of her body, and concentrated on the moment.

3

Julie and Yoshiko were holding hands and standing in front of the departure gate at Itami International Airport. Julie's plane was to take off in about ten minutes. Both were crying.

"Julie, what am I going to do without you? I miss you already." Yoshiko said.

"I know. I miss you already, too." Julie's voice started to crack. She swallowed hard. "We both know I have to go. I can't stay in Japan forever."

"I wish you could stay a few more months. The apartment will be so empty without you."

"Oh, come one, you know your mother will be coming over all the time. Please thank her and all your family again for everything they've done for me. I love them just like my own family."

"They love you, too, but not as much as I do."

"Yoshiko, this isn't the end. You can still come visit me anytime in Canada and I'll come back to Japan someday. I know it. Come here. Give me one last hug. You'll always be my best friend."

Yoshiko hugged Julie as tightly and warmly as she

32

could. Then Julie picked up her carry-on luggage and walked through the gate leading to the boarding ramp. Yoshiko watched the plane taxi down the runway and take off. She stared at the sky for a long time after the plane disappeared from sight.

*　　*　　*

Yoshiko took a sip from her third glass of whiskey, set the glass back down on the kitchen table, and looked out the sliding glass door leading to the garden behind her apartment. Outside was a wall of blackness. Inside the apartment was cold and empty.

She lit a cigarette, then picked up the birthday card from Julie and read through it once more. "Why," she said, "did you have to leave me today of all days? Now all I have is my coffee, my cigarettes, and my whiskey."

Her diary lay open before her. She wanted to write down everything that was in her mind, but her thoughts were all jumbled and the page remained blank. She began writing the *kanji* character for "righteousness." In Japan each of the five strokes was used as a counter the way westerners wrote four vertical lines with a diagonal slash through them for units of five. Yoshiko began thinking of former lovers.

There were the three Japanese boys after she had

graduated from high school and the owner of the Cocos Island coffee shop. That was before she had gone to Canada. She took a deep drag off her cigarette and another sip from her whiskey. Franz, Julie's brother, was the fifth. That made one *kanji*.

Franz was an artist who, in the beginning, gave her confidence, tried to draw out the artist in her soul by giving advice, encouragement, praise for her attempts at finding a medium to express herself, this in the time when she still spoke little English. But sex with him, like all the others, was masturbatory with little regard for her own pleasure. As she came to know him better he seemed to carry a demonic aura about him, an affected superiority, as if through his sculpting, painting, and poetry he was above the rest. The world belonged to him alone. He was always playing games, setting people up in situations where he was the sole judge of who they were, of how worthy they were, secretly sizing them up in his mind to see if they were in fact worthy of him. She despised that. She was grateful for what he brought out of her, for the confidence that emerged bit by bit, but in the end she found she could never love a man with such an enormous ego, a man who professed to have such great compassion yet was so lacking in it, a man who believed the artist was God.

There was Ron, the Scot with whom she spent nearly

a month. He had a musical character and a sweet voice. He was very intelligent. Yoshiko felt grateful to him, too, for the books he gave her, for the different thoughts so new and strange and intoxicating that came from reading those books in the cold winter of his apartment. They had good times together. He showed great tenderness in his love-making, but she did not experience orgasm. Then one day he took too many drugs and ended up in the hospital. That day frightened her more than anything else in her life.

There was Thomas, the Buddhist monk who put great existential questions to her during the time she had first grappled with a new belief in God. She respected him in the beginning, especially when he rejected her initial sexual advances. He seemed like such a pure man, calm, gentle with other people. But his calm posture was just a mask covering a seething volcano of inner conflicts and doubts. She eventually discovered his true belief: To rid oneself of worldly desires one had to continually punish oneself, to literally beat oneself into a submission of the spirit. She was thoroughly disgusted the day she found him with another lover, bound and gagged to the bed, welts on his body, a rubber hose in the lover's hand, a look of ethereal joy in Thomas's eyes.

Ten minutes had passed. Yoshiko had written two *kanji* characters in the diary. She poured herself another drink and lit another cigarette. Two *kanji* characters. Ten men. She was single, 23 years old today, the age when most Japanese women began to think seriously about the future and marriage. If there was one among the ten Yoshiko could have committed her life to, it was Joe, but he was far away living alone in his shack in the Canadian wilderness.

She tried again to compare Joe to Harlan. Harlan had an independent strength that was difficult to define. She knew there were deep wounds inside him that caused him to project a facade of harsh toughness, but she liked being with him, sleeping with him, feeling his gentle caresses and strong arms. It was only after she left him that she felt his coldness.

She began to speak aloud in Japanese to Harlan:

"You can have anything you want in this country, but what of me? Do I dare be alone in this world? What will I do now that Julie has left me? Will you become my one lover? Will you stay hidden behind your mask?

"I'm not strong enough. For you it's easy. You can drink your beer and read your books and have your little adventures to block your loneliness, but for me it's different. There's something more to my loneliness that even my whiskey can't erase."

Her mind was like a merry-go-round spinning in a frenzy. She felt a surge of insanity creep into it. Tears formed. She lit another cigarette, inhaled deeply, exhaled slowly, and watched the trail of blue smoke rise to the ceiling. She shook her head, as if trying to cast off the weight of her own thinking. She rose from the table, stumbled a bit, put on her jacket, grabbed the bottle of whiskey, and walked out into the night.

By the time she reached Harlan's apartment, Yoshiko's head had cleared a little. Harlan was seated at his *kotatsu*. Yoshiko sat down beside him, pulling the blanket around her legs, and looked at him intently.

"Are you OK?" Harlan asked.

"Yes, just feeling lonely is all."

"Would you like some coffee?"

"I'd rather drink this whiskey."

"I'll help you."

Harlan went to the kitchen, came back with two glasses, and poured them both half full.

"So Julie is on her way to Canada," he said.

"Yes, I miss her already."

"Crying about it won't help. Life is full of separation. You just have to accept it. There's nothing we can do about it."

"You don't believe in God, do you?"

"It depends on what you mean by God."

"God of the Bible."

"Well, if you mean the Christian God, I guess not

37

really. I suppose for a while I was an atheist, but these days I'm more of an agnostic."

"What do you mean, atheist and agnostic?"

"An atheist is someone who believes absolutely there is no God. An agnostic is someone who believes it isn't possible to know whether God exists."

"They both sound the same to me. I don't understand the difference."

"I guess they do seem almost the same. To me, an atheist would think that man is alone in the universe, while an agnostic would think it's possible there's a God, but he won't find out until after he dies. That's how I feel. I've seen too much misery in the world to think any decent God could create this mess, but I've also had several experiences that were maybe spiritual and made me think there must be someone looking after me. I simply don't know. I'd like to believe in God, but I can't accept organized religions the way man has made them."

"What kind of spiritual experiences did you have?"

"Things like when I should have died, but didn't. You know, if I had been one foot to the right or left of where I was at a particular moment or a second or two earlier or later. Or people or events that came out of nowhere to save me or guide me. It's hard to explain. All I can say is that I survived sometimes because of something more than just luck."

Yoshiko thought about what Harlan had said. The way he expressed himself was enigmatic and bothered her. She wanted him to say something more direct, something concrete to reveal himself. He was too evasive. Always at the point of revealing some clue about his past, about the reasons and the forces behind his entering her life, he would suddenly cast a cloak over himself and withdraw from her.

"Julie always said that we have to have faith in God. God doesn't show himself to us because he wants to test our faith." Yoshiko said.

"I don't believe that. If God is like that, he's a mean and terrible creator. The only real faith I have is in myself."

"You're not sad that Julie went back to Canada, are you?"

"No. She had to move on, that's all. Like I said before, life is full of separation and we just have to accept it and get on with our lives. Maybe if you had the experiences I've had, you would feel the same way."

Harlan was becoming weary of this tedious dialogue. He picked up the bottle of whiskey and poured two more drinks. Yoshiko sat holding her glass and staring into it, absorbed in the privacy of her own mind. Harlan knew she was reaching out to him for an answer to the confusion of her existence, but he was powerless to provide it. He knew only that people never knew enough about other people and their sufferings to have the right response at the right time. The more people spoke to each other, the more wretched and self-conscious they became.

He wanted somehow to explain everything about his life to her, every little detail and how each experience, each thought, each relationship he had accumulated in the course of his 33 years was connected to who he was and how he saw the world. But words always failed him, always complicated things. That was probably the force behind his need to write. He had a deep need to express himself, to explain himself and try to make sense of the kaleidoscope of life-experience images that constantly ran through his brain, but he could not do it with a stream of spoken utterances. He needed time to examine and reexamine his thoughts before putting them down on paper. Even then it was an impossible task. It took years to find the right words to explain a single experience to himself, let alone to another human being.

This is what had amazed him about Sachiko. She was the first one who had ever responded to his written words, the first to show some inkling of understanding. She seemed to have an intuitive sense of what was inside him. It was as if she were the one reader he had been writing to all his life. Her letters to him were the voice and the response he, like Yoshiko, had longed for, yet the duality of her nature was impenetrable. When in her presence, there was a wall between them. He felt no stir of emotions. She was a block of stone. Her own passions, like his, seemed confined to too much intellectual scrutiny and exposed themselves only in bits and pieces.

Yoshiko had more of the animal instinct. She was tormented by the same questions of self-examination, but her questions were closer to the surface and had an urgency to them. She required immediate answers that could not be given. Her emotions and yearnings were out in the open. There was also a sense of urgency to her love-making, as if in calling forth and focusing all her passion she could exhaust her suffering.

Harlan reached out to put his hand on her shoulder. She moved closer to him. They finished the bottle of whiskey. Harlan pushed the *kotatsu* away and spread out the futon.

"Do you want me to give you a massage?" he asked.
"Please."

Yoshiko lay face down on the futon. Harlan began kneading her back, shoulders, and neck. Her head was spinning from the whiskey. The tightness dissolved and she felt herself floating. Later, in the middle of the night, she woke with a start. She had been dreaming. She had been in the Canadian wilderness searching frantically for Joe's shack. There had been wolves chasing her. She had called for Joe, but he had not come.

Harlan stirred and put his arm around her. Yoshiko snuggled closer for warmth. Tears started, but she willed them away. She had come to Harlan tonight wanting his support and an affirmation of her faith. It had not happened. She wondered if she would be able to change him, change his negativism. A sudden pattering of rain outside disturbed the silence.

4

Harlan laced up his running shoes and headed out the door and down the stairs. He turned left at the narrow road leading to Route 171, passed the police station and Itami City Hall, crossed Route 171, and ran up the incline leading to Koya Park. He entered the park, a refuge for ducks, swans, and other birds that spent every winter on the man-made pond, and started jogging on the two-and-a-half-kilometer path that circled the park.

He was in a rhythm, legs and arms pumping, heart beating, images and abstract thoughts racing through his mind. He had started running regularly again about a month ago and was getting into better shape. The beer belly he had put on in Maui was gone. Japanese phrases he had learned recently flashed in his mind as he headed through the stretch of cherry trees, now nearly in full bloom and looking like a mass of cotton candy. On the right and across the street was a row of high-rise apartment buildings with long lines of brightly-colored laundry flapping in the breeze. Beyond the apartment buildings were three baseball diamonds. Two softball games were in progress. On the third field fathers and sons were playing catch.

Inside the park and lining the edges of the pond were dozens of birdwatchers with their cameras. A group of school children in uniforms squealed in delight and waved and shouted encouragement as he passed by them. Now he was on the back stretch, running past a hospital. Several construction workers in the parking lot stopped to watch him. Then he ran through a back entrance to the park and up a slight incline where a few families were eating *bento* lunches. He completed two more laps and returned to his apartment.

At the end of these invigorating and therapeutic runs Harlan liked to drink a beer and sit down to think and write in his journal. He was feeling healthy and energetic these days. Things were going well. He had recently met an interesting American who was running his own conversation school.

They had met about ten days before. Harlan was walking to the UCLA school from the Nishinomiya train station when he bumped into another American whom he recognized from some pictures he had seen at the school. Rick Stratford was a rotund man who was in his early fifties and had a broad smile. He had quit UCLA two weeks before Harlan had started working. He had set up his own school in Mukonoso. Harlan had a half hour before his first class started and they agreed to have a cup of coffee together. Rick said he had too many students to handle by himself and wanted to hire a couple of teachers. He invited Harlan to go out to discuss the possibility of working for him.

They met again a few nights later at a *yakitori* grilled chicken shop near the Mukonoso station. Over beer and chicken Rick told Harlan about his school and how he had started with two students and now had 35, about his life as a photographer in the States, and about meeting his Japanese wife when she was a homestay student on an exchange program that he had been involved in in Seattle. He talked about the changes Japan had undergone from the time he was a serviceman stationed in Japan in the 1950s to the last few years after he returned to settle permanently. He warned Harlan about the need to stay clear of schools like UCLA that exploited both teachers and students. He talked about the importance of the conversation teacher creating a relaxed atmosphere in which the students could do the majority of the speaking. He brimmed over with confidence and enthusiasm, and gave Harlan many tips on teaching and surviving in Japan.

Harlan took an immediate liking to Rick's good-natured personality and engaging smile. He liked the way Rick joked and bantered with the cooks and other customers at the *yakitori* shop. He had decided that night he would go to work for Rick as soon as he could. The next day he gave his notice to UCLA. He planned to start at Rick's school at the beginning of May.

This plan suited Harlan well. He would extend his tourist visa in a few days for another three months. That would carry him as far as the beginning of July. Rick had told him that beyond that it would not be difficult to get a six-month culture visa. All he would have to do is claim he was studying Japanese at Rick's school. His salary at the school would be considerably less than what he was getting at UCLA, but he would have to teach only in the evenings and would have plenty of time to study. The long hours at UCLA were starting to wear him down and he wanted more time to himself. Besides, by the end of April he would have the key money on his apartment paid off and would not be burdened by the ¥80,000 a month he was dishing out for that.

He looked forward to a new change, to having more time. His Japanese studies were going well. He had started taking lessons a couple months before. He had seen an ad in a local English newspaper, called the teacher — a woman named Nishimoto who spoke English well — met her in a coffee shop in Umeda, and continued meeting her at the same coffee shop twice a week in the morning before going to work. Rick had said that when Harlan started working at his school, Harlan and Nishimoto could use the school for their lessons.

Nishimoto was stiff and nervous in their first lesson. She had just graduated from a six-month training course in teaching Japanese to foreigners. Harlan was her first student. She gradually began to relax and grow confident, and now they were often joking with each other. Whenever Harlan made a particularly glaring mistake in pronunciation or grammar, they would both have a good laugh about it.

Nishimoto prepared extensively for their lessons. She brought in pictures, maps, graphs, charts, props, anything she could think of to make a point clear and help him remember a new expression or pattern. She always related the material to his personal life. She taught him baseball expressions, literary expressions, vocabulary to explain where he came from, what his life history was, where he had travelled, what he had seen, what he wanted to order in restaurants. She drilled him in correct pronunciation and the time length of Japanese vowels. She insisted Harlan use standard Japanese rather than the Kansai dialect, although she took the time to point out the differences in intonation, verb endings, reduced speech, and male and female patterns. She

47

always listened patiently with interest to Harlan's tales of misadventure with the language. She counseled perseverance and effort when he told her of his frustration about not making fast enough progress and not understanding what people were saying. She consoled him by explaining how she had studied English for over eight years and still had trouble understanding a conversation between two native speakers.

Studying Japanese induced Harlan to see more clearly the difficulties of his own Japanese students studying English. He had often wondered why so many Japanese students were reticent in the classroom. Now he was beginning to understand the obstacles involved in constructing a simple sentence in a language totally unrelated to one's own. There was no concept of singular and plural in Japanese, the subject was often omitted, the verb came at the end of the sentence. In addition, the Japanese had a way of responding three or four times to a speaker's single sentence. If this response was not given, the speaker seemed to have difficulty continuing. A native speaker of English responded to entire thoughts or opinions. If a student could not think in the second language, and had to grope through a tension-ridden thought process of internal translation — clause by clause and sentence by sentence — from one language to another, it was no wonder so many classes were filled with silence and confusion. Harlan's empathy went out to those students. He resolved to make himself a better teacher, a teacher as committed as Nishimoto.

It was time to get moving. He had promised to meet Sachiko at Ashiya Station at seven o'clock. He put on a kettle of hot water, washed and shaved at his kitchen sink, and changed into a clean shirt and pants. He had mixed feelings about this meeting. Since that day Sachiko came to the door when he and Yoshiko had been making love, he had vowed to cut off any further development of a sexual relationship with Sachiko. He had explained to her that he wanted theirs to be strictly a business relationship. She had agreed, but her letters increasingly revealed a passion born of desperation. That bothered him. Yet he wanted to find out what had happened in Tokyo. She had actually found an agent who might be interested in representing his book. He had to admit that her commitment to and understanding of his work inspired him. He was already making notes in preparation for a new book. She was the only one he could talk with honestly about it. He hoped that time would diminish her attraction to him and they could settle into a friendship based on mutual interests.

* * *

Sachiko's head swirled with excitement as she walked from her home to Ashiya Station. Much had happened in the last two months. She had graduated. She had started her new job as an office worker in a foreign trading company in Osaka. She had gone to Tokyo as Harlan's representative and met the secretary of a Japanese literary agent she had found out about. She was anxious to meet Harlan and tell him about the trip. She also wanted to show him the cherry blossoms along the banks of Ashiya River.

This was Harlan's first April in Japan. Throughout the Kansai area the cherry blossoms along Ashiya River were among the most famous. It was a popular spot for young lovers. Every year Sachiko went there alone and watched the couples stroll arm in arm. It always made her feel envious and lonely. Perhaps tonight she would know what it was those lovers felt. She believed happiness demanded a certain boldness. She would try to put her arm in his, to hold his eyes in hers. She was in love with his eyes. She wanted to feel again his warmth, his kisses.

A coldness passed through her. She knew she was deceiving herself, but she could not help it. Every time she thought of him she experienced a sickness of heart, a tenseness of the body. She knew it was better for her not to send her letters to him. She revealed too much of

50

herself. She imagined that he and his soulmate, his other lover, sometimes read Sachiko's letters while in his futon and perhaps even laughed at her confessions. The thought depressed her.

He had told her he did not want to be emotionally involved with her, but she found it impossible to separate her roles of lover and agent. She wanted him for herself. If he became famous, she would confess to the world that he was the first man with whom she had had sex.

She wished she had the courage to speak to him directly. He never wrote back. He said nothing about her letters when they met. He usually spoke only about writing and books. She wanted to hear him talk about his feelings, confess his love for her. Perhaps he was like her in that respect. He saved his feelings for his writing.

Harlan arrived promptly on time. The walk to the downtown area of Ashiya took only ten minutes. There were many fashionable shops that Sachiko liked, but, remembering his reactions to the fancy restaurant she had taken him to before, she took him to a Mosburger hamburger shop. They ordered and sat down.

"So how was Tokyo?" Harlan asked.

"I have some good news."

"That's nice."

"I didn't meet the agent, but I met the secretary and she was very nice."

"What happened?"

"Well, at first I was a little nervous when I approached their office, but I was composed when I entered."

"And then?"

"The agent was out, but the secretary agreed to have lunch and look at your manuscript. We spent two hours together and became friendly with each other. She said she would like to meet you, but they weren't selling many literary manuscripts. They did a lot of literary work in the past, but now most of their business is from representing models and actors. She said it might be better for you to approach an American publisher first. She said most of the English books published in Japan have already been published and successful in the United States or England."

"I tried sending it to several American publishers before, but no one was interested. Do you suppose she knows any other agencies or publishers in Tokyo who might look at the manuscript?"

Sachiko felt her confidence growing as she spoke. Always before she had been tongue-tied and tense when she met Harlan, but now she had his full attention and her story was not just about her own history and thoughts and feelings that were so hard to explain but about something that involved them both. She luxuriated in the warmth of his look, the strong interest he was showing in her.

"I don't know," Sachiko said, "but the important thing is we made a contact, and that contact might possibly lead to something else. I think we should go to Tokyo together this summer. Just to meet her and see what happens. She might introduce us to another agent if she likes the book. What do you think?"

"I wouldn't expect too much. Maybe it's best just to chalk this up as another failure. An artist or writer can't expect success. After all, constant failure is an important source of inspiration to the artist."

They laughed and Sachiko felt happy.

"Let's go anyway," she said. "I want to show you Tokyo. I know you'll like it very much. There are so many things to see. We can stay in my father's apartment in Nagata-cho. He only uses it when he goes to Tokyo on business. It's located in a convenient place. It's also very quiet even though it's in the center of a lot of government buildings, hotels, and restaurants. If you want, you can go jogging and see the Diet Building or Prime Minister Nakasone's residence or even the Imperial Palace. There are always many joggers on the streets. And the agent's office is near the next subway station. What do you think?"

Harlan hesitated. "I don't know."

"Please, Harlan. The secretary said she wants to meet you. I'm sure you'll make a good impression on her. We can't give up. I'll continue to work hard for you. Maybe if I can translate the book into Japanese, we will have a better chance."

"Well, OK, but you know I don't have any money to pay you. And translating the book will take a lot of time, probably wasted time."

"I don't need money. Besides, it's the kind of work I love. Maybe I understand your book better than others. I want to do it."

"Thank you. If you really want to do it, then you have my blessings and appreciation."

After eating they walked along the banks of Ashiya River. The cherry blossoms were in an earlier stage of blooming than those in Itami. The moon glittered on the surface of the river. Sachiko took Harlan's arm as they walked back to the station. Harlan stiffened. Several times she seemed to bump his side intentionally and he felt the fullness of her breasts press against him.

Sachiko suddenly began talking about the works of Hieronymous Bosch and El Greco. She talked about how she was attracted to Bosch's portrayal of man's insanity and to El Greco's emaciated saints. It seemed strange to Harlan that she would shift their conversation in this direction. He wondered what she was really trying to tell him, if her words revealed a true interest in those artists' works or if she was repeating what he had written in his book about the artists who had stirred his imagination during his initial journey to Europe years before. He wondered if this were not some ploy to push her way into getting closer to him and resume the affair he had chosen to cut off.

At the station they said good-bye, agreeing to meet again soon. In the meantime, Sachiko would make a plan for going to Tokyo in the summer and continue trying to translate the book.

On the ride back to Itami Harlan thought deeply about both Sachiko and Yoshiko. He wondered how far he should allow himself to get involved with either one. He was more attracted to Yoshiko. Her gritty, independent rebelliousness, tough intelligence, and love of down-trodden people were much more to his liking than Sachiko's higher-class aloofness and intellectual fanta-sies. He also preferred Yoshiko's hard, athletic body to Sachiko's soft fullness. Yoshiko seemed to understand better his need for time alone. He often went for days without seeing her, then she would show up at his apart-ment late at night, as if possessing an intuitive sense of when he wanted to see her.

Back in Itami his thoughts dwelled more and more on Yoshiko as he walked the silent, dark streets back to his apartment. Grey-white clouds, illuminated by a near full moon, drifted quickly across the sky. The realization of how much he was starting to care for her came to him. Recently he had found himself going for long midnight walks to escape the confines of his small apartment. At the end of these walks he would invariably pass by Yoshiko's place, stare up at the light coming from her bedroom window, and wonder if she were in bed with one of her lovers.

Harlan moved through the silence and coolness of the night. He passed along the back street leading to Yoshiko's place. There was a car he had not seen before parked near the back of the house. Her bedroom light was on. He paused a moment. A rush of wind struck his face. He headed home.

5

Yoshiko sat at the counter of the Cocos Island coffee shop in Mukonoso drinking her coffee. It had been her favorite hangout since her high school days when she often skipped school and came here to drink coffee, smoke cigarettes, and read favorite books. The owner of the shop had been her confidant in those days and still was now. He was the first man she had slept with and they still occasionally went to a love hotel. She felt easy and safe with him, with his sense of humor, his advice. There was no need to worry about attachment. He was 12 years older and married with two children.

Recently, however, she had been feeling the need to have a stronger anchor in her life, one special person who could fill the empty space in her heart. She wanted to go crazy over someone, someone like Harlan. She had gradually become used to life without Julie, but there was still something missing. She needed direction, a reason for which to live. Thoughts of her future flooded through her brain nearly every minute of every day.

Above all, she needed to get away from her parents.

She had to find a way to become independent of them. She would take the STEP test, the national English proficiency exam, in June. If she could pass that, she would be qualified to teach English to children. That was one possible avenue toward financial independence, but she doubted her ability to pass the exam. She needed to buckle down and study hard, to change her life and get out of the rut of dissolute behavior into which she had fallen.

She knew her parents were worried about her. She hated the way they watched over her. They had made it a point to spend increasingly more time with her since Julie had left. Her mother was coming over three or four times a week to cook and conduct knitting classes in the apartment. Just the other night her father had come over while she and Harlan were alone in the apartment at night. He had laid down the rules. She was not to allow any male visitors without her parents there. She remembered his exact words: "It is not the Japanese custom to visit an unmarried, young woman in her own home unless she is accompanied."

It was easy and almost natural to argue with her mother, but she had never been able to oppose her father. He seldom spoke, but when he did it was with a stony finality that carried the weight of absolute authority. She loved him greatly, but resented his control over her life.

He was the one who paid the rent and gave her an allowance every month. He was the one who had allowed her to go to Canada. He was the one who had allowed Julie to return to Japan and live with her. Yoshiko bit on her gratitude and took another drink of coffee.

She looked at her watch. She still had another hour before Harlan would get off work in Nishinomiya and she would meet him at the station. They had been getting along well recently. Their relationship had become more clandestine since Julie had left. Yoshiko could not show any affection in front of her parents when Harlan came to her apartment. That frustrated her because when she saw him she often wanted to wrap her arms around him and devour him on the spot. She thought of the day last week they had spent at Koya Pond.

It had been a sunny day. They took a bottle of whiskey with them. They spent most of the day at the park watching the birds, taking surreptitious sips from the bottle, making fun of the other people, and laughing in the warm sunshine. They returned to his apartment in the early evening and, half drunk, made wild love. It was as if they were unable to get enough of each other. She explored his body with her hands and tongue and mouth with unconscious abandon. When finished, they had lain exhausted for several hours.

She was good at pleasing her men. For that she could thank the Cocos Island owner. He was the one who had first shown her how to make a man feel good. He had taught her where the most sensitive areas were and how to stroke them lightly, teasingly, lovingly. She liked to give pleasure to men. She liked watching and feeling them respond. She liked the feeling of control. It was the one thing in her life that made her feel powerful. But the men she had made love to, including the owner, were invariably takers. They did little in the way of caring for her body. After they ejaculated, the act and her control were gone and she was always left with an empty feeling.

Harlan was different. Although he did not express it verbally, his body told her that he cared. What she loved most was the way he held her in his arms silently after he was finished. No one had ever done that before. It was a warm and secure feeling when the world seemed to be a good place, almost like when she had been four years old and fallen asleep in her father's lap. The last time with Harlan had been the best.

The owner finished serving the other customers and came over to her spot at the counter. He began washing some cups and saucers. "Another cup of coffee or are you ready to switch to whiskey?" he asked.

"No, thank you. It's time for me to go."

"Got a date?"

"You could say that."

"With your foreign boyfriend?"

"Yes."

"How are things going with him?"

"Good, I guess."

"Poor Yoshiko. Always confused. Always looking for something new. You should settle down one of these days."

"I know. I know. You sound like my father."

They laughed. The owner took her ashtray and replaced it with a clean one.

"Are you still looking for a job?" he asked.

"Sometimes. I could use the money and I need to do something to keep me busy now that Julie is gone. You know me. I get bored easily and when that happens I start drinking."

"I might be able to find something for you. I have a few friends who are looking for some part-time help. I'll ask around."

Yoshiko smiled. "Would you? I'd really appreciate it. I've got to go. Thanks."

She got up to pay, but the owner waved his hand and said, "It's on the house today."

Yoshiko tried again to pay, but the owner refused to

accept any money. Finally, they agreed she could treat him when she started working.

Yoshiko arrived at the Nishinomiya station a few minutes early and waited for Harlan near the ticket turnstiles. She wanted to talk with him, to explain about the changes she was going through. She saw him approaching. He had a happy look on his face.

He passed through the turnstile. Yoshiko took his arm and they walked together to the platform and got on the next train. He said he had received a three-month extension on his visa that morning. Yoshiko was relieved to hear it. She would not have been able to bear losing both Julie and Harlan one after the other.

They switched trains at Tsukaguchi Station to the Itami line. On the walk from Itami Station to his apartment Harlan explained his plans about quitting his job and going to work for his American friend in Mukonoso in May. When they arrived at his apartment, Yoshiko made some coffee and they sat together at the *kotatsu*.

"I'm going through a lot of changes," she said.

"What kind of changes?"

"I'm going to take the STEP test in June. If I can pass it, I want to teach English to children."

"That's great. I hope you do."

"I really need to get away from my parents. I want to make my own life. Maybe go someplace else."

"Where would you go?"

"I don't know. Maybe I can go to Nagoya. My uncle lives there. I can stay with his family until I find a place of my own. I just need some kind of change."

"I hope you find what you're looking for."

They were silent for a while, then Yoshiko asked, "Do you ever think about death?"

"I don't think about it much anymore. I used to be obsessed by it. But that didn't do me any good. There's not much we can do about it anyway. We're all going to die someday and when our time is up we have to go. Why do you ask?"

"I feel confused a lot these days. I'm always thinking about the future and the past. When I came back from Canada, I found out about three people I knew in high school who died. They were too young. It isn't fair."

"Did you know them well?"

"Pretty well. All of them were boys in some of my classes."

"What happened to them?"

"One had — I don't know how to say it in English — he had a bad sickness. One was in a car accident. And another was suicide. He was very smart, always had the best grades, you know. But his mother was what Japanese call an education mama. She was always pushing him to do better. He was very sensitive. I guess he couldn't take the pressure anymore. I'm not sure. Now no one talks to the mother. I understand about his wanting to kill himself."

"I've lost a lot of friends, too. Most of them in Vietnam. It's tough."

"I understand why he wanted to die. I was the same way before I went to Canada. I wanted to kill myself. I even tried it twice."

"You don't want to die now, do you?"

"No. I'm better now. But I still think about death a lot. I think about my grandmother. She's 89 and will probably die soon. I want her to be happy. I think about all the bad things I've done and how I hope I'm forgiven before I die. I want to live and be happy and make someone happy. I think I'm ready to change. I really want to love someone with all my heart and go crazy over him. I think I'm ready for that."

Yoshiko looked expectantly at Harlan. He turned his eyes away for a second, seemingly weighing her words, then looked back at her.

"Well," he said slowly, "I'm sure you'll find that someone someday."

There was a long silence. Then Yoshiko got up and said, "Yes, maybe someday. I better go home. My mother is probably there waiting for me. I'll see you later."

TORAWARE

Yoshiko started to walk home, then decided against it. She took a taxi to the Cocos Island coffee shop. The owner would be closing up about now and no one else would be there.

6

It was a clear May day with a refreshing breeze. Sachiko was on her way to Itami. She had stopped by Harlan's apartment, knowing he would be in Mukonoso teaching, the evening before on her way home from work. She had left a note on his door telling him she would visit today. She did not want a repeat of the last time when she had interrupted his love-making.

She had seen him only once since the night they strolled along Ashiya River and gazed at the cherry blossoms. She had been very busy with her job and her translation of his book. She had now finished 50 pages of rough draft and wanted to show him. Also, her father's apartment in Tokyo would be unoccupied the first weekend in June and she had made most of the arrangements for setting up a meeting with the Tokyo agent's secretary. She hoped Harlan would agree to go with her.

Sachiko loved this time of year when the azaleas gave color to every street and the muggy rainy season still seemed far away. The shops in Kobe and Ashiya were crowded with throngs of women in the latest fashions.

Children filled the parks and cried out with sounds of joy and laughter. Many shops and homes displayed the colorful *hina-matsuri* dolls. And, it seemed to Sachiko, everywhere lovers could be seen walking together.

She had bought a new dress and sported a new, shorter hairstyle just for this meeting. In addition to the copy of what she had translated, she carried two pairs of running trunks and a bouquet of flowers to add cheer to his apartment. The one pair of running trunks he used now was old and torn. She knew he abhorred ostentation and preferred practical things. She had settled on plain colors for the trunks.

She approached the apartment. None of his neighbors seemed to be home. She climbed the steps and knocked on his door. There was no answer. Her own note had been taken down, so he probably knew she was coming. She looked at her watch and saw that she was about 15 minutes early. The door was unlocked, so she let herself in. His room was in typical bachelor disarray: clothes scattered about and dirty dishes in the sink.

She sat down to wait at the *kotatsu*. She looked about the room and saw some Japanese novels in English translation: Osamu Dazai's *Setting Sun*, Yukio Mishima's *Thirst for Love*, Soseki Natsume's *Kokoro* and *Botchan*. She was impressed by his taste in authors and his desire to learn about Japanese literature. Sachiko had recommended Natsume to him. She wondered if the other woman had introduced him to Dazai.

Next to his futon, which was folded and placed in the near corner, lay two notebooks. A sudden temptation seized her. Inside those notebooks were recorded, no doubt, his most secret thoughts. A powerful curiosity rose within her. Had he written anything about her? About her letters to him? About his other lover? Sachiko wanted to find out. She wanted to know what he really thought about her.

She reached over to pick up the notebooks. Her hand trembled as it hovered a moment above them. Would reading them be an invasion of his privacy? Would he be angry if he knew she had looked at them? Two voices spoke to her. One said yes, go ahead, you are his agent and have a right to know what he thinks. The other said no, you will be deeply hurt by what you read.

She could not control herself. She picked up the notebooks and opened the one on top. She thumbed through it quickly, taking in random notes on Japanese grammar, *hiragana* and *katakana* practice exercises, vocabulary lists. Here and there were passages copied out of the novels he was reading. She put that notebook down, picked up the second one, and turned to the first page. It was his diary. Her heart beat quickly as she read. The first week's entries contained only descriptions of his job, apartment, and the local neighborhood. She skipped a few pages to February's entries. Her eyes froze on one word: Yoshiko.

She heard footsteps at the bottom of the stairs. She hurriedly replaced the notebooks next to the futon, picked up the Osamu Dazai novel, and was looking through it as Harlan entered the apartment.

"Hi, how are you doing?" he said with a smile. "Sorry I'm late. I was at the *sento*."

"No. I was early. I hope you don't mind. I came in because the door was open."

"That's OK. I always leave it open. Nothing here to steal. Have you read that book before?"

"Yes, when I was in high school. I think most young people like Osamu Dazai."

"I'm not so young, but I thought it was a great book."

Sachiko put the book down and stood up. She handed him the flowers and running trunks. "These are for you. I thought the flowers would be nice for your apartment. Maybe you need new running trunks, too. I hope the colors are all right."

"Thanks. That's really thoughtful of you."

Harlan went to the kitchen, found an empty beer can, filled it with water, put the flowers in it, and placed it on the *kotatsu*.

"There. How's that? They do brighten up the place, don't they? Sorry I didn't have a chance to clean up much."

"That's all right. It looks like an artist lives here."

Sachiko gave him the work she had done and explained about her translation. Harlan could not read *kanji*, but she was pleased to see how impressed he was with the amount of work she had done. She asked many questions about the following chapters and how she should approach the translation. She was especially interested in one chapter where the main character took LSD while in Vietnam.

"Have you ever taken LSD?" she asked.

"Yes, many times. I was quite the hippie several years ago."

"Was it because of Vietnam?"

"I don't know if it was just Vietnam. A lot of people in the 1960s and 70s took hallucinogens like LSD and smoked marijuana. I suppose we were looking for a different reality or a different consciousness."

"What was it like? Was it frightening?"

"Not for me. I never had a bad experience with it. It's hard to explain in words. It made me feel things I'd never felt before, think things I'd never thought before. It made all my senses more alive, more acute might be a better word. I wouldn't recommend driving or having to carry out any day-to-day responsibilities while on it. Time seemed to be distorted and music was wonderful to listen to. Some people became very paranoid and couldn't handle being around other people, but that never happened to me. In fact, one time I took LSD and played in a basketball game and had one of my best games ever."

"Is it true that you can see the world through the artist's eyes like a Bosch or Monet like you wrote in your book?"

Harlan laughed. "I borrowed that idea from Aldous Huxley, the famous scientist and writer. He experimented with hallucinogens back in the 1950s and wrote about his experiences in a couple of pieces called *Heaven and Hell* and *The Doors of Perception*. Jim Morrison's rock group The Doors supposedly took their name from that book. If you're really interested, you should read it. I think that would answer your question better than I can. Would you like some coffee?"

"Yes, please."

Harlan got up to make some coffee. Sachiko thought about his life, his adventures. He had seen many places, done many things. She wished he would take her away with him, carry her off to some faraway place where they could have an exciting life together. Maybe she would be brave enough to take LSD with him and understand his mind, see the things he saw, feel the things he felt. She wondered what sex would be like on LSD.

Harlan returned with two cups of coffee.

"Sorry I don't have any sugar. I always use honey," he said.

"That's all right. I like honey." Sachiko stirred a spoonful in her coffee, took a sip, and hesitated a moment before speaking. "Are you free the first weekend in June?"

"I think so."

"Let's go to Tokyo. The agent's secretary can meet you that weekend and we can give her the translation I've done and see what she thinks. It's a good chance. And we can stay at my father's apartment. There will be no one there and we can have the place to ourselves. I can show you many nice museums and book stores, too."

"I suppose I can go, but I don't have much money. This has to be strictly a business trip."

"Don't worry. I have money. I can buy both Shinkansen tickets."

"No. I insist on paying for my own ticket."

"Then you'll go?"

"Yes, but I have to be back on Sunday night."

"Great. I'll buy the tickets next week and call the

secretary. We can take an early morning train Saturday and return Sunday on an afternoon train. We'll have a nice time. I know you'll enjoy Tokyo. Please leave everything to me."

*   *   *

After Sachiko left, Harlan sat at his *kotatsu* for a long time drinking coffee and smoking cigarettes. He had mixed feelings about this trip to Tokyo. He had few hopes for his book and, although he had no idea if Sachiko's translation was good or bad, he doubted her work would meet with any approval. The work did seem to be good for her in the sense it gave something positive to her life, but he wondered if he were not just stringing her along.

On the surface she seemed stable enough, but he believed her superficial calm was merely a mask hiding many strange and complex emotions. Although she had not written him many letters recently, she had in her earlier letters revealed that side of herself. He worried about her romantic fantasies. He could not reciprocate. It would be unfair to continue to give her any hope for a future with him. He had told her before he did not want to enter into a love relationship with her, but perhaps he had not been clear enough. He resolved to emphasize again that theirs was to be a platonic, business relationship. He had to be gentle, but firm, in stopping this thing before it got out of control.

He thought about the many changes that had taken place in the last few weeks. Things were going well at Rick's school. Harlan was much more relaxed than he had been at UCLA. After the last class each night Rick and his wife often treated Harlan to a sumptuous supper and lively conversation. He enjoyed their companionship and the way Rick always rubbed his belly and said "To hell with the diet" when they sat down at the table. The way Rick mispronounced nearly every word over three syllables amused Harlan greatly, but he had to admire how Rick's enthusiasm, bubbly nature, good humor, and gift of applying teaching theories he could not pronounce made him a hit with the students.

Aside from Rick, there were the other two friends he had made: Ishimine and Sugiyama. Ishimine had been a student at UCLA and switched to Rick's school when Harlan started teaching there. He was a bureaucrat who worked for the Hyogo prefectural government and also lived in Itami. His hobby was talking to people overseas on his ham radio set. His English was good and he was one of the most polite men Harlan had ever met. He had invited Harlan for dinner at his home twice. His wife had prepared a feast on both occasions and his two little girls had sat shyly at a distance listening to their father and Harlan converse in English. Ishimine had visited Harlan's apartment the night before and brought a used television as a present. He had also offered to be the guarantor for Harlan's next visa application. He always gave Harlan a lot of encouragement.

Harlan had found Sugiyama's business card in his mail slot one night about three weeks before. On the back of the card Sugiyama had written a greeting in English and offered his services if Harlan wanted to open a bank account. Sugiyama worked for one of the local banks. His job was riding a motorbike around Itami every day collecting deposits from businesses and individuals while also trying to meet a monthly quota for soliciting new accounts. Two days later Harlan met him near the *sento*. They visited for a few minutes and agreed to have a beer sometime.

A few nights later Sugiyama showed up at Harlan's apartment with some beer and snacks. He had just gotten off work. They stayed up until three in the morning drinking and exchanging life stories. Sugiyama's dream was to become a professional painter. He had not used English since graduating from university two years before, but he was adept at articulating abstract ideas. He had belonged to a translation club in university. He loved John Lennon and could recite the lyrics to many of Lennon's songs.

Sugiyama had stayed over twice since that night. The dormitory he lived in was an hour-and-a-half commute from Itami and he often missed the last train when working overtime at the bank. Harlan had offered his apartment as a kind of atelier for Sugiyama. On the previous weekend, Sugiyama had brought some canvases, paints, and brushes, and spent the two days working feverishly in the three-mat room while Harlan studied Japanese in the six-mat room. He and Harlan had surveyed the painting — a colorful, surrealistic depiction of a forest seen from a distance — from different angles, commented critically, and sat down to more beer and life confessions.

Sugiyama was interested in Harlan's travels, experiences, and writing. He wanted to help Harlan adapt to life in Japan. Their conversations were a mixture of Japanese and English. Their dictionaries were becoming dog-eared. Harlan saw a lot of his earlier self in Sugiyama, in his passion for life and art.

Harlan's life had changed dramatically during his first few months in Japan. For the first time that he could recall, a sense of stability had entered his life. He had a job he enjoyed, the blessing of new friends, the stimulation of learning a foreign language, and the challenge of again adapting to life in a foreign land. He had much for which to be thankful. There were, of course, many uncertainties, particularly concerning how long he could stay in Japan and what direction his relationships with Yoshiko and Sachiko would go, but for the time being he was content.

It was late. He had run out of cigarettes. He got up, stretched his legs, and walked outside. He bought a pack of cigarettes at a nearby vending machine, gazed up at an eerie half-moon with an orange circle around it, and listened to the dull hum of dead night.

7

Harlan was disoriented as he and Yoshiko exited the Umeda movie theater. It was as if he had entered a time warp while watching "Gandhi" and now was groping to return to the reality of being in Japan again.

"I need a cigarette and a beer," he said.

They found a small, uncrowded Chinese restaurant near Hankyu Umeda Station, sat at a table for two, and ordered a large bottle of Kirin beer and two plates of *gyoza*.

"It was a great movie, don't you think?" Yoshiko said.

"Yes, I was impressed. Ben Kingsley is a great actor."

But it was not the acting he was thinking about. It was India itself and the experiences and changes in his own life associated with that country that had come rushing back to his mind over the last two and a half hours inside the theater. It was all the death and disease and horror of human existence that had nearly driven him mad over five years ago when he had slept in the streets with the lepers and prostrate death-forms. It was the feverish hallucinations of his sickness and the lying in the sticky warmth of his involuntary excretions while some unknown benefactor poured water over his head. It was the puking in a Calcutta street the morning after he had drunk himself silly with rotgut wine and passed out and woken up next to an abandoned dead baby whose skin had been parched and cracked and ants had been crawling in and out of the nose and ears and mouth.

He guzzled down the rest of the beer, ordered one more, lit another cigarette, and watched Yoshiko eat her *gyoza*. He had no appetite and pushed his plate toward her.

"Go ahead and have mine, too. I'm not really hungry."

He thought about their last time together. She had asked him if he ever thought about death. All he had been able to respond with was some nonsensical remark about there being nothing anyone could do about it. How could he possibly explain everything he had seen and thought about death? It was about the only thing he had thought about for years since his experiences in Vietnam and India. Somewhere along the line he had managed to push those thoughts and the insanity they invoked back into a corner of his mind, but they were always close to the surface and now they had come back again.

Robert W. Norris

It had started last night with the news on television of
the worst earthquake in 35 years that had rocked
northern Japan, a tremor that triggered tidal waves and
killed over 100 people, 45 of them school children
swept away to sea from a beach near Akita. The
dramatic music, the scenes of everything moving, the
cars wrapped around boulders, the boats beached on
high ground, the collapsed buildings, the gaping cracks
in the roads and ground had all triggered his apocalyptic
visions and given him nightmares. And now the scenes
of India in the movie had given him more flashbacks
and he felt again in the deepest recesses of his soul the
utter helplessness of man and the vanity of his life.

At the root of his despair was the unanswerable *why*
of it all. He had grappled with that one for way too long.
The death he witnessed in Vietnam had started all the
questioning, but at least there had been some tangible
reason for all that misery. War. A war he had known
was wrong, but war nonetheless. As his wandering took
him in later years to other parts of the world, he
somehow managed to rationalize the poverty and
sickness and cruelty and inhumanity. That is, until he
found himself in India, in Calcutta. As much as he
wracked his poisoned brain there, there was no
discernible or valid reason for the deplorable human
condition he witnessed. That had jolted him beyond his

limits.

Yoshiko had finished eating and was staring at him. "Are you OK? You look lost in another world."

"It's nothing. I was just remembering when I was in India. Movies always seem to take me back to one place or another. Sorry. Let's get out of here, OK?"

It was dark when they got back to Itami. A light was on in Yoshiko's apartment. Her mother was probably there waiting for her. Yoshiko did not want to go inside just yet. She had stopped attending mass after Julie returned to Canada and no doubt her mother would bring up the subject again.

"Let's go over to the park for a while," she said.

They sat in the swings and rocked back and forth silently. Harlan intrigued her with the way he was comfortable in passing time together and not always having to talk. Sometimes she liked that, sometimes not. There were many things she wanted to ask him, to tell him, to confess to him. It was almost impossible to figure out what he was thinking, like earlier today when he had blanked her out completely and immersed himself in his own private world. He rarely initiated conversation with her. She usually did most of the talking.

Today was the first day they had seen each other since she had met him at the Nishinomiya train station and later tried to explain her readiness to make a commitment. His refusal to acknowledge her feelings had hurt her and she reacted by returning to her old ways. Then he called her two days ago and hearing his voice was enough to forgive everything, to blame herself for not getting through to him, to feel ashamed of her own behavior.

When he asked her what she had been doing since the last time, she felt an urge to say, "Well, I've slept with the Cocos owner and two other men since I saw you and you rejected my feelings. One of them I can't even remember because I was drunk in a bar and he picked me up and I woke up in a strange place with a bad hangover."

Instead she said, "Oh, nothing much. How are you?" and he laughed softly and asked her to a movie. Now here they were and she was feeling good. In fact, she was feeling grateful at this moment, not least of all for his nonjudgmental attitude toward her. She had many mixed feelings about him, but the one thing she appreciated most was that he never made her feel guilty about her behavior. He seemed to accept her for who she was without placing her under any obligation. The others always expected sex from her, which she gave too willingly when she had been drinking. With Harlan she could be both sober and comfortable. She felt no shame about her past, about her molestation. With him it was her choice if they slept together or not, but sometimes she wished he would take the lead.

She stopped swinging and turned to him. "I feel very happy right now."

"I'm glad you do."

"I think I'm learning about patience and about accepting myself."

"How's that?"

She told him again about her time in Canada, especially the first year when she could only smile at everyone while they were treating her like a child and then returning to the convent every night and drinking whiskey and crying herself to sleep. She told again about the importance of her friendship with Julie and what Julie had taught her about honesty and God and being independent.

"You know, sometimes I just want to say thank you to something, to someone, to God when I feel this happy."

Harlan smiled at her. "I think I know what you mean."

They sat motionless in the swings, looking at the moon.

"So, you'll be going to Tokyo with Sachiko next week," Yoshiko said.

"Yes, just for a couple of days."

"What will you do?"

"She's set up a meeting with this agent's secretary. I don't expect anything to come from it, but there's no harm in going. I guess we'll check out some book stores and museums, too. Nothing exciting really. I've never seen Tokyo before, so I'm kind of looking forward to it."

"Where will you stay?"

"Her father has an apartment somewhere near the agent's office. He won't be using it, so we'll stay there."

"Are you going to sleep with her?"

"No. That would ruin everything, the whole business relationship."

Yoshiko believed him. If she had asked the same question to any other man she knew, she would have assumed immediately the answer was a lie. From Harlan, however, it had to be the truth. Despite his taciturnity and unresponsiveness, he had an air of honesty about him that she admired.

"I better go back home. Thanks for the date. I had a nice time. See you again sometime soon."

Harlan lingered for a few minutes after Yoshiko disappeared, then headed home himself. He had many things to write in his diary.

Yoshiko's mother looked up from her knitting as Yoshiko entered from the back door. "Where did you go tonight, dear?"

"To a movie with Harlan."

"Did you have a nice time?"

"Yes. I'm a little tired, though. I think I'll just take a bath and go to bed."

"The bath's ready. There's some fish and salad in the refrigerator if you're hungry." Yoshiko's mother went back to knitting.

Yoshiko immersed herself in the tub, feeling relaxed and thinking about the day. There had been something sad about him today, something the movie had stirred in him. She wished he would forget about India. Whatever had happened there was too private, too deep for her to penetrate. She wanted him to think more about the future. She was glad she had asked him about his trip to Tokyo with Sachiko. She liked the answer he had given. He had not kissed her good-bye, but he had communicated something very important to her tonight.

* * *

It was a heavy, muggy day, neither stormy nor clear, typical of the weather that came before the June rains. Sachiko and Harlan were on the Shinkansen seated next to each other as the train headed toward Tokyo. Harlan was reading an English newspaper. Sachiko was watching the monotonous array of rice fields and factories speed by outside the window.

A tumult of emotions raced within her breast as she tried to consider what course of action would be the most appropriate after they arrived. She was stirred to a happy tremulousness thinking that at last she had him all alone to herself for the next two days. Her impatience and imagination painted the coming night together as something of unlimited joy.

The announcement over the loudspeaker that the train was approaching Tokyo snapped Sachiko out of her self-absorption. They took the subway to the station nearest her father's apartment, then walked the rest of the way. The apartment was small, but clean — two rooms, a kitchen, a toilet, and a bath. They set their bags on the floor. Harlan noticed there was only one bed.

The appointment with the agent's secretary was not until two o'clock. They still had two hours to kill. They decided to eat lunch in a cheap restaurant and do some window-shopping. They arrived at the agent's office at the appointed time. The secretary served them iced coffee and some sweets.

The secretary spoke English well and was friendly, but she restated what she had told Sachiko before about the agent not handling manuscripts anymore as it was more profitable to work with actors and models than with writers. She had read Harlan's manuscript and thought he was better off sending it to an American publisher. She accepted Sachiko's translation and said if she came across anyone who might be interested she would pass it on. They talked about different American and Japanese writers for an hour, then the secretary said she had to get ready for another appointment. She wished Harlan good luck with his life in Japan, apologized for the absence of the agent, and gave him her business card.

Harlan had not expected anything different from the treatment they received, so he was not disappointed. It was still hot and muggy outside on the streets and they stopped at a small shop, drank two beers, and talked about the secretary and how nice she had been in taking time out of her busy schedule to see them.

"Is there any place you want to see now?" Sachiko asked as they finished their beers. "We can take a walk around the government buildings."

"To tell the truth, I'm really not so interested in sight-seeing, especially in this weather. If you know of any used book stores around here, I'd rather go to a place like that. It's the one thing I miss about the States. I haven't been able to find any good used book stores in Osaka or Kobe."

"There's one a couple of blocks from here I can take you to. After that, let me treat you to dinner. There's a nice little Italian restaurant not far from my father's apartment."

"That sounds fine, but I can't let you pay. We'll go 50-50."

They spent over an hour at the book store. Harlan seemed to retreat into his own world as he browsed through the rows of titles on the dusty shelves. Sachiko pretended to look for books, too. She mainly watched him intently out of the corner of her eye. When she was with him, he often disappeared into that private area where no one could reach him. She understood his need for those impenetrable walls, but it caused a deep loneliness in her. She did not want him to retreat from her now, not after all the plans she had made. Finally, he decided on two hardbound novels he said he had been looking for for a long time.

At dinner he was quiet. Sachiko did her best to keep up a patter of conversation, but every avenue she explored met with a dead end. He did ask her how her job was going, but seemed bored with her descriptions of her coworkers. He spent a lot of time gazing around the restaurant at the other diners. She made a few attempts at cryptic humor, but he did not laugh at her jokes. He drank an entire bottle of wine by himself. She wondered if she had done something to make him angry.

On the way back to the apartment, he stopped in a liquor store and bought some cans of beer. He said, "This weather makes me thirsty."

At the apartment Harlan excused himself and said he wanted to read. Sachiko tried to read a magazine she had bought, but she could not focus her attention on it. Her eyes kept returning to his direction. He took no notice.

Midnight came and she grew tired. Sachiko had told herself to be bold and yet here they were again at a distance. Why was he ignoring her? Had he not told her that one night he liked her? Was she destined always to be alone? She could not accept that. She went to the bathroom, brushed her teeth, changed into her pajamas, then got into bed.

"Aren't you tired?" she asked in a pleading voice.

Harlan put his book down, got up, took a blanket and pillow from the closet, and lay down on the floor.

"I think I'll just go to sleep here," he said.

A hard lump came to Sachiko's throat and, with a sense of helpless urgency, she found herself begging, "Won't you please come to my bed. I want to sleep with you."

Harlan switched off the light, said good night, and closed his eyes. Several times during the night, he woke to the sounds of soft, muffled sobbing.

On the train back to Osaka the next day they spoke
few words to each other.

8

Harlan was into his third lap on the running path surrounding Koya Pond. He was thinking about how lucky he was, about how well things were going for him. Last weekend he had flown to Korea and been granted a six-month culture visa from the Japanese consulate. Rick's idea about putting Nishimoto's name on the school's books as a Japanese teacher and Harlan's as a student had worked. The next time he could apply within Japan for an extension of the same visa.

The school now had about 100 students and Rick had hired another teacher. Harlan enjoyed his classes and the many students he was teaching. There was one student in particular with whom he had become friendly. Inoue was a 44-year-old copy writer whose literary ambitions had been thwarted by the necessity of providing a steady income for his wife and two daughters. He was stocky and animated, and gave the appearance of a Japanese bohemian with his neatly-trimmed beard and corduroy trousers. His English ability was minimal, but on the occasions he had invited Harlan out for a drink he had shown an ability to communicate effectively with basic verbs and nouns. He spoke Japanese very slowly for Harlan's benefit and somehow they managed to understand each other through a mixture of the two languages.

Inoue had encouraged Harlan to read the work of Ango Sakaguchi, a contemporary of Osamu Dazai. Inoue thought Sakaguchi was one of the greatest writers Japan had produced. He lamented Sakaguchi's work being unheard of by the outside world. Harlan had been able to find only one Sakaguchi story translated into English: *The Idiot*. It was the story of a writer who was forced during World War II to produce propagandistic copy for the government and who survived the Tokyo fire bombings with a mentally retarded woman. The woman was the "idiot" from the title and a symbol of man's insanity. Harlan had been so fascinated by the story and Sakaguchi's style that he was hungry for more. That one story came as close to describing his own feelings about what he had undergone in Vietnam and India as anything he had read.

He had talked a lot about Inoue and Sakaguchi with Yoshiko, who had also discovered Sakaguchi when she was in Canada. She seemed eager to meet Inoue sometime. She had surprised Harlan by saying that he should also invite Sachiko and make a party of it. Harlan had told Yoshiko about the weekend in Tokyo and she had expressed sympathy for Sachiko's feelings. Harlan had not had any contact with Sachiko since that time and he was feeling a little guilty about not having been gentler with her. He would arrange for all of them to go out sometime soon.

He finished the lap, sprinted past the fire station and city hall, and arrived back at his apartment. The rice field across the street glimmered in the afternoon sun. Sweat was pouring off him. He was thirsty. He grabbed a few coins off the *kotatsu* and headed to the liquor shop on the narrow street that ran past the *sento*. He stopped in front of the liquor shop, put the coins in the vending machine, and pushed the button for a 500-milliliter can of beer.

A burst of laughter came from inside the liquor shop. Harlan peered around the vending machine. Seven men — all seemingly in their thirties and forties — dressed in softball uniforms were seated on empty beer crates, drinking, joking, and obviously taking an interest in Harlan. He recognized one of them as a regular customer at the *sento*. Suddenly, all of them got up, came outside, and surrounded him. He could not understand much of what they were saying.

One of the men, whose name was Hashimoto, thrust a softball and a glove into Harlan's hands. Harlan stared back, unsure of what to do. Hashimoto made some exaggerated motions of throwing and catching a ball.

"Kyatchi booru yaroo. An'ta to bokura."

The others laughed heartily. Harlan put on the glove and tossed the ball to Hashimoto. They began to play catch. Hashimoto moved back a few paces until he was about 20 meters away. Harlan began to cut loose with some strong throws and heard exclamations of approval from the onlookers. A smile spread across his face. He had not played any ball since his high school days, but the simplicity of the ritual that had been such a big part of his youth had not lost any of its thrill. Hashimoto threw Harlan some ground balls, which he fielded smoothly and fired back as if to nip a speedy runner by half a step. Now there were fly balls to catch. Harlan settled under them, caught the ball one-handed, and fired strikes back to Hashimoto, who applied the tag to an imaginary, sliding runner trying to score. One of the other players signaled the runner out or safe.

The players motioned Harlan inside. They poured him a beer. The group drank, joked, clapped one another's backs, and carried on a lively conversation with much gesturing and single-word exchanges.

"Namae?"

"Harlan."

"Kuni?"

"America."

"*Shigoto?*"

"English teacher."

"*Kanojo?*"

"No, no girlfriend."

"*Toshi?*"

"I'm 33."

"*Yakyuu ga suki?*"

"Yes, I like baseball."

From the scraps of conversation Harlan could understand, he learned the team was comprised of local players who had played together for 12 years. In their younger days they had captured several local fast-pitch softball championships. They were now playing at a lower level of competition, but were still near the top of their league. Although most of the teams in the local leagues were made up of members from a single company, the members of their team, the Sasa Club, worked at a variety of jobs. Some worked at Itami City Hall, some at the fire station, some at the nearby hat factory, and the remainder seemed to have their own businesses. The team sponsor was the liquor shop. No foreigner had ever played in the leagues, but they needed a first baseman. Hashimoto, who was a bureaucrat at the city hall, was sure he could pull the necessary strings with the town officials to allow Harlan into the league. Today had been their final league game, but there would be a practice game next Sunday. The new league would not start until the fall.

The party lasted into the night. Harlan was given a team uniform and an autographed softball. Everyone shook his hand firmly when he finally departed. A pleasant buzz hummed through his head as he stumbled home.

The following Sunday Harlan arose early. He had been too excited to sleep well. He drank a cup of coffee, put on his uniform, and began applying some oil to the glove he had bought the day after meeting the team. It was starting to loosen up and take shape from the numerous coats of oil he had applied and from the three-hour practice he had taken part in with the team yesterday.

He felt good about finally making a connection with the people in his neighborhood. He had been too isolated his first few months to try to make many friends. He had been unable to express himself beyond a few basic pleasantries. Until he had met the Sasa Club members, it had seemed most of the Japanese he met — aside from the students at Rick's school, Sugiyama, Inoue, Yoshiko, and Sachiko — were always waiting for him to take the first step toward a relationship. He wondered how he would perform today, if he would live up to his billing as the first foreigner to play in the Itami leagues, if he would be accepted as just another player or looked down upon by the other teams and the fans. He had read more than one story about foreign professional baseball players who had not been able to cope with Japan.

He heard a car horn. It was Ikeda, the 41-year-old, power-hitting left fielder. Ikeda had been the first to greet him at the team practice. He had taken Harlan under his wing and made sure Harlan understood where to be and what to do during the practice. Afterward, the two had gone out to a *yakitori* shop for some beer and grilled chicken. Ikeda's manner and speech were gentle and full of cheer and encouragement.

Most of the other players were already warming up when Ikeda and Harlan arrived at the park. Everyone greeted Harlan with smiles and shouts. Harlan warmed up with Hashimoto on the sidelines before taking some batting practice. The players on the other team watched him take his swings. Most were smiling, but Harlan noticed a couple of them mimicking his swing and laughing. Players' wives and children and assorted spectators gathered on the sidelines and began spreading out box lunches and thermoses of tea.

Sasa Club took the field. Harlan tossed grounders to the infielders. It was wonderful to hear the chatter of the players and fans, to watch the pitcher take his warm-up throws, to feel the summer sun on the back of his neck, the pop of the ball meeting his glove, the dust on his hands, and the competitive jitters churning once again in his stomach.

The umpires signaled for the game to start. Sasa's pitcher went into his motion and fired a fast ball. The umpire pivoted to his right, shot out his right arm, and bellowed, "*Sutoraiku!*" On the next pitch the batter bounced a slow roller to the shortstop, who scooped it up and side-armed a perfect throw to Harlan at first. Harlan threw the ball to the catcher, Hashimoto, as he had been told to do on an out at first base, and revelled in the satisfaction of a well-executed play. The next two batters flied out to Ikeda in left field.

Harlan batted seventh in the order. The game was still scoreless when he came up to bat in the bottom of the second inning with one out and a man on first base. He entered the batter's box and tapped the head of the bat on the rubber plate. Harlan took the first three pitches, then stepped out of the batter's box and asked the umpire for the count.

"*Tsuu wan,*" the umpire said, showing Harlan one finger with his left hand and two fingers with his right hand.

Harlan thought that was strange. If the count was two balls and one strike, the umpire should have indicated two fingers with his left hand and one finger with his right hand. Everything seemed reversed in Japan.

The pitcher delivered the next pitch on the inside corner. Harlan swung, but did not make contact. The catcher threw the ball to the third baseman. The ball continued around the infield. Harlan stepped out of the batter's box again, bent over to grab some dirt, wiped his hands on his uniform, adjusted his cap, and stepped back in the box. The first baseman tossed the ball to the pitcher, who turned around to face the plate. A look of astonishment crossed his face when he saw Harlan still in the batter's box. A suspended moment of confusion ensued. The catcher and umpire looked toward the Sasa Club bench, gesturing frantically.

Ikeda jogged toward the plate, grabbed Harlan's arm, and pulled him to the sidelines.

"What're you doing? I've got one more strike."

"*Haaran-san. Auto datta.*"

"What do you mean out? The umpire told me two balls and one strike. That was only the second strike."

"*Chigau. Tsuu sutoraiku wan booru datta yo.*"

Harlan realized his mistake. Strikes were given in the count before balls, not the other way around as in American baseball. He suddenly felt deeply embarrassed. He turned to the umpire and players in the field, shouted, "*Gomen nasai!*" and bowed deeply. The umpire laughed, tipped his cap, and signaled for the next batter, who grounded out to second base.

After three innings the score was tied 1-1. Ikeda had blasted a long home run to right field for Sasa Club's lone run. In the top of the fourth the other team put its first two runners on base with a single and a walk. Harlan had seen enough Japanese baseball on television to know the next batter would bunt. He moved ahead three paces and kept his weight forward on his toes, ready to charge the ball if it came his way. The batter laid down a hard bunt that bounced into Harlan's glove. He whirled and unleashed a powerful throw to cut down the lead runner at third. The instant the ball left his hand he knew it was into orbit. He watched in disbelief as the ball sailed above the third baseman's outstretched glove, continued in a straight line before falling to the ground some 15 meters beyond, and finally came to a halt in a distant ditch. By the time Ikeda had retrieved the ball, all three runners had rounded the bases and stood at home plate, waving at Harlan and shouting, "*Gaijin-san ookini!*"

Harlan's face flushed. Nothing was going right. The whole world was staring at him. Hashimoto was having a heated discussion with the home plate umpire, who eventually signaled the batter back to second base and the runner ahead of him back to third base. The rule was only one extra base on an overthrow. The score was now 2-1.

The next batter attempted a suicide squeeze bunt toward first base. Harlan again charged the plate and caught the ball on one bounce. The runner on third was streaking toward home. Harlan's momentum propelled him forward. There was no time for a throw. He dove toward the plate, his gloved hand outstretched, and tagged the sliding runner.

"*Auto!*" the umpire cried.

A loud cheer erupted from the Sasa Club bench. Harlan jumped up, making sure the other runner would not try to score. He tossed the ball back to the pitcher, dusted himself off, and returned to his position. The next batter lofted a fly ball to center field. The runner on third scored easily. The last batter struck out.

The score remained 3-1 throughout the fifth and sixth innings. Harlan led off the bottom of the seventh inning with a line drive single to left field, but was left stranded as the next three batters flied out. Sasa Club had lost the game. Several of the other team's players came up to Harlan to shake his hand and say, "*Naisu geemu.*"

The Sasa Club players gathered together at the liquor shop. They were discussing the game amid more joking and laughter. Morita, the owner of the shop who had retired from playing but still attended the games, poured

Harlan a beer.

"*Yoku ganbatta. Naisu battingu, Haaran-san.*"

"I played terribly. It was my fault we lost the game. I'm really sorry. I'll do better next time."

Morita, Ikeda, Hashimoto, and the others would not accept his apology. They kept talking about his base hit and play at home plate on the suicide squeeze attempt. They told him not to worry about the throw. It was just a practice game and they would have much time for more practice before the league started again in the fall. Harlan felt among friends, a regular team member. There was much he wanted to tell them about his life, much he wanted to learn about them. He would have to renew his study efforts.

Later Ikeda and Harlan went to the *sento*. The hot water dissolved all his stiffness and the tension of the day. Ikeda was talking to the other bathers about the game. They shot approving glances at Harlan. As they left, Ikeda patted Harlan gently on the shoulder.

"*Otsukare-sama. Kondo mo ganbaroo.*"

Harlan walked home. It had been an exhausting day. He folded his uniform and placed it in the closet. He put his glove on top of the uniform, paused for a moment, put the glove back on his left hand, pounded the pocket a few times with his right fist, then replaced it on the uniform. He could not wait for the next game.

9

S achiko got off the train at Mukonoso Station and checked her watch. She was early for her appointment with Harlan, so she stopped in a coffee shop near his school and ordered an iced coffee.

Harlan had called her two nights before and asked if she would like to go out with him, one of his students, and Yoshiko. After the weekend in Tokyo, she thought she would never hear from him again. She had not been able to believe that Harlan wanted to introduce her to Yoshiko. The possibility of the three of them meeting together in the same place had not occurred to her before.

Sachiko's hand trembled a bit as she poured some cream into her coffee. She wondered how Yoshiko would appraise her, if they would cast daggers at each other with their eyes. She would try to remain calm. They might even become friends. She needed a friend now that Yumi had gotten married so hastily and moved back to the States with Terry. She wanted to talk with Yoshiko about Harlan.

Sachiko finished her coffee. It was time to meet

Harlan at the school. He would be finishing his last lesson about now. She walked hurriedly to the school, climbed the flight of steps, paused at the door to catch her breath and compose herself, then entered. The secretary asked Sachiko to sit down.

Harlan was smiling as he emerged from the classroom. He introduced Sachiko to Inoue as the other students filed out the door. Inoue looked similar to what Sachiko had imagined: bright eyes, intelligent face, a neatly-trimmed goatee, and wearing a corduroy jacket with patches on the elbows. Harlan did not mention anything about Tokyo.

"Shall we go over to the coffee shop?" Harlan said. "Yoshiko should be there by now."

Yoshiko was seated at the counter talking to the owner when Harlan, Inoue, and Sachiko entered. She stood up to greet them and introductions were made. Sachiko and Yoshiko were face to face for the first time.

"It's nice to meet you. Harlan has told me many nice things about you," Yoshiko said. There was no trace of vindictiveness or sarcasm in her voice. "Let's sit at the table by the window."

Harlan sat between Sachiko and Inoue, and across from Yoshiko. They ordered American beer and pizza. Inoue apologized for not being able to speak much English. He and Yoshiko began speaking in Japanese.

Sachiko interpreted for Harlan.

Inoue and Yoshiko were talking about Sakaguchi's books. Yoshiko said she had discovered Sakaguchi when she lived in Canada. She liked his rebellious nature and urgent search for meaning in the midst of Japan's collapse, but she was sometimes put off by his condescending style. She preferred Osamu Dazai, who also wrote about the same themes as Sakaguchi but with a humble, self-effacing humor and a more human touch.

Inoue said he understood her opinion and that in his youth he had also preferred Dazai, but age had changed him and he now saw Sakaguchi as the more mature literary figure. He thought Dazai's appeal was limited to younger people, whereas Sakaguchi's work had to be digested and appreciated over time. Sakaguchi's criticism of authority and social values was more universal. He lamented that Sakaguchi's work was unknown outside of Japan. His hope was that someone like Harlan would one day be able to introduce Sakaguchi to the outside world.

As they continued to drink, the conversation turned to philosophical and religious matters. Yoshiko was getting slightly drunk. She insisted on the need for mankind to have a faith in God in order to live a meaningful life. Harlan expressed the opinion that Yoshiko was being naive. He criticized Japan and the western world's rampant consumerism. He explained how his experiences in India had drained him of whatever spiritual beliefs he might once have had and that he would like nothing better than to transport all the people of the United States and Japan to India for a few days, dribble their heads like basketballs in the squalor and misery, and see if they could retain their faith in a benevolent creator.

Sachiko was noncommittal, preferring to act instead as Harlan's interpreter. It had been a long time since she had been in the middle of such a rapid-fire, intellectual debate. It excited her greatly, but she lacked Yoshiko's confidence in arguing a point. She found herself admiring Yoshiko's grit. She wished she could express herself in the same way. For now, however, she was content to serve as the English voice of both Inoue, who seemed to be taking great delight in exploring the debate from both the spiritual and secular sides, and Yoshiko.

Three hours passed. The owner told them he had to close the shop. Harlan and Inoue decided to go to another bar. Yoshiko invited Sachiko to spend the night at her place in Itami. Sachiko readily accepted. Later, at the second bar, Inoue tried to explain to Harlan his impression of Yoshiko, but Harlan could not understand Inoue's Japanese. Finally, Inoue took out his dictionary, looked up a word, pointed to it, and said, "Yoshiko is this."

The word was "nihilist."

* * *

Yoshiko and Sachiko had finished taking a bath and were seated at the kitchen table. Yoshiko poured them both a glass of whiskey and water, then lit a cigarette. She offered Sachiko one. Sachiko took it. She had never smoked before and felt a childish pleasure in her new boldness.

"Did you have a good time tonight?" Yoshiko asked.

"Yes, it was very exciting for me. I haven't been in the middle of that kind of discussion in a long time. I really admire the way you express yourself. I wish I could be that way. I'm always so passive and keep my opinions to myself."

"You shouldn't wish that. It's probably better to be quiet. That way you don't get in trouble. It seems I'm always fighting something or someone."

"But I agree with everything you said. It was as if I was watching myself speaking the words that I don't have the courage to speak. It was very exciting. I think you might be a kind of alter ego for me."

"I don't know about that, but it was a stimulating conversation. I enjoyed talking with Mr. Inoue. It was an intellectual challenge. To tell the truth, that was the first time I've heard Harlan express a strong opinion. Most of the time he's so difficult to engage in a debate of any kind. Sometimes I wonder if he has any opinions at all."

"I know what you mean. He doesn't talk about himself very much."

"He can be very exasperating at times. I never know what he's thinking."

Sachiko took a puff, blew a long stream of smoke into the air, and tapped her ashes in the ashtray the way she had seen Yoshiko do. "Have you read his book?" she asked.

"No. I'm not sure I want to know what he's written. I would prefer to hear what he's thinking about and feeling now. The present is more real to me than the past."

"He writes very passionately. He must have deep feelings to write that way. When I was reading his book, I could sense that he's really deep down a caring and sensitive man."

"I wish he would show those feelings in real life."

"I know exactly what you mean. I think he saves all his passion for his writing. He must exhaust it all when he writes and doesn't have any feeling left over for his personal life. He's like an observer all the time."

"You're right about that."

"He's taken LSD before, you know."

"Yes, and that's one thing that scares me about him. I don't need any drugs to see demons. I need whiskey to drive them away." Yoshiko poured them both another drink.

"Do you really see demons in your dreams?" Sachiko asked.

"Sometimes."

"I do, too."

They stayed up until early in the morning talking about many things. They talked about their experiences overseas, their families, unrequited love, their favorite writers. Sachiko believed she had found a new friend to take the place of Yumi. It was hard to believe she was becoming close to her rival. If she could not have Harlan to herself, it was not a bad option to share him with Yoshiko. She went to bed with a smile on her face.

* * *

Yoshiko lay in bed listening to the sound of Sachiko's breathing. Yoshiko was still wide awake and thinking. She had enjoyed visiting with Sachiko. She had been curious about what kind of woman Sachiko was. Now they had met and strangely she did not feel any jealousy or animosity. There was an odd attraction that she did not fully understand. Perhaps it had something to do with recognizing that Sachiko, too, was another lost, searching soul.

Yoshiko had explained many things about herself, but she had stopped short of any full confessions about her most private secrets. She could not tell anyone that the demons she saw were not in her dreams but in her waking consciousness, particularly at the moment before sexual climax with Harlan or any of her other lovers. The demons always appeared at that moment and prevented her from going beyond it. She could not admit that she had never achieved orgasm with any man.

She knew why the demons appeared. It was her punishment. She had sinned. Terribly. If she had had the baby, it would have been three years old now. Perhaps the Cocos Island owner would have divorced his wife and married Yoshiko if she had had the baby. But that was speculation. Even if they had married, she had still sinned and in the eyes of God had to be punished.

The demons had frightened her in the beginning, but she had learned to accept them. By now they had become almost familiar. Yoshiko knew every detail of their horrible faces. Always they appeared at that precise moment. They lingered and made her feel guilty. Most of them were old people, ugly, dripping with some putrid liquid. They never spoke. They just stared in a mocking manner. She would hear the sharp crackle of fire and see many dramatic things, as if in an apocalyptic painting that has come alive. There was always one without a face, a baby, her baby, stretching its puny, little arms out toward her and making muffled, pleading sounds. Whenever the baby appeared, Yoshiko would lose her concentration, open her eyes, and look into the face of an uncomprehending lover.

She got out of bed slowly so as not to wake Sachiko. She crept down the stairs and into the kitchen. She poured herself another glass of whiskey and sat for a long time in the still darkness.

*   *   *

A few nights later Yoshiko went to Harlan's apartment. He was watching a baseball game on television. He turned the game off and got a beer from the portable refrigerator he had found recently in a garbage pile down the street and hauled home. He opened the beer and poured two glasses, then sat down with Yoshiko at the *kotatsu*. Her face was a little flushed from drinking.

"Where did you and Inoue go the other night?" Yoshiko asked.

"To a snack bar near Mukonoso Station. He said he enjoyed visiting with you. He said he thought you were a nihilist."

Yoshiko laughed. "Maybe he's right."

"So how did you and Sachiko get along?"

"We got along fine. I was very surprised. I think the timing was right. I couldn't have done it before, not while Julie was still here. I probably would have hated Sachiko. There's something about her, though, that I like. She's not like the others. We talked a lot about you."

"Oh?"

"Yes. We both agreed you're a puzzle."

"A puzzle?"

"You put all your emotions on paper, but you never tell anyone what you think. Do you ever think?"

"Of course I think."

"When do you think? The other night was the first time I heard you actually express a strong opinion. All you want is for everyone to go to India! I never know what you're really thinking. I never know if you're serious or not. You don't give a shit about anyone but yourself, do you?"

"I suppose you're right. I've gotten too used to being alone for most of my life."

"Oh, forget it."

Yoshiko took off her clothes and got into Harlan's futon. She made love with an aggressiveness she had not shown before. There was a desperation about it that excited Harlan. Afterward, she got up, lit a cigarette, sat on the window sill, and stared out at the August night. Harlan watched her from the futon, enraptured by her naked figure. She was like a little succubus who would come at night to enchant him, then leave him alone after he fell asleep.

Yoshiko crushed her cigarette in the ashtray and turned to look at Harlan. "You know, you can't love others unless you love yourself."

Harlan wondered if she was talking about herself or about him. He said nothing. Yoshiko returned to the futon and snuggled against him. An hour later, she got up and dressed.

"I have to go now."

"Thanks for coming over."

"Will you go anywhere during *Obon*?"

"No. I get about a week off, but I think I'll just stay here and do some writing and studying. Sugiyama might come by, so we'll just hang out. How about you?"

"I'll be with my family all week. I probably won't see you for a while."

"That's OK. I'll see you when I see you."

"Bye."

Yoshiko leaned over, kissed him, and was gone.

* * *

For the next three weeks Harlan kept himself busy with his writing and studies. The August heat was suffocating. Sometimes, when seated at his *kotatsu* in the nude with an electric fan cooling his sweaty body, he would break away from his *hiragana* and *katakana* lettering practice to smoke a cigarette and stare out his window at the wide, pellucid sky. An occasional plane would float across this canvas. He would watch the shadows grow in the glare of the sun on the colored, tiled roofs, listen to the sound of carpenters hammering and sawing at a far-off apartment building, and think of his youth and watching his father, a logger and excellent carpenter, work.

That had been the happiest time for him. His had been an idyllic childhood, growing up on the outskirts of a small logging town on the northern coast of California. It had been the perfect world, but all the sanctity and security of that world came crashing about his family the day his father was killed in a logging accident.

Harlan remembered the day his mother gathered him and his brother Danny together to tell them what had happened. He was ten years old and Danny twelve. Their mother's head was hung low, her arms limp at her sides. Her eyes were red and puffed, her face pale. Her lips quivered as she spoke the words that would shatter their lives: "Your father is dead." Then she wept shamelessly, her head held in her right hand and her body shaking in spasms of grief.

The news of his mother's death came years later when he was in Vietnam. The words in the letter said that cancer had claimed her body, but Harlan knew that was not true. She had died of a broken heart. Danny? He joined the Marines after high school and Harlan had not seen him since.

10

The sweltering heat of August passed into September. The insistent scream of cicadas faded, then disappeared. The days were still warm, but the nights grew increasingly cooler. By the end of September, the rice fields had turned yellow-green. The colors of autumn were sharp and vivid. There were several quick evening showers that left the streets and tiled roofs of houses glittering in the fading light. A violent typhoon swept through the Japanese archipelago and many areas were flooded. In mid-October the rice fields were harvested. In the early evening dusk the long poles on which the rice plants were hung to dry looked like rows of straw soldiers standing at attention.

* * *

Sachiko had now been working at the foreign trading company in Osaka for over half a year. Her life had changed greatly in that time, yet much remained the same. She and Yumi had gone their separate ways. She did not think she had lost Yumi's friendship. That could not be taken away. Their paths had simply intertwined for a period of time before again forking off in different directions.

Her brother Hiroshi was now in the United States studying engineering. Sachiko envied him his courage in rejecting their father's desire that he take over the family construction business. There was an emptiness in the house with Hiroshi gone. Sachiko rarely spoke with her parents. Even when she was home she spent most of her time in her room reading, writing in her diary, or listening to music. She had not done any translation on Harlan's book for two months. There had been no letters or calls from the agent in Tokyo and the project seemed futile anymore.

Her relationships with her fellow office workers were distant. Everyone got along well enough during office hours, but Sachiko did not like socializing with them after work. She did not like to take part in their petty gossip. She preferred to keep her private life to herself.

Sachiko's time with the company was limited. Working for a large company did not suit her. Working as a career woman did. Something connected with the arts would be best. Perhaps she could one day manage an art gallery or a boutique. She wanted to use her creative instincts, not have them stifled in a place that treated its workers as automatons, its women as adorn- ments useful for only a few years until the age they should get married.

She had begun researching information about study programs in the United States. If her brother could study there, so could she. She had taken the TOEFL test in June and scored 520. She needed a score of at least 550 to enter a master's program, but she was close enough to know she could achieve the required score if she prepared hard enough for the next test.

She had not seen Harlan since the night with Inoue and Yoshiko. She had waited for another call from him, but it had not come. She was still writing him an occasional letter, but she could not bring herself to confess her deeper feelings the way she had in the beginning. Thinking about all the things she had written him embarrassed her. She had never exposed her private self to any man the way she had to Harlan.

If there was anything promising that had happened to her this year, it was the unexpected friendship with Yoshiko. Since the night she had stayed at Yoshiko's they had gone out for coffee together once or twice a week. Sachiko had never dreamed of meeting someone who understood her so well. There was no pretentiousness to Yoshiko and she seemed sincerely interested in Sachiko's thoughts and feelings and problems. Yumi had been a bit too critical of Sachiko's behavior at times and there had always been an unspoken rivalry between them, particularly concerning men. Yoshiko was unabashed when talking about men. She had a wide range of experiences and spoke honestly about them. She, too, had suffered a lot of guilt, but had a deep faith in her religious beliefs and thought there was something meaningful about every experience. She was a good listener and frequently offered practical advice. Yoshiko was the one who had encouraged Sachiko to continue her studies.

Sachiko was astounded at first when Yoshiko showed no signs of jealousy about Harlan. She had expected Yoshiko to be possessive and guarded. Instead, Yoshiko was open about her own feelings, her own frustrations, her own hopes and fears about her relationship with him. Sachiko felt so close to Yoshiko that she had shown Yoshiko her diary. Yoshiko reciprocated by showing parts of her diary, too. They had giggled when they found similar entries concerning Harlan.

Yumi had never opened herself up as honestly to Sachiko. Yumi had described her sexual experiences in detail, but had rarely mentioned her feelings about them. It was as if Yumi had wanted to brag about her experiences and criticize Sachiko's lack of experience. Sachiko had always felt excited when listening to Yumi's descriptions, but she had also felt inadequate and lonely. With Yoshiko there was a warmth and understanding that encouraged Sachiko to trust and believe in herself. For the first time in a long time she was beginning to like herself a little.

*   *   *

Yoshiko had spent the *Obon* holiday with her family. It was her favorite time of year because there always seemed to be harmony in the family. Whatever present problems existed disappeared as everyone paid homage to their ancestors and all conversation revolved around good memories and stories of people from the past. There was much laughter and good food. The local *Obon* festival was especially enjoyable. Yoshiko loved to join the children in their colorful summer *yukata* robes and lose herself in the traditional dancing.

Of all the people she met again every year during *Obon*, Yoshiko loved her mother's mother best. Obaa-chan was a delight to be around. She was 89 years old, losing her eyesight and hearing, and becoming senile, but she emitted an aura that had the light of life in it. Every year at *Obon* Yoshiko would spend hours at a time with Obaa-chan, listening to her stories about life 70 and 80 years ago, asking her dozens of questions about what it was like when she was Yoshiko's age, giggling like a school girl when Obaa-chan talked about her love affairs before she finally married Yoshiko's grandfather. Yoshiko would massage Obaa-chan's neck, shoulders, and feet and wonder about the aging process and how it seemed to bring about a youthfulness of the mind. When she was with Obaa-chan, she felt a particular return to a time-lost innocence. She always lost this feeling during the rest of the year.

Obaa-chan had been staying with Yoshiko's aunt and uncle in Nagoya for the past two years. They had grown weary of the responsibility of taking care of her and brought up the subject of shifting the responsibility to others in the family. Yoshiko's parents' place was too small. Yoshiko offered to have Obaa-chan come live with her. Julie had returned to Canada and Yoshiko was still searching for some part-time work, so the timing was right. Besides, Yoshiko was a little lonely living by herself. The company would be nice to have. She would not mind taking care of Obaa-chan. When Yoshiko was away from home, her mother could stop by and make sure everything was all right. Everyone agreed it was a good idea. Obaa-chan would move in with Yoshiko around the beginning of November.

Winter was not far away. Always in the past the biggest changes in Yoshiko's life had occurred in the winter. She wondered what would come this year. Whatever it was would probably change her life forever. She felt a little anxiety about this premonition, but at least Obaa-chan would be there to provide the humor and wisdom Yoshiko needed to survive the change.

* * *

The coming of September brought the beginning of the autumn softball league. Harlan performed well, even hit a game-winning home run in a practice game. He was spending a lot of time at the Morita liquor shop. Morita, as well as the players and their families, made Harlan feel welcome and a part of things. He appreciated this a lot.

Morita was a small man with a sharp wit that kept everyone in stitches. Although he had retired from playing, he was still the team organizer and decision-maker who had the final word in all the plans and activities of the team. His shop was small — only a few customers could stand and drink together at the same time — but it was usually filled with regular customers. There was a friendly atmosphere to the place. Harlan felt he could learn a lot about Japan from hanging out at Morita's. It was also a good place to practice his Japanese.

Morita had introduced Harlan to many customers and friends. Harlan was, in many cases, the first foreigner they had met face to face. He was often besieged with questions about the United States, his family, his life, his impressions of Japan, the differences between Japan and the outside world, and why he had come to Japan. His Japanese was too limited to explain much, but this did not seem to matter. He was Morita's friend and that seemed to be enough. Morita took it upon himself to be the person responsible for Harlan's well-being. Morita had the ability to intuit what Harlan wanted to communicate. He would act as Harlan's interpreter, despite knowing no more than a few words of English, to the barrage of questions that were invariably invoked by Harlan's presence at the shop. Sometimes Morita took Harlan on delivery runs around the city and introduced him to shops where he would be treated well. Morita's wife and two children adopted Harlan as one of their own.

One of the highlights of the summer for Harlan was the Saturday night in late July when the team had an informal party at a wealthy patron's home in the hills above Itami City. With its magnificent woodwork, spacious, matted rooms, and large, neatly-manicured garden, it was the most beautiful home Harlan had been in in Japan. In the main room five tables — complete with bundles of sukiyaki pans and ingredients, plates of sashimi, and lots of beer — had been set. The team members and other guests changed into *yukata* and Harlan was introduced around. They then went into the main room, where an introductory speech was given by the patron. After the speech, the beer and food flowed. Harlan made the rounds from table to table. There was much laughing and toasting of drinks. After dinner there were more speeches. Harlan stumbled through his own speech in drunken and broken Japanese. At the end of the evening, he was chosen to lead the team in a banzai yell and accidently knocked over several beer bottles with his outstretched arms. No one seemed to mind. They laughed uproariously. Later he returned with Morita to Morita's shop for more drinks and food. That night he felt for the first time fully accepted as a member of the community.

He had seen little of Yoshiko during August and none of Sachiko. In September he and Yoshiko saw each other two or three times a week. One day they took a train to Hirakata near Kyoto to see the life-sized chrysanthemum dolls that depicted famous scenes and characters from the Kansai area's past. Sometimes they went to Osaka to see a move, and again a strange vicariousness that transported him back to the past would consume him.

Near the end of September the worst typhoon Harlan had ever experienced drenched the area. The streets in the neighborhood flooded over. The rain and wind continued for two days. He was forced to stay in his apartment and listen to what sounded like the end of the world. The following days were magnificent. There was a stillness and clarity that contrasted sharply with the violence of the storm.

He was still running four or five times a week and felt in good shape. Rick's school was growing at a fast pace and another teacher had been hired. Overall, things were going well for him. The only thing he was plagued by was not knowing how long he would be able to stay in Japan, as well as whether or not he wanted to settle into the life of a permanent expatriate. This made it difficult to determine how to deal with his relationships with Yoshiko and Sachiko.

He decided to focus his attention on a new writing project. He had followed the Japanese baseball season in detail and thought he could write an interesting magazine article about foreign baseball players in Japan.

He spent a month working on the article. He poured over English newspaper stories from the past season. He read a book called *The Chrysanthemum and the Bat* that detailed the history of baseball in Japan with a focus on the foreign players who had helped shape it. He filled a notebook with information from various sources. He watched an hour-long baseball news program on television every night, copying quotes from foreign players and picking up a lot of new Japanese vocabulary

Robert W. Norris

in the process. By the time the Pacific League Seibu
Lions climaxed a dramatic Japan Series championship
with a 3-2 win over the Central League Tokyo Giants in
the seventh game, he had put together a 20-page story. It
was the first piece of work he had done in a long time
about which he could confidently say he had done a
good job. He sent off a copy of the story to a sports
magazine he hoped would publish it.

11

Yoshiko and Harlan were lying together in his futon. The kerosene heater he had found in the garbage pile down the street cast dancing shadows about the room. Nights were definitely colder lately. Winter was approaching.

"You know something?" Yoshiko said.

"What?"

"It's been over 13 months since I came back to Japan."

"Is that right?"

"Yes. September 23rd was the day Julie and I came back from Canada. That date is very important to me."

"In what way?"

"It's like a birthday. I think I'm a different person now, a new person. When I first came back, I hated everything about Japan. I criticized everything and everyone, even my family and friends."

"And now?"

"Now I think I'm more accepting and more patient. I didn't think I could live without Julie, but now I can.

127

I've learned to think about other people more and consider their wants and needs. I'm not so selfish anymore. I want to help people and give more of myself. I have many new dreams."

"That's good."

"Don't you have any dreams?" Yoshiko asked.

"In a sense, I'm living my dream right now. I've always wanted to live, work, and study in a foreign country. That's what I'm doing."

"And what about the future? Don't you have any dreams for the future?"

"I don't know about the future. I just try to live each day as it comes. As far as Japan is concerned, I want to become better at Japanese. I'd also like to finish writing another book. It's hard to say because I don't know how long I can stay in Japan. There's no guarantee about getting a new visa every six months."

Yoshiko looked at Harlan for a long time. She was feeling especially good tonight. She had not drunk too much before coming to his apartment, just enough to make her feel warm and talkative. Harlan's taciturnity did not bother her at this moment. Instead, it captivated her. Because he demanded nothing from her, she wanted to give him everything.

"I love you, Harlan."

For a moment Harlan was not sure he had heard her

correctly. He looked at Yoshiko. The features on her face and body were heightened in the glow from the heater. It seemed to him that for the first time he was able to appreciate her strange beauty fully. He thought he could spend hours lying there and gazing at her perfect, immutable face. Then words that seemed horrible even as they were forming themselves escaped from his mouth. It was as if they had an existence of their own and could not be stopped.

"You'll probably never hear me speak those words." A sharp pain of remorse gripped Harlan the instant he spoke.

Yoshiko looked at him uncomprehendingly. His eyes had a sudden, vacant gaze and shone in the dim light. She started to say something, paused, then thought better of it. She rose, went to the toilet, relieved herself, and washed her hands at the kitchen sink. She returned to the six-mat room and began dressing. Harlan was staring out the window at the faint glow cast by the neon lights of Route 171 on a horizon of darkness.

"I should be going," she said. "Obaa-chan is moving in with me tomorrow and I need to clean the apartment. I probably won't be able to leave her alone at night, so if you want to see me you'll have to visit my place."

"OK. I will."

After Yoshiko left, Harlan lay in his futon staring at the ceiling. He wondered if he would ever learn to say the right thing at the right time.

* * *

Harlan was busy throughout November. He went to the immigration department in Osaka to apply for formal permission to work while on a culture visa. He hated having to rationalize his existence to a faceless bureaucracy. There was always too much paperwork to fill out. If only one frivolous form was forgotten or filled out improperly, he was made to feel like a boy who has been caught lying or cheating. He especially hated having to sweat through the period of waiting for an answer.

The softball season came to a close. He had done well, batting around .300 and handling nearly all his chances in the outfield or at first base. After his disastrous debut when he had thrown the ball away on that important play at third base that had let in the winning run, Harlan had settled down and was once again experiencing the joy of playing catch on the sidelines, digging his cleats into the batter's box, running the bases, catching a long fly ball to the outfield, and bantering with his teammates at the after-game drinking sessions at Morita's.

He was also spending a lot of time at Rick's in the evenings after work. The school had grown rapidly and now had nearly 200 students. There was much planning to be done and Rick had rented another large apartment and converted it into more classrooms. There were now four full-time teachers, but another one was needed and Rick was relying heavily on Harlan to take up some of the slack for the rest of the year. It would be easier to find someone after the winter holiday. Rick also planned to have a big Christmas party for the students. Harlan had volunteered to help with the cooking and preparation.

He usually got home too late to stop by Yoshiko's place. He would light the heater, sit at his *kotatsu*, and study Japanese until his eyes became heavy. As the days became colder he began sleeping until noon, preferring to skip running and stay beneath the warm cover of his futon. His classes usually started at two or three o'clock. He felt immensely relieved when he received a letter of permission to work from the immigration department.

During this time Harlan rediscovered the work of Henry Miller. He had been fascinated years before by Miller's writing, but perhaps he had been too young to appreciate it fully. After the last time with Yoshiko, Harlan had experienced a tendency to fall into a remorseful depression sometimes late at night. Reading

Robert W. Norris

Henry Miller kept that tendency at bay. Miller excited him about life. Whenever he picked up Miller's books, everything was finished for the remainder of the day. His apartment remained like a hermit's dwelling, his laundry sat unwashed for another day, and the letters he intended to write were put on hold. The only thing that mattered was the joy of the moment, the flow of Miller's intoxicating language.

Harlan often copied favorite passages in his notebooks. When he did fall into a melancholy mood, he would reread those passages to snap himself out of it. The best of the passages was from Miller's *The Cosmological Eye:*

Just as a piece of matter detaches itself from the sun to live as a wholly new creation, so I have come to feel about my detachment from America. Once the separation is made a new orbit is established, and there is no turning back. For me the sun had ceased to exist; I had myself become a blazing sun. And like all the other suns of the universe I had to nourish myself from within.

* * *

The party at Rick's school was a big success. Over 250 people attended. The day before the party Rick, his wife, several students, the other teachers, and Harlan

132

had spent all day cooking and setting up everything. The night after the party Harlan stopped by Yoshiko's place. Yoshiko had taken a trip with her family in early December to Shikoku to attend a special mass for Japanese Christians. Harlan noticed a new serenity about her. She seemed to take a special delight in caring for Obaa-chan.

Obaa-chan's silver hair was coming out in patches. She had lost most of the use of her legs. Yoshiko said Obaa-chan would crawl on all fours to the toilet seven or eight times a night. She was also going blind, but there was a calmness and brightness about her that reminded Harlan of some of the cripples he had seen in India. They had carried themselves with great dignity and an acceptance of their fate.

Obaa-chan took Harlan's hand and motioned for him to sit down with her at the *kotatsu*. She lapsed into a patter of language Harlan could not understand. Yoshiko interpreted for him. Obaa-chan was telling a story from her youth. At regular intervals she broke into an infectious giggle that had all three of them laughing.

Yoshiko later gave Obaa-chan a moxa treatment for her arthritic hands. Obaa-chan asked Harlan if he wanted to try the moxa treatment. He hesitated, but Obaa-chan insisted. Yoshiko prepared the moxa ball, put it on a spot at the base of Harlan's right thumb, and used a stick of incense to start the ball burning. There was a sharp sting when the ball burned into his flesh. Obaa-chan burst out with a sardonic giggle. At length, she fell into a deep sleep.

Yoshiko made some coffee and talked about the happiness she felt with Obaa-chan. Yoshiko's life was now one of simplicity: bathe with Obaa-chan in the mornings, listen to her stories all day, drink tea together, give her moxa treatments in the evenings, and pray to God and the Buddha with her before going to bed.

They did not talk about what Harlan had said the last time together. He was grateful for that. He was not good at apologies, but he wanted somehow to make it up to her. He also felt the need to show some kindness to Sachiko. He knew both Yoshiko and Sachiko would appreciate books as Christmas presents. The next day he went to a book store in Umeda. He decided on a Bible written in simple English for Yoshiko. For Sachiko he bought Anais Nin's *Winter of Artifice* and Aldous Huxley's *The Doors of Perception/Heaven and Hell*. Sachiko had often talked about Henry Miller and Anais Nin's relationship and had shown much interest in Harlan's stories about taking LSD.

On Christmas Eve Harlan stopped at Yoshiko's with her present. Her mother was seated at the *kotatsu* knitting a sweater. Obaa-chan was sleeping. When

Yoshiko read the card, which Harlan had signed "Love, Harlan," her eyes glistened. She kissed him on the cheek. Her mother cast them a disapproving glance.

* * *

Sachiko hung up the private phone in her bedroom. Yoshiko had just called to invite her to a small party and spend the night. Sachiko was free and had accepted the invitation. Harlan and one of his friends would also be going to the party.

Things were going well. She had taken the winter TOEFL test and, although she would not find out the results until January, she thought she had done better than before and would probably score over 550. Today, December 30th, was her sixth day off in a row. Her company's winter holiday would last until January 8th. It was one of the few benefits of working for a foreign trading company. Most Japanese companies did not recognize Christmas as an official holiday. They usually gave their employees less than a week off for the New Year's holiday. She had been tired of late and appreciated the extra time.

A few days earlier Harlan had called and she had gone to lunch with him. She had not expected a Christmas present from him. His choice of books told her he had thought deeply concerning what she would like. She loved the sensuousness of Anais Nin's writing and often read herself into the Nin character of the diaries. She had not yet read *Winter of Artifice*, but she liked the title. The Huxley book might give her an insight into Harlan's mind and LSD experiences.

Harlan's giving of the books was an important gesture to her. He never seemed to notice that she was desperate for even a simple smile from him. There was rarely a smile on his face when they were alone, only when there were other people and music and conversation. He had smiled when he gave her the present. She could not believe that he had ever meant to be cruel to her. She decided she would continue her translation for him.

Sachiko wrote for an hour in her diary, then spent much of the afternoon reading. She packed a change of clothes and her make-up, stopped at two shops to buy some flowers and melons to give to Yoshiko, and took the train to Itami. She arrived at Yoshiko's at six o'clock. Harlan and Sugiyama would come about eight.

Yoshiko put the flowers in a vase on the kitchen table and the melons in the refrigerator. She asked Sachiko which she preferred, coffee or whiskey. Sachiko said coffee. She was a weak drinker and anything more than two drinks made her giddy. She would have her two drinks later. Yoshiko poured herself a glass of whiskey and water. The two sat at the table and lit cigarettes.

"How have you been?" Sachiko asked.

"Better than in a long time now that Obaa-chan has moved in with me."

"Where is she now?"

"She's at my parents' apartment. I'll be going over there tomorrow and will spend three or four days with them over New Year's. How about you?"

"I'll be with my parents, too. It's a little sad and lonely this year because my brother is in America and won't be home for the holiday. I suppose we'll eat *osechi* and watch TV and maybe visit a shrine for the year's first prayer. It'll be a quiet time. I can do what I want for a while because I don't have to go back to work until January 8th."

"That's nice. You should use the time to rest. How about the TOEFL test? How do you think you did on it?"

"I don't know yet, but I think I did well enough to score over 550."

"That's wonderful. I really hope you did. It would open up many chances for you."

They continued visiting. Yoshiko told about her going to Shikoku for the special mass and how she had gained new spiritual nourishment. She told about taking care of Obaa-chan, about how Obaa-chan had a calming influence with her humorous stories, her practical advice, her own faith in and prayers to the Buddha. She said it was much easier to be with Obaa-chan, who never criticized, than with her mother, who always found fault with Yoshiko's behavior. Sachiko envied Yoshiko her relationship with Obaa-chan. Sachiko's grandparents had died several years before.

Harlan and Sugiyama arrived shortly after eight. They brought beer and whiskey and some snacks to eat. They were already a little drunk. All of them hungrily devoured the curried rice Yoshiko had prepared and the melons Sachiko had brought.

They drank and talked about various things. There was much laughter. Yoshiko and Sugiyama seemed especially friendly with each other, but Sachiko could not detect any jealousy from Harlan. He was in high spirits and kept pouring them all more drinks. He and Sugiyama were to visit Sugiyama's hometown of Kasumi, a small fishing village on the Japan Sea, the next day. This was Harlan's first New Year in Japan and Sugiyama wanted to introduce him to some of the Japanese traditions of the season.

Everyone became excited when they looked outside and saw a heavy snow falling. It was the first snowfall of the winter. After watching the snow fall for a while, Yoshiko and Sachiko decided to go to bed. Harlan and Sugiyama would sleep downstairs under the *kotatsu*.

Yoshiko and Sachiko would sleep upstairs in Yoshiko's bedroom. Sachiko could use the bed in which Julie used to sleep.

Harlan and Sugiyama continued to drink downstairs. Sugiyama finally laid his head back. He said his head was spinning and he was going to sleep. Harlan could not get comfortable stretched out under the *kotatsu*. He had a sudden desire to get into bed with Yoshiko. It was the inappropriate thing to do with Sachiko in the same room, but a devilish temptation to demonstrate to Sachiko that their relationship was still platonic and that his sexual favors belonged to Yoshiko alone came over him. He would not go so far as to take off his clothes and make love to Yoshiko. He would merely get into her bed with his clothes on. His muddled brain told him there was nothing wrong in this.

Sachiko could not sleep, either. She had not drunk as much as the others and her thoughts were still clear. She listened to the rush of wind outside and pulled her covers tighter around her. Her heart suddenly froze when she heard the sound of footsteps on the stairway. She kept still when she saw Harlan's figure enter the bedroom and get into bed with Yoshiko.

Yoshiko stirred when she felt Harlan put his arm around her. "Harlan," she whispered. "What're you doing? Are you crazy?"

"It's cold downstairs and I wanted to sleep with you."

"You should go back downstairs."

"It's OK. I just want to lie together for a while."

Sachiko's throat tightened. She got up and tip-toed down the stairs to the kitchen. The only warm place to lie down was beside Sugiyama, who seemed to be asleep with his legs under the *kotatsu*. She lay down beside him and tried to get comfortable. She was near tears. Suddenly, she felt a hand on her breast.

* * *

The scream from downstairs catapulted Harlan and Yoshiko out of bed. Harlan glanced over at Sachiko's bed, saw she was not there, and knew immediately what had happened. They rushed downstairs. Yoshiko switched on the kitchen light. Sachiko was sitting straight up, her head in her hands, and sobbing uncontrollably. Sugiyama was on his hands and knees, bowing and groveling and apologizing repeatedly like a man pleading for leniency before a judge who has sentenced him to death.

"I'm sorry. I'm sorry. I have no excuse. I didn't mean anything," he repeated over and over in Japanese.

Yoshiko turned to Harlan. Her look was as piercing as a newly sharpened blade. "God damn you, Harlan! God damn you to hell! You two get out of here."

Harlan had never seen her this angry. He tapped Sugiyama, who was still on his hands and knees, forehead touching the floor in a profound display of self-reproach, and said, "Come on, let's go."

They dressed hurriedly. Harlan looked back as they exited through the back door. Yoshiko was holding Sachiko and brushing the tears from Sachiko's eyes. Sachiko's body was shaking in spasmodic convulsions. He caught a sidelong glance from Yoshiko that pierced him to the bone.

It was freezing outside. He and Sugiyama tramped quickly through the new snow to Harlan's apartment. They warmed themselves by the kerosene heater.

"What exactly did you do back there?" Harlan asked.

"I don't know. I woke up and you were gone and Sachiko was lying next to me. I thought perhaps she was interested in making love. I reached over and touched her breast and she screamed. I'm sorry, Harlan. I'm really sorry."

"Forget it. It was my fault. I shouldn't have gone upstairs and gotten into bed with Yoshiko. It was a stupid, idiotic thing to do. I don't know what I was thinking. I guess I just forgot how sensitive Sachiko is."

"I shouldn't have touched her."

"There's nothing we can do about it now. Let's forget it. Who can understand women anyway? When you think they want you, they don't. When you think they don't want you, they do."

"Do you think they will forgive us?"

"I doubt it."

"What should we do?"

"I don't know. Let's go to sleep. We have a train to catch tomorrow."

They both had hangovers when they woke the next morning. A brilliant blanket of white lay on the streets and fields as they left the apartment to head toward the train station.

12

I t was snowing when the train pulled into the Kasumi
station. Sugiyama's father was waiting for them. He
smiled and bowed deeply as Sugiyama introduced
Harlan. Then he led them to his car, an old Toyota. The
drive to the house took only a few minutes.

The house was located on a narrow side street. It was
flanked by other houses of a dark hue. They entered the
two-storey structure, which had been built by
Sugiyama's grandfather 50 years before, took off their
shoes, and were led into the main room. Sugiyama's
mother greeted them with a deep bow and motioned for
them to sit at the *hori-gotatsu*, a table set over an open
hole in the floor where they could warm their feet by a
coal footwarmer. They visited, ate sushi, and drank beer
until near midnight. Then they got up to walk to the
Kasumi shrine.

They walked through dark streets toward the highest
hill overlooking the village. The faint sounds of a New
Year's Eve temple bell reached their ears with a soft
resonance. They entered a larger street alongside the
railroad tracks. From out of the various streets came

groups of people in twos and threes, some carrying umbrellas, some hooded. The entire village seemed to converge as they approached the hill. The streets were now more lighted and they saw more clearly the people shuffling through the snow. They passed through the Shinto shrine gate, guarded on both sides by stone dogs, and began their ascent of the stone steps. Japanese cedar covered the hill. A steady stream of villagers, laughing and chattering, was going up and down the steps. The main shrine was at the top. On their left were three smaller wooden shrines. They paused at each one, rang a bell, threw some money in the offertory boxes, clapped their hands twice to call forth the gods, and said a silent prayer. This was *hatsumode*, the first prayer of the new year.

They descended the steps, passed again through the gate, and walked past the village graveyard — where fresh offerings of fruit, incense, and flowers were placed on the various headstones — until they reached the village Buddhist temple. They took off their shoes, entered the temple, lit sticks of incense, and again performed *hatsumode*. Outside they stopped in front of the huge temple bell. A line of people was gathered, each person waiting to strike the bell once until it had been rung 108 times.

"Why 108 times and not another number?" Harlan

asked.

"That's the traditional number signifying man's evil desires. The bell is rung to ask the gods to cast away those desires." Sugiyama said.

"Do you suppose we'll be exonerated for last night if we ring the bell?"

"I don't know, but we can try."

After striking the bell, they returned through the dark streets. The sounds of the bell grew fainter as they passed Sugiyama's father's garden, which had an assortment of vegetables to be sold in Tottori, about 50 kilometers to the west. Back at the house they drank some celebratory sake, warmed themselves at the *hori-gotatsu*, took a bath, and went to bed. Sugiyama and Harlan slept upstairs on comfortable futons. There were no sounds of traffic, only the stillness of the night.

They were called to breakfast the next morning, New Year's Day, at eight o'clock. Sugiyama's mother served *osechi-ryoori*, the traditional food prepared for the holiday. Sugiyama explained that all the various foods had a symbolic meaning. The herring roe symbolized having many children, the burdock good fortune, the black beans diligence, the sea bream celebration, and the chestnuts victory. They were also treated to a fish broth soup with pounded rice cakes in it. Before beginning the meal, they toasted one another with a cup of sake and exchanged New Year's greetings again.

After the meal, they entered the room where the family ancestors were worshipped. In one corner of the room was a shelf on which was placed a miniature Shinto shrine made of cypress. Inside the shrine were small tablets with *kanji* lettering on them. Hung above the shrine was a rope of rice straw. Pendant paper cuttings, fern leaves, a glossy green leaf, and a *mikan* orange were attached to the rope. Harlan had seen the same kind of decorated rope above the doorways of homes and businesses everywhere he had gone the previous few days. Set before the shelf were two earthenware jars. A cup of sake, a small candle, and some offerings of flowers, pine sprigs, and ferns were placed inside the jars.

In a separate alcove was the family Buddhist altar. Inside the altar were offerings of flowers, boiled rice, incense, and five ancestral tablets made of a richly-lacquered black wood. Throughout the morning friends and relatives dropped by to greet Sugiyama's family. Each greeting was done the same way: a deep bow performed on the knees, palms flat on the floor facing inward, and the forehead touching the floor while exchanging the words of greeting.

Sugiyama and Harlan took the noon train to Kinosaki, a small tourist village 25 kilometers east of Kasumi and built at the foot of a gorge cut by the Maruyama River, which emptied into a large bay. Harlan had many questions for Sugiyama about Shintoism, Buddhism, and family worship.

Sugiyama patiently explained the symbolism of everything Harlan had seen. The paper cuttings on the rice straw rope represented offerings of white cloth that had been made to the gods in ancient times. The fern leaves were symbols of the hope for posterity. Many Japanese prayed their families would increase and multiply in the same way as fern leaves branched and rebranched. The *mikan* oranges were called *dai-dai*, which stemmed from the Chinese words meaning "from generation to generation," so the fruit, too, had become a food of good omen. The glossy green leaf was called *yuzuri-ha*. The verb *yuzuru* meant "to yield in favor of another," the noun *ha* meant "leaf." The leaf came from a tree off of which none of the old leaves ever fell before a new one, growing behind it, had almost fully developed. The leaf symbolized the hope that the father in the family would not die before his son had become a grown man able to succeed as head of the family.

They walked along the Maruyama River with other Japanese tourists dressed in kimonos and wooden clogs. They took a tram to the top of the highest hill overlooking Kinosaki. The boats in the bay looked like white streaks on a placid, blue canvas. They could see resting on a lower hill Kinosaki's largest temple, its roof covered with a thick layer of snow. They took the tram back into the village and visited a museum where hanging scrolls, paintings, and folding screens with etchings by famous Japanese writers, artists, and poets were displayed. They later went to a hot springs bath.

That evening Sugiyama's mother served crab and vegetables cooked in a large pot. Sugiyama's cousins joined them for dinner. There was much laughter and animated conversation. Near midnight Sugiyama and Harlan took a walk along the Kasumi waterfront. A strong wind chilled their faces. The boats, most of which were streaked with rust, were moored in their dockings. Cables and ropes creaked loudly as the boats rocked up and down. Waves thundered and crashed beyond the breakwater. Everything was dark except for the dim lights in the harbor. They could barely discern the black outline of the mountains in the near distance. Sugiyama talked about the severity of the fisherman's life, the harsh winters, the lives lost at sea every year.

They passed by a concrete seawall. Along the seawall were great lengths of rope coiled into a long line of circles. Sugiyama pointed out a *kanji* character written on the bows of nearly all the boats.

"See that character," he said. "It is *maru*. *Maru* means 'circle.' It is a special character to me. I believe that life is a series of interrelated circles. Like the tides and the seasons, we always return to where we began. Birth. Life. Death. A complete revolution. I know I will return someday to the sea, to my birthplace, to complete my circle of life. These ropes make me think of my life and my father's life and my grandfather's life, even my future son's life."

They returned to the house. Sugiyama showed Harlan some of the paintings he had done as a child and teenager.

"When I was a boy, I had a bad heart. Everyone thought I would die. I began painting and gave many of my paintings to my friends and family because I wanted them to remember me."

There were many circles in the paintings: moons, suns, oranges, faces.

The next morning they ate a sweet, red-bean soup with rice cakes. Later Sugiyama borrowed his father's car and they drove on a winding road that rose at times into wooded hills, then descended to a rugged coastline. They went through grey fishing hamlets perched beside stony, emerald-green bays. They passed many channels and gorges where houses were nestled tightly together, their black, slate roofs gleaming in the sun. They passed stretches of flat ground where barren rice fields were covered in a pristine white. Above the fields forests of pine, cedar, and bamboo climbed the flanks of snowy mountains. An occasional hawk hovered over the landscape.

They returned in the afternoon for their final meal. Near dusk they bid good-bye to Sugiyama's family. They boarded the train, their arms filled with gifts of fruit, fish, and seaweed. The word *maru* was on Harlan's lips as he fell asleep to the clattering rhythm of the train tracks. He dreamed of playing catch with his father and Danny in their Jacoby Creek backyard.

* * *

The following day Harlan took a train to Takarazuka to visit Inoue, who had invited Harlan to spend the day with his family. Inoue was dressed in a man's kimono and wooden clogs when he met Harlan at the station. He led Harlan back to his house and introduced him to his wife and two teenage daughters.

Inoue proudly showed Harlan his collection of Ango Sakaguchi's works. Most were original prints in leather binding. The wife and daughters cooked and served a large feast of sukiyaki and poured cup after cup of hot sake for Inoue and Harlan. They were not shy about asking questions. Harlan was surprised at how much

Japanese he was beginning to understand and how much more smoothly he was beginning to express himself. It was as if all the passive vocabulary and grammatical structures he had crammed into his head were suddenly becoming active in a mysterious process of the brain. Perhaps it had something to do with the sake and feeling relaxed and comfortable around people who were sincerely interested in what he was trying to say. He felt no nervousness or need to worry about mistakes with people like Inoue, Sugiyama, and the softball team.

After all the dinner dishes had been cleared away, Inoue brought out brushes, charcoal ink, and some large sheets of rice paper so they could do what he called *hatsugaki*, the first calligraphy of the new year. Inoue said he liked to write a poem every year that reflected his hopes for the coming year. He still had all the *hatsugaki* he had written over the last 25 years. He handed some paper to Harlan after showing how to put the ink on the brushes. Harlan wrote the *hiragana* lettering of the Japanese word for "congratulations." He gave it to Inoue's wife as a present. Inoue wrote the *kanji* for "do your best in your writing" and gave it to Harlan. Everyone was pleased.

Inoue walked Harlan back to the Takarazuka station. Harlan thanked him many times for the wonderful day. As he returned to Itami, Harlan reflected on the friendships he had made in the past year. He often heard other foreigners complain that the Japanese were inhospitable and never invited foreigners to their homes. He had found the opposite in his own experience. In the last few days he had experienced a warmth, kindness, and closeness with Japanese families that laid those stereotypes to waste. He felt fortunate to have met the people he had. It was almost as if he were a newborn child of Japan and these strangers had, in the course of a single year, adopted him and taken it upon themselves to raise him as their own.

He thought suddenly of Danny, the remaining member of his American family. He could not picture him exactly. It had, after all, been 16 or 17 years since Danny had gone off into the world. Only a hazy image and a youthful voice came to mind. Harlan had a feeling Danny was out there somewhere, had somehow forged a life of his own. Even as a child he had been skilled with his hands and had always been building things. Maybe he had a wife and children. There was no way to be certain. Harlan said a silent prayer, his personal *hatsumode*, for Danny, hoping that he, too, might be experiencing the same kind of happiness that Harlan felt at this moment.

13

Sachiko opened her eyes. For a moment the unfamiliar surroundings confused her. Then she remembered. She was in Yoshiko's bedroom. She looked at the clock. It was 10:30 in the morning. Her head felt heavy and her eyes burned.

She heard Yoshiko downstairs in the kitchen. She got out of bed slowly, wishing this were her own room where she had her own toilet and would not have to face the embarrassment of confronting someone in front of whom she had made a spectacle of herself the night before. She put on her dress and sweater, quietly descended the stairs, and spent 15 minutes in the toilet washing and putting on her make-up.

She brightened a little when she saw coffee, salad, and toast on the kitchen table.

"Are you hungry?" Yoshiko asked.

"A little."

"Please sit down."

"Thank you."

The two ate in silence. When they finished, Yoshiko cleared the table and washed the dishes. Sachiko offered to help, but Yoshiko said she could do it herself. When Yoshiko finished, she sat down again at the table, poured them both another cup of coffee, and lit a cigarette.

"Cigarette?" Yoshiko held out the pack to Sachiko.

"No thank you." Sachiko watched Yoshiko take a puff, then said, "Yoshiko, I'm really sorry about last night."

"Forget it. Nothing serious happened. We were all a little drunk. If anyone is to blame, it's Harlan for being so insensitive."

"No, it was my fault. I acted badly. I never seem to do the right thing around men. My imagination controls me too much."

"What do you mean?"

"I've never told anyone about this before, not even Yumi, but when I'm with men I often get transported back to earlier experiences, bad experiences. You don't think I'm crazy, do you?"

Yoshiko regarded Sachiko for a moment. "I don't think you're crazy, but I'm not sure what you mean by getting transported."

"Do you think I could have a cigarette? Maybe I do need one."

Yoshiko took a cigarette out of her pack, handed it to Sachiko, and lit it for her.

154

"The thing is that I'm not sure which is the real experience, the one at the moment or the one in my head," Sachiko said. "Last night when Harlan came upstairs and got into your bed I was suddenly in Mexico. I swear I could smell the smells and hear the sounds of that horrible night in Jose's farmhouse when he made love to his wife while I was sleeping beside them. It was just horrible, Yoshiko, with the pigs grunting outside and the two of them grunting beside me.

"Then when Sugiyama touched my breast, it brought back all the fear and horror of the time two years ago when I went to a movie in Osaka. A yakuza threatened me. It was a small incident, but again I lost control. He was sitting behind me. He touched me. I hit him and ran. He chased me. Finally, some people coaxed him away. Even now when I see gangster types on the streets a paranoia consumes me. I become nauseated, weak, and afraid. I was afraid last night."

Yoshiko made no reply. Sachiko crushed her cigarette in the ashtray and got up.

"I really should go. I'm sorry I caused you trouble. Thank you for everything."

"I think you should go home and just rest today. It's the last day of the year, so maybe all the bad things will go away and you can start the new year with a fresh mind."

The two said an uncomfortable good-bye and Sachiko disappeared out of the back door.

* * *

It was the coldest January Yoshiko could remember. It had snowed a lot, strong winds had blown, and everywhere people seemed worn and ragged and ready to bicker. There was no snow today, but a transparent mist hung over the world like a vast umbrella. Yoshiko stared at a row of birds perched silently on a telephone wire outside the kitchen window.

After the New Year's holiday with her family there had been rapid changes in her life. The Cocos Island owner found her a job as a dental assistant for one of his friends in Mukonoso. She now worked weekdays and had weekends off. Her mother looked after Obaa-chan while Yoshiko was away. The work itself was boring: filling out paperwork, handing the dentist his tools, sticking a suction pipe in patients' mouths, and cleaning up. She would rather be doing something else, but, because she felt obligated to the Cocos Island owner for finding the job, she could not quit.

She had been drinking a lot and was tired. Obaa-chan was usually asleep by seven. The apartment would become deathly quiet. Yoshiko would drink and stare mindlessly at the TV for a couple hours, grow bored, turn the TV off, and try to study English. She could not concentrate and her thoughts would return to Canada and Joe. She would bring out all his letters, reread them, and try to envision his face.

Every time she thought of Joe, Harlan's image would also appear. The thing Harlan lacked was what Joe had and she longed for most: a spirituality that went beyond physical love. Every time after she had sex with Harlan he would disappear into that secret world of his. She would feel shut out. He had intrigued her for a long time, but lately she had grown weary of trying to penetrate his armor.

She was also growing increasingly irritated at Sachiko, who had been calling nearly every night since the year-end party. Conversation was becoming trivial and boring. Sachiko talked about Harlan too much.

She felt a need to get away from both Sachiko and Harlan. She thought perhaps she could gain strength again in Canada if she saved enough money to go back. She had to find out once and for all how she stood with Joe, if there was any potential future with him. She took out a piece of paper and a pen and began to write. Her thoughts flowed onto the paper. Within an hour she finished a four-page letter that confessed and asked all that was on her mind.

Obaa-chan was at Yoshiko's parents' place tonight.

Yoshiko had agreed to meet Harlan in Mukonoso at a cheap bar around nine o'clock. She had resolved to be honest with him, to tell him everything that was bothering her. She had always had difficulty breaking up with her lovers in the past. Sometimes they had become angry, sometimes had cried. She had usually come away from those partings with feelings of guilt and disdain for the man's weakness. She knew it was better to be honest, but she was still afraid of what Harlan's reaction would be.

It was getting late. She put on a heavy coat and wrapped a muffler around her neck. She passed a post office on the way to the station, dropped the letter in the overseas slot, and headed for the bar.

* * *

Yoshiko had already had two drinks by the time Harlan arrived. She looked a bit dishevelled and tired, as if she were carrying a heavy burden, but he did not say anything about her appearance. He sat down beside her and ordered a beer. Yoshiko ordered another whiskey and water.

"It's freezing outside," he said.

"Switch to whiskey and maybe you'll warm up."

The bartender brought their drinks. A group of four people at a corner table was singing karaoke songs.

Others at the counter were joking and laughing with one of the hostesses.

Yoshiko took a long drink, set her glass back on the counter, looked deeply into Harlan's eyes, and said, "Harlan, I have to tell you something."

"What is it?"

"You have to find another lover."

Yoshiko felt as if someone else had spoken. She had mulled over how to break the news to him for two days. It had taken three drinks to build up the courage to say it. Now the words had been spoken. It had been surprisingly easy. She felt a certain relief, but there was still a tension in her neck and back. She waited for a look of disappointment to appear on his face, but she detected no change. He had a look about him that reminded her of the Catholic priest she had befriended before going to Canada. He smiled at her.

"I thought you might say something like that. Are you having problems? Going through changes again?"

"Yes, too many. They're driving me crazy. It's not just you. It's everything. Everyone. I think I need to get away again."

"Where to?"

"I think I have to go back to Canada. I just can't forget about Joe. I have to find out what my true

159

relationship with him is. I think I still love him and I have to make sure if he loves me or not."

"I think I can understand that."

"You're not angry or disappointed?"

"No. I understand that you have to find out things by yourself."

"I really care for you, Harlan. I really do. I had to have you in the beginning, but I just haven't learned the patience to understand you. I don't know how to say it. It seems to me you're too simple. You don't seem to think very much. I don't want to read your books to find out your feelings. I want to hear them from you. Sachiko is always talking about how you said this or wrote that in your stories, but I want to hear the words from your mouth."

"It's not you. It's me. I like sleeping with you, but I don't want to have sex with you anymore. I'm not fulfilled mentally. I don't think I ever will be with you. I'm sorry."

"Don't be sorry. It's natural you feel as you do. It's like what Kobo Abe writes about in *Woman of the Dunes*. He used the imagery of sand to describe life. There's always a constant movement and shifting and changing. There's a power to it that can't be resisted no matter how we try. Your changes are probably like that."

They ordered more drinks. The bar became livelier as more customers filled the place. A din of music, laughter, and the clink of ice in glasses surrounded them. It was one of the stranger aspects of Japan that Harlan had noticed: The more noise there was, the easier it was for people to escape into privacy. At the moment it seemed he and Yoshiko were completely alone.

Yoshiko continued drinking at a fast pace. A stream of confession spilled from her lips. She told Harlan again of her need to find an independence away from her family, of her worries about the future, the boredom and tediousness of her job, the need to be nourished through love and faith, the guilt that always came when whatever nourishment she did feel was too short-lived and she would begin drinking again. Harlan listened patiently.

The other customers drifted off. Yoshiko was drunk and could barely stand. They had missed the last train. Harlan had the bartender call a taxi. During the ride home he put his arm around Yoshiko and she leaned against him.

"Thank you, Harlan."

"For what?"

"For not being angry at me. For understanding and being my friend. I feel much better now. I think I feel closer to you tonight than ever before."

Robert W. Norris

The taxi stopped in front of Yoshiko's place. Harlan paid the driver and walked Yoshiko to her back door. She stumbled once, but he caught her and she giggled. Then she pulled his head toward her, kissed him once passionately and deeply, stepped back, and passed her hand through his hair.

"Please find another lover," she said.

"Will you be OK?"

"Don't worry about me. Good night." She opened the door, stepped inside, turned to face him, waved good-bye, then closed the door and the curtains.

14

Harlan was returning on a train from Osaka. He had spent the morning and afternoon attending a teacher-training workshop. He had picked up some useful teaching techniques and materials, but had felt uncomfortable with the group of foreign English teachers who had also attended. They had seemed like obsequious sycophants in the presence of the famous linguistics expert who had put on the workshop. A constant patter of pseudo-intellectual discussion on the merits and drawbacks of various teaching theories and methodologies had filled the room all day. Harlan was interested only in what worked and what did not work in the classroom. The group members seemed to him more interested in displaying their own knowledge before the others and sizing up where they stood within the hierarchy of that world. Who was teaching at what famous university? Who had published a paper in what well-known journal? Who had met so and so at the last national teachers' conference? As far as Harlan was concerned, they had been speaking a foreign language.

He was also painfully aware of his own standing

within their world: at the bottom. He did not understand the language they used because he had not specialized in the field of linguistics. He had no college degree. He was a teacher in a conversation school, a low minor leaguer in status. When he had answered those who asked where he was working, the conversation had come to an abrupt halt as if the others had suddenly realized there was a leper in their midst and there was nothing to be gained from associating with him.

Then there was the linguistics expert himself. The way he had floated condescendingly about the room in his guru outfit, explaining all the humanistic elements of each particular teaching technique, had caused Harlan almost to retch in front of everyone. Whenever someone had asked a question, a look of weary patience had come over the expert's face and he responded with a nonsensical Zen koan that forced the questioner to retreat into embarrassed silence. Throughout the entire day Harlan had been desperate for a cigarette and a beer. As soon as the workshop was over he rushed to the nearest pub to escape the crowd, most of whom had lingered in hope of catching more words of wisdom from the master.

Harlan's thoughts turned to matters closer to home. He had not seen Sachiko since the night of the party. She seemed slowly to have withdrawn from him. He felt some relief about this. The relationship with Yoshiko had become complicated. She was obviously going through changes and he did not know what to expect from her each time they met.

He had not been surprised the night she told him to find another lover. He understood her confusion, her inability to define and focus on a future course. When he had first met her, she had seemed to thrive on the hatred she had for Japan and her past. There had always been an unmistakable air of loneliness about her. That was one of the reasons he was attracted to her. Lately, that loneliness had taken on a self-destructive quality. Hers was a beauty that filled him with a vague premonition that it had been born to be a target for the forces of destruction. It seemed that all her own reflections, self-examinations, and guilt that followed each journey into soul-searching could be obliterated only by the large amounts of whiskey she consumed. He knew too well this tendency in himself. She had looked worn and ragged the last few times he had seen her. Lines were beginning to appear on her face.

The last time he had seen her was five nights ago. He had returned after midnight to find her drunk in his futon. She had received a letter from Joe telling her he would like her to come back to Canada, but to be realistic he could not provide any security for her. She had to realize that theirs could never be more than a platonic friendship.

Harlan told her she had to rely on herself for her own happiness. No one else could provide it for her. She had cried. She had seemed to feel very old, depressed, and hurt. They lay in each other's arms for maybe half an hour. He started to undress her, but she said she could not make love. She was afraid of her weakness. She had gotten up, stumbled out the door, and gone home.

The train arrived at Hankyu Itami Station. Harlan decided to stop by Yoshiko's place. Obaa-chan had been taken to the hospital a few days before because of some difficulty in breathing. Yoshiko would probably appreciate some company, someone with whom to visit. It was a rare warm February day. Harlan hoped spring would come soon. It would be nice to see people in a more cheerful mood. It had been a long winter for everyone.

Harlan knocked on Yoshiko's back door. She was making a pot of coffee and invited him in. She looked as if she had just gotten up. There were dark circles under her eyes and a droop to her shoulders.

"Rough night last night?" he asked.

"Yes. I was out with the Cocos owner and some other friends. I didn't get home till six this morning. I just got up. Want some coffee?"

"Sounds good."

Yoshiko poured them both a cup of coffee and sat down at the kitchen table with Harlan.

"How is Obaa-chan?"

"Better. Her breathing seems back to normal, but the doctors want to keep her in the hospital for another week or so to keep an eye on her. I don't know how much more time she has, but she's in good spirits."

"That's good to hear. It must be lonely here for you with her gone. Are you getting along OK?"

"My mother drops by almost every day, so it's not so bad. It's really strange though, our relationship."

"What do you mean?"

"Whenever she is here, I wish she was gone. And when she's gone, I wish she was here. I think we both have many guilty feelings about each other and it's hard to talk with her about anything important."

"What do you feel guilty about?"

"About the times I tried to commit suicide."

"You never have told me much about that."

"The first time was in high school. Some of my friends were arrested by the police because they were working for one of those telephone sex clubs. The police found out about what they were doing and arrested them because they were under 18. I was arrested, too, because I was one of the group. I wasn't involved in the telephone sex thing, but I was arrested anyway. The police called my father and he came to the police station to pick me up. When we got home, he punched me in the face. My family didn't believe me when I said I wasn't involved. A couple days later my brother got drunk and went crazy and tried to kill me. I wanted to die. I was really depressed. About a week later when everyone was out of the house I cut my wrists with a razor and passed out on the floor. I woke up in the hospital and everyone was staring at me. I felt even worse because I hadn't been able to kill myself."

"What happened the second time?"

"The second time was after high school. I had tried to go to a business college, but hated it. I hated all the little groups and the way they always gossiped about others. I always wanted to be alone. I didn't like anybody, and I hated myself. My family and I were probably at the worst part of our relationship. I didn't know what to do and they didn't know what to do with me.

"It's quite strange, you know. I had failed to kill myself the first time. I had cut my wrists in the wrong place and didn't bleed that much. The doctor who took care of me was a very gentle and strange man. He told me why I hadn't been able to kill myself and then showed me how to kill myself if I wanted to try a second time. Maybe he was just trying to scare me or maybe he was just joking. I don't know. Anyway, one day my mother started criticizing me and I couldn't take it anymore. We got into a big fight. I punched her several times and broke one of her ribs. Then I locked myself in the bathroom and cut my wrists the way the doctor told me to. My mother called some neighbors and they broke down the bathroom door and got to me before I could bleed to death. That was not too long before I went to Canada and met Julie."

"I had no idea about all this. You seem to get along OK with your family now, though."

"Yes, we get along pretty well, but we never talk about those things. It's very, how do you say, stiff?"

"Maybe awkward is the word you're looking for."

"Very awkward. But there's no hatred anymore, just a kind of sadness that's there when we're together. We're careful about not saying anything to hurt each other or remind each other of those days."

Harlan finished his coffee and set the cup back on the table. Yoshiko poured him another cup.

"Aside from that, how are things going for you?"

"After I got that letter from Joe, I thought about going to see Julie in Canada, but I decided against it. I think I would probably rely on her too much and fall back into that. I have to find something on my own, some way for myself. The only thing I have is English, so I want to continue to study. I think I might do a homestay in America. It would be the best way to improve my English. I don't want to continue working at the dentist's, but I have to for a while because he's a friend of the Cocos owner and the owner got me the job. Maybe I'll do the homestay in the summer. I'll have to wait to see what happens to Obaa-chan."

"Are you doing anything later tonight? You're welcome to come over if you want."

"No thanks. I have to meet some people."

"The door is open anytime. I think you know that."

"I know, but it's better that I don't. I still want you to find another lover."

"Well, thanks for the coffee. I'm going to go to the *sento*, then home to study a little."

Yoshiko looked out the back door for a long time after Harlan left. She was glad she had told him about her suicide attempts. She always felt better after telling him a secret about herself. She ran a bath. The hot water took away the tightness in her neck and shoulders. Her hangover went away. Later, when she looked at herself in the mirror, she noticed an older woman staring back at her.

Before leaving the house she put a condom in her purse. She didn't often see the man she was to meet later, but she remembered the last time they had drunk together. She had not used any protection and had been worried until her period came two weeks later than usual.

*　*　*

Harlan went straight home, collected his towel and razor, then headed to the *sento*. Yamaguchi, the youngest member of the softball team, was there. He was in an unusually depressed mood. Harlan asked what the matter was. Yamaguchi said that another team member, Matsumoto, had committed suicide the night before. There had been no note left behind, but apparently Matsumoto had owed a lot of money to loan sharks. His wife and daughter had found him that morning in his car with a rubber hose running from the exhaust pipe through a small crack in the driver's window. There would be a team wake for him in about two weeks.

That night as Harlan lay in his futon he thought about the last time he had seen Matsumoto. Near the end of January the softball team had had a meeting and party that lasted well into the night. Harlan had drunk too much. The last thing he remembered about the night was drinking in a snack bar with two of the older members of the team, men in their fifties who rarely played anymore but still attended the team parties. One of them was Matsumoto. Harlan remembered him as a good-natured man who delighted in playing practical jokes. Every time Harlan had met him, Matsumoto had made it a point to sit next to Harlan and pour drink after drink for him. Harlan had always felt comfortable in Matsumoto's presence, despite understanding little of his strong Osaka accent.

Something someone had once said to him in India suddenly entered Harlan's mind: "The constant work of one's life is the making of one's death." No matter how hard he tried to ignore it or refrain from thinking about it, there was always a cloud of death-imagery hovering over him. Yoshiko's story of her suicide attempts and Yamaguchi's story about Matsumoto's suicide accentuated the darkness of that imagery. He wondered if he would ever be able to escape from it. A long time passed before Harlan fell asleep. After he did, he had frightful nightmares in which he was jumping into burning lakes to try to save friends who were drowning. They were screaming, but there was nothing he could do for them.

*   *   *

Sachiko was home resting in bed. She had a cold and had taken the day off from work. She usually could not sleep late, so, despite her slight fever and stuffy head, she felt a sense of luxury as she pulled the bed cover tighter around her shoulders. It was the middle of March and still very cold.

She had been exhausted lately. Every night for a week she had gone to a library after work to research information about graduate courses in the United States. She had narrowed her choices to five schools, but was intent on studying American literature or art history at either University of Michigan or University of California at Berkeley. She had put together several resumes and planned to send them in the next few days. If she was lucky, she would be able to start school again in the fall.

She felt pleased with herself in having made a decision on her own to do something about her future. She had received the results from the TOEFL test she took near the end of last year — 610. Her parents had agreed to her plan and would support her while she lived abroad. The idea of living and studying abroad gave her new dreams to consider, positive thoughts to cancel out the depression that had taken hold of her after the last time spent with Yoshiko and Harlan.

Harlan had not called since the party. Over a year had

now passed since that night in his apartment. She wondered how she could have been so naive as to fall once again into a futile relationship. She had only herself to blame. She had known from the beginning how things would end, but she had allowed herself to plunge willingly into that abyss of despair.

She had called Yoshiko several times, but the warmth and closeness she thought they had found was now gone. Yoshiko was cold and distant on the phone and did not call back. Sachiko did not like the way Yoshiko drank too much. Even Yoshiko's beliefs seemed hypocritical now. If Yoshiko was so pious in her Christian faith, why did she sleep around so much? At least Yumi's love and sex with Terry had been pure.

Sachiko looked out her bedroom window at the dismal sky. It was another hazy, oppressive day. She hated this time of year, the period between winter and spring that was damp and leafless and had a raw chill that bit to the bone. She wanted to stop thinking about Harlan and Yoshiko, but her brain kept pumping out more images of self-torture.

She thought of all the letters she had written to him. How could she have been so foolish to have laid bare the most private and guarded secrets of her soul? She hoped he had thrown them all away. She did not ever again want to reveal herself so completely to someone.

What had she been thinking then? She knew herself to be suspended between two existences: one of the mind and one of the body. It seemed the two could never merge. She had been a fool to think otherwise. Her letters at that time had become her very life, and in the writing of them, she now realized, she had begun to suffer from a curious sense of distorted reality that marked the way artists often behaved when dealing with real people. The Harlan she had addressed in her letters and the Harlan she had met in the physical world were two entirely different entities.

Her thoughts were beginning to irritate her. She had to do something to keep her mind occupied. She threw the bed cover aside and got up. She felt faint for a moment and steadied herself at her desk. Her body was stiff from lying in bed too long. She went to the toilet, then washed her face and brushed her teeth. She went to the kitchen. The house was empty. Her mother was probably out shopping.

She poured herself a glass of orange juice and had some tofu and miso soup. She thought briefly about having a cigarette, then dismissed the idea. It was a filthy habit. She was disgusted at herself for having smoked those times with Yoshiko. What an imbecile she must have appeared, trying to act as if she were one of them.

She felt a little better after the juice and soup. She returned to her room and sat down at her desk. The last letter she intended to send to Harlan was still lying face down on the desk. She picked it up and read it once more.

Dear Harlan,

How are you doing? I'm fine. I'm writing you listening to Mexican pops. Some are really emotional and romantic. I'm going to go to the U.S. in the fall to do my master's degree. Please wish me good luck in my study. I guess, Harlan, it's time for me to disappear from the people around you. As a matter of fact, I was thinking of it when I was at Yoshiko's party. I have no plausible reason to say, but I wish you could read me. I suppose you were relieved to read that. Anyway, I won't go to your place anymore.

Of course, you can send me on a literary errand. I'd like to cooperate with you in the literary matters. I need your advice, too. I'm just your literary friend, and I wouldn't like to disturb your private life. I think it's better for me not to have anything to do with the people around you.

Well, I'll close now. See you later.

Sachiko

Sachiko thought for a moment, then made up her mind she would send the letter. She wrote Harlan's address on an envelope, put the letter inside, and sealed the flap. She would send it the next day.

She decided to do some painting. She had not painted in a long time. She mixed some paints together and cleaned her brushes. She picked up the smallest brush and held it poised above a small canvas. The brush felt heavy in her hand.

When she looked again at the clock on her bedside table nearly an hour and a half had passed. It was as if she had fallen into a coma. She had no recollection of what had occurred in that time. She could recall no thoughts that had come to her mind. She looked at the canvas. In the background were several figures with no distinctive features. They looked like individual wisps of smoke. In the foreground was a large snake that seemed almost to be hissing. Its head was raised, its jaws open and fangs exposed, and its green eyes scintillated with a sleek, venomous stare. A trail of blood had been left behind in its wake.

Sachiko rose from her chair, went to the toilet again, got back into bed, and fell into a deep, undisturbed sleep.

15

Near the middle of March Sasa Club had its first
game of the year. Although the team lost 7-3,
Harlan had a good game. He had a hit, stole a base,
scored a run, and handled all his chances in center field.
He also threw out a runner trying to score on a sacrifice
fly. After the game, the team members, still in their
uniforms, gathered at Matsumoto's house. At first
everyone took turns kneeling in front of the family altar
with Matsumoto's picture on it, ringing a bell to call
forth Matsumoto's spirit, and saying a silent prayer.
Then Matsumoto's widow and daughter began serving
food and drinks. The mood became festive. Everyone
got drunk. There was much singing and laughter. Morita
and Matsumoto's widow capped the evening by reading
the sutras.

The next night Harlan went out with Morita and
Yamaguchi to a snack bar. He drank too much and at
one point, feeling rather cocky with his improved
Japanese, responded loudly and cynically to what he
thought was a stupid question by another customer
asking if he was really an American: "Am I

American? Am I American? I don't know. What do you think? I think I'm German. No, wait. I think I'm Chinese. Are you Japanese?"

All conversation in the bar stopped and everyone was staring at him. Morita grabbed him, paid the bill, and drove him home. Feeling guilty about his behavior, Harlan went to Morita's shop the next day to apologize. There were no other customers, so Harlan and Morita sat on some beer crates and warmed themselves by the kerosene heater. Morita told Harlan that the snack bar owner's parents had been killed by Americans during the war and that Harlan should be more sensitive about others' feelings.

A dark cloud of remorse enveloped Harlan and he felt compelled to talk about his frustrations in dealing with some Japanese. He was tired of all the same questions constantly being put to him as if he were the sole representative of the outside world and what it thought about Japan. He was also suspicious of all the kindness he was receiving, the way people were always paying for him and wanting to take him places. He wondered if there were not ulterior motives behind these acts and if he would be expected to pay everything back somewhere down the road. He was worried that he was being used.

Morita thought for a while, then said, "You think too much. Don't worry about it."

The weather remained cold throughout March. It snowed several times. Although the first day of spring arrived, Harlan felt as though winter would never end. One night Sugiyama showed up at Harlan's with the owner of a local art gallery. The owner was going to allow Sugiyama to display some of his paintings. They were hopeful the paintings could be sold. The farmer next door spent one day rototilling his *hatake* garden. It was the first activity in the field since new dirt had been dumped on it in December.

The team continued to play games on weekends. Harlan was playing with confidence, hitting the ball well and making all the plays in the field. He was in the best shape he had been in years. In addition to the softball games, he was running nearly 50 kilometers a week around Koya Pond.

Spring finally arrived. The cherry blossoms burst into fullness, then disappeared to be replaced again by the brilliant colors of azaleas. Harlan often stood outside his front door watching the neighbor and his wife diligently weed and water the plastic-covered rows of vegetables in the *hatake* field. Sachiko had disappeared from his life. He saw Yoshiko only sporadically, but it seemed she had forgotten her desire for him to find another lover. Sex with her had taken on a deeper dimension. She was insatiable. One night she showed up drunk and, after they had finished making love, she lay in his arms and said, "Do you still like me? You're the best man I've ever had."

A few uneventful weeks passed. One day there was a phone call for Harlan at Rick's school. It struck him as strange because he had given the phone number to only two friends from his high school days with whom he still stayed in touch through occasional letters. He had just finished a Japanese lesson with Nishimoto. Hiroko, a new secretary at the school, handed Harlan the phone.

"I think it is from America," she said.

An air of heightened expectancy seemed to fill the room. Harlan was aware of everyone's attention. Yasuhiro, a young friend of Rick's who had become the school's promotion manager, and Rick were seated on the couch adjacent to Hiroko's desk. Their faces brightened as they listened for Harlan's first words. Hiroko moved out of his way to join Nishimoto and two students.

Harlan felt a poignant sense of unreality as he held the phone. It was as if he were in a cage in a zoo where the onlookers were smiling in smug satisfaction at a newly-discovered aberration of the human race. The clarity and nearness of the voice on the other end frightened him.

"Is this Mister Harlan Cooper of Arcata, California?"

"Yes, it is."

"This is Father Lowry of the Arcata Catholic Church. I've been trying to locate you for several weeks now and only recently received your address and phone number from a friend of yours."

Harlan felt rather than saw the nods and smiles around him. He felt a vague irritation. Hiroko and Nishimoto started a conversation about him in Japanese. He found himself listening to their conversation. Why wouldn't they shut up? Didn't they realize this was a long distance call?

"...and I thought it my duty to inform you that your brother Dan was killed in a car wreck two months ago and..."

"*Hontoo?*"

A burst of laughter filled the room. Harlan did not realize he had responded in Japanese. Everyone but Rick doubled over, pointing their fingers at Harlan. Rick's face was red. It seemed he alone understood what had happened. About a month before he had received a similar call after one of his best friends was found strangled to death in Seattle. A hot flash of anger passed through Harlan. The laughter grew so loud he could not hear Father Lowry. He glared at the others, motioning frantically for them to be quiet. He heard Rick tell Yasuhiro, "Someone has died."

Later, at a noodle shop with Rick, Harlan tried to remember Father Lowry's exact words, but all he could remember were the bare facts. Danny had been working as a mechanic in a small town in Louisiana. He was divorced with no children. It had been a head-on collision with a big truck late at night. He may have been drunk. He had died instantly. He was now buried next to their mother and father in the Arcata Catholic Church cemetery.

Harlan ordered a beer. Rick lit a cigarette. Blue smoke floated above their heads in a flickering stream. The grill in front of them sent off a wave of heat. Harlan was sweating. The mama-san brought the beer and two glasses. Rick poured Harlan's glass full, then filled his own. Harlan emptied half the glass in two swallows. Rick filled the glass again.

Harlan drank in silence while Rick talked about death. A few years before, his first wife had lost five family members in the same year. She had lost her grip on life after that and became bitter and misanthropic. They had then divorced. Rick sighed.

"That was a long time ago," he said. "There's no reason to go back to the States."

The States were far away for Harlan, too, but the phone call had brought back the past with a suddenness that was unnerving. He felt helpless and guilty. Why had he never made an attempt to find his brother? He had spent several years roaming about the States and the thought had rarely crossed his mind. Shame and remorse reared their heads inside him.

"We better get back to the school," Rick said.

Three empty bottles were lined up on the counter.

"You go ahead. I'll be along in a few minutes."

Rick rose, paid the bill, and left the shop. Harlan ordered another beer. He still had 15 minutes before his first class. He was glad Rick did not mind his drinking. He seemed to understand Harlan's need to be alone.

As he finished the last of the beer, Harlan realized Rick was another in a long line of father figures in his life. Perhaps, Harlan thought, it was his own silence, his refusal to judge others' lives, his ability to listen, that attracted these older men to him, men who had literally or figuratively lost their own sons and saw in Harlan a chance to pass on the scraps of experience and knowledge they had acquired, pass on in effect what they had failed to pass on to their own sons, as if to atone for their failures and leave a lasting mark on the world. Harlan had always readily accepted what they had given him. He wished his real father had lived long enough to pass on to him some tangible legacy.

It was time to return to the school. The students would be waiting for him by now. He walked the narrow street leading back to the school. Two women on bicycles passed by him. He nodded a greeting, recognizing them as mothers of children studying at the school. The humid day, coupled with the beer he had drunk, made him feel dizzy. He thought how nice it would be just to forget about all responsibility. He felt himself on the verge of a binge.

By the time the last class was over, he had sobered up. Everyone had gone home. He locked up the school, went downstairs to where his bicycle was parked, and started to ride home. He was thirsty again. He looked forward to opening the bottle of scotch he had at home. He took his usual route through some back streets and past the Mukonoso rice fields that were now flooded for the planting of the rice. A warm stillness was in the air. He passed a lumberyard. The freshly-stacked lumber gave off a strong smell. It reminded him of his childhood in the Jacoby Creek forest outside Arcata.

He passed a stretch of shops and the Shinkansen bullet train overpass. A train sped along, sending blue electric sparks into the night. He headed along a straight stretch. On the left were some onion fields that ran into a series of rice fields. The first summer frogs were croaking away. A solitary man, hands in his pockets, looked longingly out across the flooded fields. Moonlight flickered on the water.

He pedaled up the last uphill section of the road. This part of the ride always took his breath away. He was sweating when he reached the traffic light at the peak where the road ran into a T-junction. There was no traffic, so he crossed against the red light and turned into the dark side streets of his neighborhood. The fields gave off a coarse, sweet odor. He arrived at the apartment, parked his bicycle under the shed with the other tenants' bicycles, and climbed the stairs.

He was home. The word stuck in Harlan's mind as he unlocked the door. Had he finally found a place to call home after nearly 15 years of rambling? It seemed suddenly inconceivable to him, yet he had lived in this same apartment for about a year and a half, longer than any other place he could remember living in since graduating from high school. He filled a glass with ice, grabbed the bottle of scotch off the kitchen floor, sat down at the *kotatsu* in the six-mat room, and poured himself a drink. The first swallow burned his throat. A warm flash passed through him. He gritted his teeth and took another drink. He fell into a reverie. Countless scenes, real and imagined, took possession of his thoughts.

There was a knock at the door. It was Sugiyama. He had missed the last train. He smelled of whiskey. His suit was rumpled. He wore his characteristic smile.

"Sorry for bothering you. Too much drinking."

"Come on in. There's a pillow and some blankets in the closet. Have another drink?"

"No, thank you. Too much drinking with Fukuyama-san."

Sugiyama's face was red, his eyes droopy. He stripped to his underwear and passed out on the floor of the three-mat room with his glasses still on. Harlan took the glasses off and put them in the closet. He returned to the six-mat room to continue drinking alone. He left the sliding panel doors between the rooms open and watched Sugiyama sleep. Against the wall was the canvas Sugiyama was currently working on. It was a big canvas, about three feet by five feet. Sugiyama liked working with big canvases. This one had changed many times in the last two weeks. It had started out as a distant city seen from inside a dark forest. Now it was a jungle and ocean scene with an island in the distance. He had started with dark colors, then switched to light greens, oranges, and reds. Sugiyama had an over-abundance of energy when he painted. He had not yet learned discipline and control.

Harlan envied Sugiyama, envied his dedication and optimism, his innocence. He thought Sugiyama was still in the stage of artistic growth when all is new and fresh and there are still heroes to copy and follow. He wondered how long it would be before Sugiyama discovered that continually exploring the imagination, the unknown, would lead him to a kind of madness. Harlan became quite drunk, plunging willingly again into a dark loneliness. Yoshiko's image flashed before him. He wanted to touch her, to feel her warm, silky body next to his, but he could not move. He slept a fitful sleep filled with strange dreams.

Harlan stayed drunk for two days, holed up in his apartment in a quagmire of remorse. Danny's death weighed upon him more as a symbol of all Harlan had lost than as the loss of his only brother. He realized suddenly, fully, that the year and a half he had spent in Japan was but a transitional limbo now drawing to a close. All the joy and discoveries he had experienced lost their glitter. What lay ahead was dark and foreboding. The relationships he had entered into seemed surreal. He became immersed in the imagery of his past. Strangely, it was of grave importance to reexamine that past. His body was still attached to the present, but the people who inhabited that world were no more than apparitions to him.

16

Yoshiko was in her backyard harvesting the heads of cabbage she had planted several weeks before. The last few days had been warm and muggy, a prescience of the coming rainy season, but today there were few clouds in the sky. A light breeze stirred the leaves on the trees across the street. Yoshiko paused to wipe the sweat off her brow. She liked being in her garden and watching the wonder of nature at work.

More changes had taken place in her life. She had quit working for the dentist when she found a job teaching English conversation to elementary and junior high school students at the ECC school in Osaka. The new job did not pay as much as the other, but she did not have to feel obligated to anyone and she liked being with children. It made her think about the future and someday becoming a mother herself.

She was now living alone again in the apartment. Obaa-chan had died about a month ago. She had not suffered. She had simply gone to sleep one night and not woken up. That night Obaa-chan had come to Yoshiko in the form of a butterfly in a dream. Yoshiko had not felt afraid. There had been a radiant light around the butterfly and it had spoken to her. Yoshiko could not remember the exact words, but they were something like "Don't worry about me. I am happy and with Grand-father again and it is very peaceful in this new world. You go ahead now and live your own life. Thank you so much for your love."

Yoshiko had woken the next morning in a happy mood. When her mother called with the news about Obaa-chan, Yoshiko had not been surprised. She had cried, but her tears were those of happiness. She knew Obaa-chan was where she should be and would be waiting for Yoshiko when it was Yoshiko's turn. There had been a small family wake. After Obaa-chan's cremation the family had collected the ashes and remaining bones. When Yoshiko visited her parents' now, she always lit a stick of incense and prayed before Obaa-chan's picture on the family altar. She felt something spiritual when she prayed to Obaa-chan, something deeper than any Christian or Buddhist or Shinto ritual could give her. She could not articulate it in words, but there was a feeling that Obaa-chan was her guiding spirit. She felt a calmness she had not felt before.

Yoshiko uprooted another head of cabbage and picked out two caterpillars. She held them in her right hand. They, too, were one of God's miracles. She stroked their fuzzy, soft bodies and they curled up into small balls. It was as if she held Obaa-chan's warm, reassuring spirit in her hand. Soon they would transform themselves into butterflies and bring a new joy and beauty to the world as they flittered here and there before ascending to Heaven. She set the caterpillars free and watched them crawl away from her into the shade of the shrubbery that surrounded the garden.

Whenever she felt a surge of happiness like what she felt now, she wanted to share it with someone. It was such a poignant feeling that it would be overly selfish to keep it to herself. The feeling was always too fleeting and unreal. It was as if she needed to share it with someone who recognized it and confirmed it in order to have it reaffirmed in her own mind as something real. Today she wanted to share the feeling with Harlan.

The relationship with him was becoming more and more confusing. She thought he had understood her the night she decided to break off the relationship. He had not gotten angry or disappointed when she told him to find another lover. His reaction, ironically, had made her love him more. She had been the one who returned to him just a few weeks later aching for his body. The image of Joe had disappeared and she had given herself wholly to Harlan that night. She had been drinking and the next day regretted having shown her weakness for him. He seemed to accept everything about her. He was the best man with whom she had ever slept.

But the last two times had given her pause again. In the last week something had happened to drive him back into that inaccessible world of his. There had been something distinctly different about him. She could not put her finger on it exactly, but she hoped it was just a minor depression that would pass. There was a new look on his face, something frightening and penetrating she had not detected before. It was as if while he sat gently staring into space a whole silent inquisition was taking place in his mind. Yoshiko had no way of knowing what kinds of questions and accusations might be unrolling in his mind, but she feared they concerned her. When she tried getting him to talk about whatever was bothering him, he retreated even further into the recesses of whatever it was that engulfed him. When he had spoken the last two times, he had muttered only some caustic statements criticizing what he called "the empty, votive symbols of organized religion."

It was all right for him to be reluctant to submit himself to the discipline of any church, but she wished he would respect the need in others to do so. Why did he have to be so critical of spiritual feelings and beliefs? How could he be so self-assured in his atheism? Or was it agnosticism? She thought these

words were merely euphemisms for misanthropy. That
was another thing that had always puzzled her about
Harlan. All the other people she knew who professed a
disbelief about the existence of God were, if the truth
were known, misanthropes, pure and simple. Harlan was
different from them. She sensed he possessed a spirituality; it just had to struggle to make its way to the
surface. At least that is how she had felt before the last
two times they had met. Now she was not sure. Perhaps
he was at heart a misanthrope.

She finished pulling up the heads of cabbage. She had
found several more caterpillars and set them free to join
the others in the shade. She took the heads of cabbage
inside to rinse off in the sink. She would keep three or
four for herself and give the others away. That, too,
would bring her great joy.

The feeling of happiness was still in her. She did not
want it to fade. She knew Harlan would be home now.
It was early afternoon. The *sento* would not be open for
another hour. He had no classes today. If he was not
home, he would probably be out with some of his
softball friends. In that case, she could always ride her
bicycle to Mukonoso and visit with the Cocos Island
owner.

Yoshiko straightened the apartment and changed into
a clean T-shirt and pair of jeans. Some of the neigh-

borhood children were playing in the park as she passed by it. They shouted and waved at her. She smiled and waved back. As she approached Harlan's apartment, she noticed his bicycle was parked in its usual place. She climbed the steps, knocked on the door, said a cheerful "Hello," and entered.

Harlan was lying on top of his futon. He groaned, rolled over, and looked at Yoshiko through glazed eyes.

"Are you OK?" she asked.

"Yeah, just a bad hangover. I was on the verge of getting up, but couldn't talk my body into moving."

Harlan rose stiffly and went to the toilet. Yoshiko went through the three-mat room into the other room. There were books and clothes strewn about. The place was a mess. She made room to sit at the *kotatsu* and waited for Harlan to finish. She noticed several empty beer cans in one corner of the room. Some of Sugiyama's paintings were in the three-mat room. Harlan reached into his refrigerator, pulled out a carton of orange juice, popped two aspirin tablets in his mouth, took a long drink, then took a sponge bath at the kitchen sink. He put on some hot water for coffee.

Yoshiko got up and said, "Here, let me make the coffee. You go ahead and sit down."

"Thanks."

Yoshiko brought two cups of coffee and set them

down on the *kotatsu*. "You look terrible," she said.

"I feel terrible."

"Did Sugiyama stay the night last night?"

"Yes. I guess he took off while I was still sleeping."

"That painting is interesting, don't you think?"

"I guess so. I'm not into thinking about art right now."

Yoshiko could feel him slipping away already. There was a sarcastic tone to his voice. She did not like it, but she was determined not to allow him to destroy her own mood.

"How late were you up drinking?"

"I don't know. I suppose I passed out around five or so."

"Is the headache bad?"

"Pretty bad."

"Would you like me to massage your neck?"

"Please."

Harlan stretched out face down on the futon. Yoshiko climbed onto the lower part of his back and began massaging his back and neck. His neck was particularly tight. She pressed her thumbs hard into the neck muscles and kneaded them until she felt them loosen. She applied pressure to the middle of his back and felt his spine pop several times.

"Is that better?"

"Yes. Thanks."

He rolled his neck several times, then did some stretches. Yoshiko made them another cup of coffee.

"I feel very happy today," Yoshiko said.

"Oh yeah?"

Harlan knew he should show some interest in what she was saying, but he could not focus. His mind was still in a fog of darkness, desolation, and despair. He thought what he probably needed more than anything right now was a drink, but that would lead to his wanting to vomit. He looked at Yoshiko and saw her lips moving and her hands gesturing, but it was as if someone had turned the volume down and he was now in the middle of his own silent movie. A sense of the meaningless disorder and overwhelming complexity of existence gripped him suddenly, choking him and cutting him off from any connection with the present moment.

"...and when I held the caterpillars in my hand and felt their softness and thought about how they would soon turn into butterflies I really felt deeply the wonder of nature and God. It was like Obaa-chan had come back to visit me like she did in my dream and..."

The sound had been turned up again and was now echoing in his mind. It had to be the mutterings of conscience and remorse, he thought, or maybe the memories of lost deliriums, or the voices of all the dark angels who had plagued him at various times and places in his life. Whatever they were, they were all clamoring and competing simultaneously for his attention. Danny's voice seemed to rise above the others for a second, but it was drowned out by the chorus of other pleadings and wailings. He thought he heard the cry of a soldier riddled by sniper fire, then the sound of blows in the room next to his Seattle skid-row room, then the susurrant moans of the wretched masses in the Calcutta streets. What were they saying? Why wouldn't they leave him alone? What had he done to create their suffering?

"...so that's why I feel so happy today. I just wanted to share it with someone."

Yoshiko stopped to look at Harlan. He had that look on his face again. He had never seemed as far away from her as he did at this moment. He had not heard a word of what she had said. She picked up one of his books lying on the floor and threw it as hard as she could at him. It struck him on the head. He looked first at the book, then turned his gaze slowly, uncomprehendingly, toward Yoshiko. He looked for a moment like a Lazarus climbing out of the darkness of his grave into the blinding light of the waking world.

"You don't give a shit about my stories at all, do you?"

A cold, sharp edge had appeared in Yoshiko's voice and eyes. She stared at him for a long moment. Harlan wanted to say something, but no words formed in his mouth. He just sat looking helplessly back at her. Yoshiko got up suddenly and stormed outside, slamming the door behind her.

17

The rainy season accentuated Harlan's melancholy. A haunting stillness pervaded the days: the grey skies, the somber blue of hydrangea, the rice field across the street reflecting the dark outline of the surrounding houses. Harlan looked out his window one day to see three children with a long net fishing lazily for frogs in the rice field. No sound escaped their lips. Two birds fluttered across the landscape, emitting weak warbles as if to voice their sluggishness. Black smoke rose from the smoke stack of a nearby *sento*. Harlan felt utterly isolated, faced with a growing depression that strangled him as in a nightmare.

At work he was uninspired. He merely went through the motions in the classroom. He stopped running. He fell into a slump on the softball diamonds. He quit taking Japanese lessons. All he could think about was death, separation, and loss. He had not seen Yoshiko since the day she threw a book at him and dashed out of his apartment.

He had taken up his old habit of going for long midnight walks when he was restless and could not sleep. He would often walk the street that passed by Yoshiko's place. She was usually not home yet. When she was home, there would often be a car parked outside her backyard. A wave of nausea would overcome him when he thought of her again sleeping with other men.

Sugiyama had been the one stabilizing force in his life these last few weeks. He was staying over most weekends. In the middle of June they had taken a two-day trip in his car to Kasumi, then back by way of Himeji. They had driven first past Lake Biwa and spent the night camped out at a beach on the Japan Sea side of Hyogo Prefecture. They had drunk beer, watched the stars, talked about their problems, and listened to John Lennon tapes. Harlan had taught Sugiyama the lyrics to *Working Class Hero*. They had sung the song many times.

They had spent a couple hours visiting Sugiyama's family before heading back. Passing through the wooded hills had taken Harlan back again to his youth and all his ramblings. All the shades of green had soothed his weary mind, particularly the bamboo trees bowing their heads as if in supplication, an image that seemed somehow symbolic of the Japanese people themselves. Then they had passed the golden fields near Himeji and finally Himeji Castle, which Harlan thought was much more beautiful than Osaka Castle.

The trip had been good for him, but its benefits lasted only a few days. There were problems at the school. It was growing too fast and starting to lose its original atmosphere. Rick was becoming too concerned about money. He had hired some more teachers, but they did not like him and often talked about him behind his back.

One night Yasuhiro stopped by Harlan's apartment. Yasuhiro had quit that day. He spoke of the danger of Rick's lack of business etiquette. Rick's Japanese was limited and he was too blunt when talking with Japanese about money matters. Everything was either "too cheap" or "too expensive." He always came straight to the point without establishing good relations first. The school had managed to get contracts for a few company classes, which Harlan was expected to teach in different parts of Nishinomiya and Osaka, but had lost too many others because of Rick's bad manners. Rick even did the unpardonable by counting the day's money take in front of the evening students and embarrassing them beyond belief. Yasuhiro was worried about the future of the school and thought it was better for him to quit now. After Yasuhiro left, Harlan thought about how he was always attracted to self-destructive people. He understood their capriciousness.

He received another six-month extension on his visa. From the middle of July the days became hotter. Harlan would look out his kitchen window and see the wind blow over the rich green rice field, sending off rippling waves of light. He began to take a new interest in studying Japanese at home. He bought a new textbook and tapes and spent an hour or two every day repeating after the tapes or taking dictation. He had stopped all work on his writing projects. They were all filled with too much dark and depressing imagery. At least the Japanese study helped him concentrate on something else.

Near the end of July he called Yoshiko and asked if he could see her in a few days. She consented. He finished teaching a company class in Osaka at 7:30, took the train back to Itami, stopped at a vending machine to buy a few beers, and arrived at her place about 8:30 on the appointed night. She was reading a book and drinking whiskey and water. She looked tired, but not as ragged as before.

"Long time, no see," he said after taking his shoes off and entering through the back door.

"Yes, it has been a while."

"Have you been busy?"

"Pretty busy. The ECC school has given me a few more hours. Would you like a drink?"

"No whiskey, but I brought some beer." He took one out of the plastic sack and put the others in her refrigerator. "Have you been seeing other men?"

"Yes, sometimes," she said wearily.

The answer hurt, but he was glad she had answered honestly. Over the past few months he had had the feeling she lied to him whenever he asked what she had been doing after not having seen her for a while. He opened his beer can and took a long drink.

"Are you still angry at me?" he asked.

"No."

"That's a relief."

They both laughed lightly. It was good to see her smile. She had the kind of smile that put people immediately at ease. Her whole face radiated a warmth of spirit, a sense of having suffered and survived, and an acceptance of the person who sat before her.

"I'm afraid the last time you saw me I was a bit out of sorts, not really myself," Harlan said.

"What do you mean by out of sorts?"

"A little off balance or out of order."

"Why? What happened?"

"I got a phone call from someone who told me my brother was dead. He had died in a car crash two months before and was already buried. I had no chance to go to the funeral. I guess the realization that now I have no family hit me rather hard. Not that it matters that much. I hadn't seen him since I was a teenager, but still hearing about his death brought back a lot of my past. I think I fell into a miserable state of self-pity, feeling that somehow Danny was my last link to the world I grew up in. Anyway, I'm better now."

"I'm very sorry and sad to hear that. When I saw you last time Obaa-chan had just died, too."

"I remember."

They sat listening to the wind rush through the trees outside. Harlan finished his beer and got up to get another. Yoshiko also poured herself another drink and stretched out on the floor. It was dark now, but neither bothered to switch on a light. Harlan returned from the refrigerator and lay down beside her.

"The wind always blows like this between the rainy season and the real summer," Yoshiko said.

Harlan put his beer aside and leaned over to kiss Yoshiko. She did not resist. He kissed her softly several times on her lips and neck, then removed her T-shirt and bra. She ran her fingers across his face and he kissed her breasts. He started to unzip her jeans, but she stopped him and said, "I can't. I'm on my period."

She kissed his chest, then slid down to pull down his pants. She took him in her mouth and performed the act tenderly, expertly, dreamily, but without enthusiasm. When she was finished, she wiped him off with some tissues. He pulled his pants up. She brought him his beer and handed it to him. They sat drinking silently in the darkness. Yoshiko seemed to be brooding over something.

Finally, she cleared her throat and said, "I have a confession to make."

"What's that?"

"I haven't always told you the truth about me."

"I know."

"You do?"

"Yes. A couple of times when I called you I knew someone was here with you, but you said you were here alone. I also know some of the times you said you were going to your parents you were really going to a love hotel with another man."

Yoshiko sighed heavily. "That's true. I'm sorry I lied those times, but that's not what I'm talking about."

"What are you talking about?"

"About us. About sex. I don't know how to explain it in English. I think we have no *en*. In Japanese we say *En wa arimasen*. It's not your fault. It's my fault. I can't have an orgasm. Not with you or anyone. I was molested when I was nine years old. My uncle and cousins molested me. I can never forget that. I can never forgive them or me. I want to have good sex, but I just can't. I always have to drink first. It helps me forget. It's like I want to punish myself. I haven't had sex sober

205

for a long time."

"I didn't realize. Maybe I've been too selfish myself."

"It won't work. I know the size of my Japanese vagina and your American penis. There's no *en*."

Harlan could not believe what she had said. When Yoshiko was confused, she often repeated what others had told her, but this inanity was too outrageous for anyone to believe. No doubt she had heard it from one of her boyfriends who had probably picked it up from the strange comic books that many Japanese men read. Harlan repressed the urge to challenge the ludicrousness of her statement.

"I think *en* probably means affinity. You're trying to say we have no affinity," he said.

"Maybe that's it. Whatever it is, we're not right for each other, physically and mentally."

"Where does our mental affinity go wrong?"

"Your cynicism bothers me. It's your attitude about Christianity and God. My belief is very important to me, and I don't think we can ever meet on this point. I know you didn't respect Julie either because she was a Christian."

"I liked Julie a lot. I thought she was a great person."

"But you didn't respect her belief."

"Respect has nothing to do with it. I simply did not agree with what she believed. It's OK to disagree with someone. That doesn't mean you don't like or respect them."

"Well, whatever. I still don't feel comfortable with you."

"I'm sorry to hear that. I'll try to be more positive. At any rate, I appreciate your honesty. I hope you don't lie to me anymore in the future."

"I'm a bad girl. I wish I didn't feel this way. I know God loves me, but I have a hard time loving myself. With Julie gone I have no one I can really be honest with. It's taken me a year and a half to be able to reveal these things to you."

Harlan did not know what else to say. He rose to his feet and said, "I suppose I should go. Thanks for telling me all this. I know what you said must be hard for you."

Yoshiko went to the refrigerator to get his other beers. "Here, don't forget these."

Harlan returned to his apartment. Sugiyama was asleep in the three-mat room. Harlan sat at the *kotatsu* drinking the rest of the beer, listening to the cicadas, and thinking about where he had gone wrong in his relationship with Yoshiko. When the last of the beers was drunk, he lay on top of his futon and fell into a restless sleep. He began to dream.

* * *

Sugiyama and he were in a Greyhound bus riding through the redwood country in California. They were behind the driver, who resembled one of Harlan's high school friends. They were on a logging road in a national park. The bus skidded around a bend in the road and nearly toppled into a river. Suddenly, the driver became a young punk and Sugiyama turned into Yoshiko. The punk was trying to put some moves on Yoshiko. The bus was now a dune buggy. They met three more of Harlan's high school friends. He was waving good-bye to the friends. He felt a deep sense of guilt because he could not remember their names. They stopped at a restaurant. The punk was talking to Yoshiko. He had been wearing a bus driver's uniform before, but now he was wearing jeans and a T-shirt. He wanted to go to Japan and was asking Yoshiko about job possibilities. Harlan felt a sick sense of what was going to happen next. The punk started to kiss Yoshiko. She responded with a long French kiss. Harlan broke them apart. The punk laughed and went to the toilet.

Harlan took Yoshiko into the kitchen, which turned into a big country house run by a commune of hippies who were picking up empty Kirin beer cans. Harlan shook Yoshiko and said, "This is America, Yoshiko. You could get raped if you keep acting innocent and keep playing along with any stranger you meet."

They went back to their table. Yoshiko sat opposite Harlan and stuck a cigarette up her nose in defiance of him. The punk had his arms around her. Harlan felt paranoid, jealous, helpless. The punk pulled his pants down and put his penis in Yoshiko's mouth. She was slavering and grunting. Harlan moved toward them. Someone grabbed him from behind. He tried to scream. No sound came from his mouth.

*　*　*

Harlan woke with a start. Sugiyama was seated cross-legged in the three-mat room, working on a painting. Harlan glanced at the clock on the *kotatsu*. It was five o'clock in the morning.

18

O bon came and went. Harlan was thankful to have a week away from work. It was too hot for anyone to be able to concentrate. With the increase in Harlan's working hours had also come an increase in pay, but he was tired and the time off was more important than the money. His despair about the relationship with Yoshiko withdrew to a less dominant position.

Sugiyama often stopped by his place and they would go to the art gallery owner's shop, start drinking in the afternoon, return to Harlan's for a nap, go to the *sento* after the nap, go out to a cheap restaurant, then head back to Harlan's again to drink some more while watching a baseball game on television.

One night late in the month while Sugiyama was working on some sketches and Harlan was watching another baseball game, Yoshiko stopped by. "I was out jogging and saw your light on," she said. "Do you have any coffee?"

Harlan made the coffee. Sugiyama asked Yoshiko if she would model for him. She sat on the window ledge drinking her coffee while Sugiyama made several sketches of her. The last rays of the summer sun were fading. The sky had lost its brightness and become an almost transparent blue. A slight wind had come up. Outside and high above, violet clouds scudded across the sky.

An enchanting smile played on Yoshiko's oval face as she joked with Sugiyama. Harlan sat in a corner of the room staring at the delicate rose of her cheeks, the tense nostrils of her nose, the grave and hard-set corners of her mouth. He sensed in her the patience of a woman enduring a painful illness. There seemed to be in her an unresolved inner knot that was beyond his skill as a lover to untie.

Harlan felt a sudden, sinking helplessness of yearning to possess her. He felt the anguish of love as he had never felt it before. It was an almost unbearable pressure and suffering. He was seized by a sense of destiny, a realization that he would never again come across a woman so perfectly suited to himself. He began to feel ashamed that he had been so reluctant to enter her heart, but so eager to devour her body.

Sugiyama finished his sketches. Yoshiko had not spoken a word to Harlan. She got up to leave. As she passed by Harlan on the way out, he reached out and grabbed her arm. She threw him a vicious look, yanked her arm away, and hurried outside. Harlan ran down the stairs after her, stopped her in the street, and pleaded with her to listen to him.

"Yoshiko, I can't be a no-touch kind of friend after we've been intimate for so long. Why are you like this?"

"I'm sorry, but that's how it must be. It's over between us."

"How can you say that? Look, you and I are alike. We're strangers to love. We're always running away from situations and people. We don't know how to love. This might be the last chance for both of us. If you give up on me, you'll never be able to love anyone. Can't you see that?"

The more he spoke, the more wretched and self-conscious he became. He cursed himself for being so pathetic and impotent. Tears welled in his eyes. He felt his voice cracking.

Yoshiko looked at him for a moment. "I'm sorry, but you're wrong," she said, then turned around and walked home.

*　*　*

Two days later Harlan called Yoshiko with the hope of achieving a reconciliation. He went to her place and they stayed up half the night discussing what had gone wrong with their relationship. She again admitted her

212

apprehension about his cynicism, her resentment of his attitude toward Christianity, and her confusion about love and sex. It was a repetition of everything she had tried to explain to him before. He did not respond to her words the way she wanted him to. He just sat there during her explanations, unreachable, as if he belonged to a different world that had different laws. They were like two antipodes. She wondered if the problem lay in his inability to deal with rejection or in her inability to speak English clearly.

He began stopping by her place nearly every night after work. Yoshiko's own classes were in the afternoons and finished by five or six o'clock. She would return home to rest, fix dinner, watch the grey twilight descend, and get ready to go out at night. Then he would show up around nine o'clock. The first three or four times she tried to be polite, offered him dinner, and ran a bath for him. She even washed his shirt. She knew he had been out in the summer heat battling the crowds, and his shirt was drenched in sweat. She spoke little. She would watch him silently, showing no emotion, and wait for him to finish eating and go home.

By the fifth time, she had become irritated. His presence began to repulse her. He was like a child overcome with self-pity, but possessed of a strange power over her. She was afraid of this power because she did not understand it. She knew that he, too, was a prisoner of his own past, about which she still knew little, and there was a part of her that still wanted to reach out to him. But the more she was harried by his presence, the deeper she realized their relationship had become like a ragged piece of clothing that no longer fits.

A few times during this period she received a phone call from one of her boyfriends asking her to meet at a bar later in the night. She would take the call upstairs and spend a half hour or more giggling and talking a little louder than usual, hoping Harlan would take the hint and go home. A look of disgust would be in her eyes when she came downstairs again to find him still there. One night, after another long phone call and seeing him still seated at her table and wearing the same shirt he had worn for two days, she went to the closet, pulled out one of the shirts he had left on a previous occasion, and threw it at him.

"Change shirts tonight," she demanded. "You stink!"

After two weeks Yoshiko was at wit's end as to how to deal with Harlan's persistence. She was determined to get him to stop coming to her place. She started drinking early that night and was drunk enough to be frank when he showed his face.

He arrived later than usual. She told him to sit down. She glanced at him, lowered her eyes for a moment, then reached across the table for her cigarettes. She lit one and took a drink from her glass. Harlan noticed she was drinking her whiskey straight tonight. There was a look about her that Harlan had not seen before, something slightly different yet sharp and irrevocable. She spoke quietly, but with a piercing edge.

"You have to go home. I don't want you to come here anymore."

Harlan said nothing, got up, went out the door, put his shoes on, and left her apartment. He stopped at the park, hid in the bushes, drew from his pocket a battered pack of cigarettes, lit one, and, filled with contrition, waited to see if she would leave the apartment. Fifteen minutes later she did.

* * *

Jealousy based on imagination was something Harlan had experienced many times in his life, but now he began to be consumed by something different. It was certainly a feeling of jealousy, but it was such a vivid and sharp physical sensation that he could not free himself from it. He became addicted to it. He would return home late at night and lie on his futon until the early hours of the morning, accusing Yoshiko in his fantasies of shamelessly betraying him, and the feeling would continue to grow, invading every pore of his body like a cancer. He would grow hard and masturbate furiously, but this only exacerbated the feeling. He wrote long, rambling, confessional letters to Yoshiko, then tore them to shreds. He went to the park almost every night to spy on her. The thought of losing her became symbolic of losing life itself. He was submerged in a dark, clammy helplessness. He was trapped in a deplorable state that he had created for himself.

* * *

The autumn leaves changed color. The rice fields were harvested. The sound of insects lingered for a while, then disappeared. Yoshiko was alone at her apartment drinking. It was two in the morning. She was drunk and feeling depressed. She had been reprimanded at work that day for showing up late and teaching a bad lesson. The Cocos Island owner had been too busy to pay much attention to her at his coffee shop. Her other married boyfriend, a man she had seen off and on since her high school days, had promised to meet her at a snack bar and then stood her up. She was thinking about Harlan. She felt terrible about the way she had treated him. She knew it was weak and wrong for her to seek his forgiveness, but something, perhaps her overriding fear of loneliness, prodded her to move, to go to his place, to forget everything that had been said and done. There was only this moment. She did not want to be alone.

Harlan was still awake, lying in his futon. When he heard Yoshiko's voice and saw her silhouette at his door, he thought a ghost had come. In the last day or two he had finally convinced himself that Yoshiko was lost forever, yet here she was in the flesh. It was as if his unspoken prayers to a god he did not believe in had been answered.

"May I come in?" Yoshiko asked softly.

"Yoshiko, is that you?"

"Yes."

"Sure, come on in."

Yoshiko sat down at the edge of the futon and looked at him sadly.

"Are you OK? Is anything wrong?" Harlan asked.

"I don't know."

"Do you want to get under the cover?"

"Yes."

She took off her clothes and got in beside him. They said nothing, but made love with an unrestrained frenzy. While they were rolling about, Harlan's penis slipped out of her two times and they laughed together in a way they had not for a long time. When they finally finished, they lay panting and gazing at the dim glow of streetlights outside of his window. Then Yoshiko got up, put her clothes back on, and sat for a while longer looking at him from the shadows.

"I'm confused," she said. "I don't know why I'm here. There are two voices inside me. I don't know which one to listen to. I don't know if this is right."

She kissed him once more, then left.

* * *

Harlan waited for over a week, but Yoshiko did not come back again. His jealousy was rekindled and stirred in him like boiling tar in a cauldron. He felt himself going out of his mind. All he could think about was her. Why had she come back to him like that, only to toss him aside again? What had he done to make her so vindictive? Was this her way of torturing him for some unknown sin he had committed against her? He could not understand the reasoning behind it. In all of the nightmarish experiences he had undergone in his life, he could not recall ever feeling such a depth of despair and rage. Perhaps what he felt was beyond that. Perhaps it was more of an overpowering fear. Whatever it was, he could neither understand nor control it. It had to be vented.

After waiting for ten days he called Yoshiko after

work and told her to meet him at the park. He had worked himself up to a feverish pitch by the time she arrived. He started by lecturing her on her selfishness and lack of thoughtfulness about other people, but she just sat before him on the ground with a blank look on her face. He raised his voice and found himself starting to rant and rave. His anger spilled over and he screamed at her.

"You bitch! You fucking bitch! How dare you play with me like that? How can you tell me to stay out of your life, then come to my bed and fuck me and then throw me away again like a stinking piece of garbage? Don't you know what you've done to me? People have been killed for doing such things! You're a fucking whore and a fucking bitch!"

His fists were clenched, his body shaking. Yoshiko sat motionless, head down, tears flooding from her eyes. Harlan wanted to punch her face to a pulp. He stomped on the ground around her several times like a child throwing a tantrum. She would not look up at him. He cursed her once more, turned his back on her, and stormed home.

19

After the night of screaming at Yoshiko, loneliness, isolation, and confusion invaded Harlan's mind. He had never lost control of himself in front of a woman before. He was ashamed of himself. He did not know why or how he had allowed it to happen. He knew only that he had been overcome by a powerful emotion and succumbed to it.

With the softball and baseball season over, the approaching winter promised to be long, gloomy, and filled with introspection. He began thinking a lot about his past, particularly his childhood, about which he had never written effectively. He began jotting down a montage of childhood images in his notebooks. Knowing that Yoshiko was finished with him and that he was no more than a worm in her life now, Harlan decided to use his notes as the basis for a complete written examination of his life to present to her. Since he could not communicate with her directly, his only chance of putting back together the scraps of their broken relationship was to try to do it in written form. His previous attempts at confession had been pitiful outpourings of whining self-commiseration, all of which he had thrown away. Now he had a clear focus.

He began to write Yoshiko long letters about his childhood, adolescence, war experiences, journeys around the world, and how all this related to him and her. He was trying to understand not only himself, but also Yoshiko, for she, too, was a puzzle. Even her private moral self haunted him with a sense of something he had not clearly understood or evaluated. It seemed necessary for him to explain and justify his past and his love for her. He wrote and rewrote these letters with great care. The idea occurred to him that he could use the letters as the basis for a book. He made copies of every letter. When satisfied with what he had written, he would go to Yoshiko's late at night to slip the letter through the mail slot in her front door. He did not know what her reactions were, but the writing itself did him good.

Sometimes late at night after he had finished another letter and sat warming himself at the *kotatsu*, he contemplated his future. He would get the final renewal of his culture visa in January. He would have to change the type of visa in July if he wished to continue living in Japan. He had reached the point where a fundamental decision had to be made: Did he want to return to the States, where the only work he could find would

221

probably be as a cook? Or did he want to commit himself to a life in Japan? If he committed himself to living in Japan, he would have to make some serious efforts toward a career. Teaching at Rick's was becoming the equivalent of working at a language sweatshop. He had no academic qualifications to rise above the position he was in now. The school was becoming increasingly geared toward business growth. The familial atmosphere that had existed in the beginning had lately turned into something resembling a factory assembly line with students and teachers being rushed in and out of the partitioned classrooms like so many goods. The school had become a carbon copy of UCLA. They were not educating the students. They were merely feeding off a business phenomenon that saw a greater perceived need for English on the public's part than there was a supply of qualified institutions. Harlan did enjoy teaching English, but he had reached his peak in salary and position unless he made a move to improve himself professionally.

He began to have a series of dreams that seemed to underscore his dilemma. In the dreams he belonged to neither Japan nor the United States. Characters from both the past and present inhabited the dreams. The language used was a mixture of Japanese and English. In some dreams he returned to the States as a criminal, shunned by both family and friends. In other dreams he was in Japan as a bystander observing kidnappings or murders. The criminals would approach him and he would say in Japanese that he had not seen anything. The criminals often told him to go away. He would head off into a fog and become lost.

During the winter holiday Harlan took a four-day trip with Sugiyama through the Japan Alps and on to Karuizawa, a resort area outside Tokyo where the rich and famous went on vacation. The movement of the train and the passing scenery spurred his mind to thoughts of his time in India. He made more notes on how to use his relationship with Yoshiko in the novel he would write. The first sentence would be: *The first thing I noticed about her was the scars on her wrists*. The last sentence would be: *Tomorrow I leave for India*. He would focus on descriptions of Yoshiko, conversations they had had, changes in moods, and her alienation from Japan. He would have each description lead into a narrative about his own life the way he was capturing it in his letters to her. In the background would be a recurring desire to return to India to shock himself into a new perception in which the nagging questions of what comprised life, suffering, and fate would be all but obliterated.

Perhaps that is what he really would do. Perhaps

India was the next step. After Danny's death all ties with the United States had been severed. He wondered if he had grown too complacent in Japan. Had the fact he could eat, sleep, drink, work, and live comfortably made him contentedly bovine, complacent to the point where he could no longer think clearly and feel sensitively as he imagined he once had? The consumerism of Japan disgusted him as much as that of the United States, but there was still something about Japan that attracted him. He knew he would always be an outsider here. He knew he was, for all practical purposes, a man without a country. He knew he could never conform to the group behavior of Japan nor the ruthlessness of trying to succeed in the United States. For the time being, that suited him.

January was cold and grey. Harlan saw little of the Sasa Club members and Sugiyama. He had not seen Yoshiko for about four months. It seemed most people were holed up for the winter. The only time he left home himself was to go to work. At night he would try to make notes for his projected book by envisioning all he could about Yoshiko — her eyes, her narrow chin, the sharp lines of her thighs and calves, the way her breasts bounced perfectly when she walked, her smooth arms and hands. He would reconstruct the many scenes of their love-making and stare at them for hours. He would listen to the sound of her laughter and the slur of her words when she had been drinking. Then an emptiness behind the brain would blot out everything except for the realization that he was no longer the mainstay of Yoshiko's life.

*   *   *

Yoshiko remained sitting on the ground at the park, her spirit bruised and battered, for perhaps an hour after Harlan had berated her and called her "a bitch and a whore." Then she dragged herself home, threw herself on her bed, and wept profusely until the tears ran dry.

No one, not even her family members during the nadir of her relationship with them, had made her feel as low and worthless as Harlan had. No other lover had belittled her so thoroughly or honestly. No one had ever cut her to the bone with such precision. She knew she was "a bitch and a whore," but to hear the words screamed into her ears and stomped into the earth around her had been a torture worse than any her private demons had inflicted upon her. There was no end to the self-abasement she now felt.

More frightening than the look she had seen in his eyes when he had showered his rage over her had been the stark realization that she had caused it all, had even willed it all, to take place. She felt something rotting inside her, something horrible and nameless, something putrid and ugly that had such a contagious, disease-ridden quality it could not be contained. Whatever she touched became infected with it and also began to rot. She knew she had poisoned Harlan, and this terrified her.

The next day she bought a notebook. She needed to write down what the rottenness inside told her. She knew before she began that the things she would write would be so ugly and horrific that no eyes should ever see them. That is why she put her entries in the back of the notebook rather than in the beginning. She thought she would go crazy in the writing of all her sins, but if she did not write them, confess them in her special notebook to God, she would be forever at the mercy of her rottenness. She would be condemned to the fires of Hell.

She began recording her sins, filled one notebook, and started another. During this time she began receiving Harlan's letters on nearly a daily basis. Five or six letters piled up before she got the nerve to try to read one. Each letter was at least eight pages long. Lying unopened on her desk in her bedroom, they frightened her with what she knew they contained. She could not bear to see any more words from him that would strip her soul naked and expose her any more than her own self-examining was doing to her. She thought she finally understood his need to write, to purge his own demons, but she wished he would do it privately, as she was, and not slip his letters in her mail slot like so many Pandora's boxes that had the potential to release even worse horrors into her rotten world.

She knew she should either return the letters to him or throw them away, but her curiosity controlled her. Part of her sickness was a desire to suffer even more deeply. She tried to read the first two letters, but the flood of his emotional outpouring was too great. There were too many twists and turns, too many metaphorical digressions and descriptions, and too much unfamiliar vocabulary. The reading of those two letters exhausted her in the same way he had exhausted her. She gave up trying to read them. She found an empty box and, as his letters continued to arrive, tossed the new ones in with the old until the box filled up and she had to find another.

A month passed. Harlan's flood of letters turned into a trickle. Yoshiko hoped he had spent himself and defeated what had possessed him. She had exorcised much of her own sickness on paper and was now back into her routine of working, studying English, and drinking. She was once more in a void concerning her future. Her parents did not say much anymore, but she could feel the unspoken pressure on her to start considering the option of marriage and a more stable life. Her mother often dropped such hints as referring to how cute someone's baby was she had seen recently.

The anniversary of Yoshiko's return from Canada came and went. Now, in the depth of another winter, she was again going through enigmatic changes. The rhythm of the seasons of the last year had passed by with her scarcely taking notice. She had stopped going to Sunday mass altogether. Without Julie or Obaa-chan to talk with in the evenings, she was alone in her apartment with only her whiskey and guilt-stained conscience to keep her company. Often the loneliness was too great and, if she received no phone calls from any of her boyfriends, she would leave the apartment, go to Mukonoso, wait for the Cocos Island owner to close, and go for a midnight drive with him.

Near Christmas Yoshiko received a letter from Julie. Julie wrote that she would get her nursing degree in June and would probably be able to find a full-time job in Toronto by the fall. She hoped Yoshiko would think about visiting again in Canada if it were possible. The idea took root in Yoshiko's mind. The more she thought about it, the more excited she became.

She wrote back to Julie saying she was intent on visiting during the summer. Julie's invitation had given her a plan to focus on. She would save as much money as she could and try to leave Japan near the end of July. She also wrote about the breakup with Harlan, her frustration with men in general, her shameful behavior and inability to change without someone like Julie or Obaa-chan to give her guidance, and her need to escape the enclosed walls of Itami in order to gain a fresh perspective on her life. She was sorry that she was not living up to Christian standards, but she was certain that if she visited Canada again she would regain the spiritual feeling she had lost somewhere in the past year.

Yoshiko spent much of the winter holiday with her family. Her parents agreed with her plan to go to Canada. Her father offered her a chance to earn some extra money by working in his office as a part-time secretary two days a week. His other secretary was overloaded with paperwork and could use the help. Yoshiko thought his offer was partially a way to keep a closer eye on her, but she was happy to have the chance to save more money. It would be easy to fit two days of working at her father's office around the three days of classes she taught each week at the ECC school.

Near the end of the holiday Yoshiko took a three-day trip to Nagano to go skiing with some new friends she had met at a popular bar for young people in Umeda.

She had not skied since coming back from Canada and she enjoyed herself tremendously. The group skied all day for two days and stayed up until two in the morning drinking, acting silly, and telling stories. Yoshiko made some private time with the young man, a senior at university, who had invited her. She liked him. She had spent too much time with older men who were always serious and contemplative. This fellow was more fun-loving and had a wonderful body. She looked forward to seeing more of him.

Yoshiko's mother began to spend more time with her in January. Most of the time her mother knitted and complained about Yoshiko's brother. He had been dating the same woman for six years and was intent on marrying her. Yoshiko's mother could not stand the woman's parents and refused to entertain the idea of spending the rest of her days as an in-law to such despicable people. She was dead set against the marriage and would not compromise.

Yoshiko loved her brother greatly and felt sorry for him, for the pain he was suffering. She knew Masanori loved his girlfriend and was torn between his love for her and being ostracized by his family if he married her. There seemed no way out of the dilemma. There was nothing Yoshiko could say to her mother to change things. All she could do was listen and point out any inconsistencies she heard in her mother's criticism. In the end, Masanori would have to make his own decision and live with it. If he married the woman, he could be out of the family business. Like Yoshiko, he had not gone to university and had no useful qualifications. The only thing he knew was their father's business.

The problem took some of the attention away from Yoshiko. She seldom heard any complaints from her mother about what Yoshiko planned to do about her future. There was no mention about arranging a meeting with eligible and attractive marriage prospects. That was one thing Yoshiko was determined never to allow in her life. If she could not find a love relationship, she would settle for becoming "unsold goods," the Japanese expression used to describe women over 30 who had never married. She was approaching 25. She imagined she would get married around the age of 30.

In the meantime, she would work and plan for the coming summer and hope her family problems would be resolved in their own way. One day she wrote a letter to Obaa-chan, asking for guidance for herself and her brother, and placed the letter on the family altar. She made sure the envelope was sealed tightly. After a week passed, she retrieved the letter and took it to her own apartment. She put the letter in the same box she used for hiding her notebooks of confessed sins. She knew

Robert W. Norris

this was probably strange behavior for a Christian, but it gave her comfort and consolation. She believed God would forgive her if He saw anything wrong in being eclectic in her manner of worship.

20

The November wind nipped at their faces as Sachiko and Yumi stood before Sather Gate on the Berkeley campus. Yumi had flown up from San Diego the night before to spend the week with Sachiko, who now had her own small apartment near the campus. It was their first time to see each other in over a year. They both had much to catch up on about the changes in their lives. It felt good for Sachiko to be able to speak in Japanese again.

"Doesn't it make you feel nostalgic for Kobe?" Yumi asked.

"Not really. Kobe Women's College doesn't compare with Berkeley. Come, let's go to the Campanile. We can ride the elevator to the top and do some sketches of the scenery. It's beautiful. You'll like it."

They saw many students. Some were walking to classes, others were passing out leaflets.

"I feel wonderfully anonymous here," Sachiko said. "There are people from so many ethnic backgrounds. They dress in every conceivable wardrobe and have so many different kinds of behavior. The diversity is so

233

rich. That's the main difference between here and our school in Kobe. It's wonderful. I can blend into the crowd and still have my senses stimulated by an incredible array of sights, sounds, smells, voices, and colors. I just love it."

"I see what you mean. There's not that much diversity in San Diego. Terry and I have to go to Los Angeles when we get bored."

They arrived at the Campanile, entered the tower, rode the elevator to the top, and marvelled at the expanse around them. To the west they could clearly distinguish the Golden Gate Bridge, the San Francisco-Oakland Bay Bridge, and the outline of Mount Tamalpais in the distance. The entire Bay Area stretched out before them.

"It's beautiful, absolutely beautiful," Yumi said. "Think of all the thousands of kilometers that separate us from Japan."

"That's the way I like it for now."

After making several sketches from all the viewpoints at the top of the tower, they decided to rest awhile in the shade of the trees at Faculty Glade. Many students were either picnicking or sitting on the grass and studying. Sachiko looked at her sketches. The one of the eastern viewpoint with the Hearst Greek Theater nestled into a foothill in the center and surrounded by trees was the best. She showed it to Yumi.

"Do you like it?" Sachiko asked.

"Yes, very much. You still have the same talent you had before."

"I think I might frame it and put it next to the Renoir and Toulouse-Lautrec prints on the wall in my bedroom."

They opened their little *bento* lunch boxes, which were wrapped in Japanese scarves, and ate the sandwiches and fruit Sachiko had prepared.

"Things have changed a lot in the last year and a half, haven't they?" Yumi said thoughtfully. "I can't believe we are both living in America. It's very exciting, don't you think?"

"Yes. I'm very happy now, but the day I left Japan I was more frightened than when I was 19 and got on the plane to go to Mexico by myself. I was worried about everything. Had I made the right decision? Would people understand my English? What would I do when I arrived? Would I be taken advantage of by a dishonest taxi driver? Would I be able to find an apartment by myself? Did I have all the proper documents? I was worried about everything.

"In the seat next to me on the plane there was this big black man. I was terrified by his size, but he started a conversation and turned out to be a gentleman. He had been in Japan on business and said he liked Japan and the people. He got off the plane in Hawaii, but asked an elderly couple to watch over me and help me if I had any problems when we arrived in San Francisco. I did have a few moments of anxiety at the airport, but the couple found a taxi and instructed the driver to take me to the campus here.

"The people at the Student Affairs office arranged for me to spend a week in the International House. It's a kind of dormitory. Then they helped me find my apartment. I felt grateful to everyone. And now I feel quite confident. I do all my own shopping and I know how to use the BART train. Sometimes I go walking in different parts of San Francisco. I think I'm becoming independent."

"That's wonderful," Yumi smiled at Sachiko. "I'm very proud of you."

"Thank you. But I'm talking only about myself. Please tell me everything about your life. Is it hard? Do you miss Japan?"

Yumi told the whole story of the scandal she and Terry had caused in both their families. They had waited for Terry's divorce to be finalized before he went to Japan and started working in a conversation school, but the salary was not enough and they decided to get married and return to San Diego, where he could resume his private practice as a dentist. They had not had a wedding ceremony in Japan. They had only registered the marriage at Ashiya City Hall. They had then gone to Reno for their American wedding and honeymoon.

At first, Terry's parents had seemed distant, but now that she was two months into pregnancy they had become more loving and supportive. Yumi's own family had expressed outrage in the beginning, but they too seemed to have accepted the marriage now that a future grandchild had entered the equation.

"Of course," Yumi said, "there are many things that are difficult to become accustomed to, but my English has improved a lot. Terry and I are just as much in love now as when we first met. Our marriage is the best. I still feel as if I'm in a dream sometimes. As long as we have each other I don't care where we live. I have no regrets. The only problem is that in America there's so much food and everyone eats so much. You can see how much fatter I am now. You better be careful, Sachiko. I know how much you like to eat."

Sachiko laughed. "I'm so happy you came to visit me."

"I am, too. You look very beautiful, grown-up. I think you've changed a lot. Have you made any friends here?"

"No one like you, but I've made some acquaintances.

I think at first I was a little tentative about trying to make friends too quickly. I didn't trust anyone, but everyone I meet seems amiable and involved in something meaningful. I'm patient. Eventually I'll find a confidant, maybe even a lover."

"Whatever happened with Harlan? I was always worried about you and him. I had a feeling you were in over your head with him. And then you were foolish to become friends with your rival."

Sachiko thought for a moment. The humiliation and frustration of those relationships seemed suddenly far away. "It's strange to think about," she said. "I don't feel any antagonism toward them. In fact, I think I even feel grateful for what they did for me."

"Grateful? That's a strange word to use. What do you mean?"

"Well, I think they helped push me onto a path I probably couldn't have chosen for myself. Yoshiko is the one who encouraged me to take the TOEFL test and start thinking about continuing my formal education. Shortly after I scored well on the test I rediscovered the world of painting. You know, I had abandoned that world in my teens. One day when I was sick and also depressed because of Harlan I created an extraordinary painting of a snake shedding its skin. I shocked myself with that painting, but when I thought about it later I

238

realized my subconscious had told me something."

"What was that?"

"The snake was me and I had to shed the skin of my former self before I could become a new person. Also, I realized I had a talent. I decided then to give up my study of literature and return to my artistic roots."

"But can you do anything with a degree in art or art history?" Yumi asked. "I can't imagine you as a teacher."

"Neither can I, but I have a plan. I think some day I want to run my own art gallery. I can never go back to working in a big company. Actually, the time I spent working in Osaka wasn't wasted. I learned a lot about bookkeeping and handling money. I did hate working for such common people, though. It was insulting to have to serve tea and make copies for lazy, middle-aged men who think only about numbers, statistics, sizes, amounts, and sex. I hated their babel and their trivial attitudes. In the future I think if I can combine my love of beauty and knowledge of art with my father's money and my own bookkeeping skills, I just might be able to create reality from a dream."

"You've always been a dreamer, Sachiko."

They laughed again. It was late afternoon and the sun was low in the sky. The wind had died down. A few scattered groups of students were lingering after classes.

A feeling of peacefulness settled over the campus.

"And Harlan? How are you grateful to him?"

"Maybe grateful isn't the right word. He stirred emotions in me that I had never felt before. I didn't understand them and I certainly couldn't control them. I know he never meant to be cruel to me. I suppose more than anything he helped me realize that I was unable to express myself adequately in words. I can say he played a big role in turning me back to painting as my main form of expression.

"I wanted desperately to be his mentor of Japanese literature, but I couldn't. Maybe he was looking more for a masculine point of view, someone like Mr. Inoue, the expert on Ango Sakaguchi who I wrote you about."

"Did you ever make love with him?" Yumi asked.

"That's my secret. The fact is now he's no longer a part of my life. I wish him well, but I have to make my own life."

"If I know you, Sachiko, you'll find a new obsession soon enough."

"I don't know. I doubt I have the patience anymore to wait as long as I did for all three of my unrequited loves — Jose, Tom, and Harlan. I'm going to concentrate all my energy on my study and painting. If someone comes along who can share that with me, fine. I want to be the one who dictates the terms of the relationship.

"That's the one thing I respected about Yoshiko. She was the one in control, the one who manipulated her men. She had more lovers than just Harlan. Who knows? Maybe there's more than one man in my future. Anyway, it's starting to get cold. Shall we head over to Bancroft Way? There's still enough time left to see some of the collection of art in the University Art Museum. After that I want to take you to a nice Italian restaurant near my apartment."

"That sounds like a wonderful plan." Yumi rubbed her stomach and giggled again. "Now I have to worry about eating for two."

They packed their *bento* boxes, stood up, brushed the grass from their skirts, held hands, and began the short walk to the University Art Museum.

21

Yoshiko was seated at her kitchen table, a bottle of whiskey and scattered papers placed before her. She was almost finished with the six-page translation she had been working on for three days. She had been a fool to take on the job of translating her university boyfriend's friend's term paper from Japanese into English. The money had seemed easy — ¥1,000 a page — but she had not anticipated how much time it would take. Her rough draft was hopelessly inept and she was supposed to have it ready by the next day.

There was only one thing she could do at this late stage: go to Harlan for help. She had no other choice, but the thought of seeing him again frightened her. She did not know how he would react to her knocking on his door late at night after not having seen him for five months. Would he fly into a rage like he had the last time? Would he be forgiving? Would he want to sleep with her? Would she be able to say no?

She looked down at the papers, sighed, picked them up, and put them into a neat pile. There was no more she could do with the translation. Her sentences contained too many grammatical mistakes and were mostly direct translations of the original. She would go to his place, get down on her knees and beg if she had to, plead for his forgiveness, and ask for just this one favor. He was, after all, a teacher, and the proofreading that needed to be done was not for her alone, but for a student of English. If he would not do it for her sake, he might do it for the student.

She picked up the pile of papers, put on her jacket, and started out the back door. She hesitated a moment, then returned to the kitchen table and grabbed the bottle of whiskey and a new pack of cigarettes. If Harlan decided to do the proofreading, she would need something to keep her occupied while she was waiting.

His light was still on when she reached his apartment. A sudden panic swept through her. What if he was inside with another woman? Yoshiko had no idea if he had another girlfriend. If someone was with him, particularly in bed with him, it would further complicate things and prove embarrassing. He would probably misread her coming to his place at night. She quickly dismissed the thought. She would have to risk his having company. She climbed the steps and knocked softly on the door.

Harlan opened the door and stood transfixed. "Yoshiko. What are you doing here? You're about the last person in the world I expected to see tonight."

"May I come in?"

"Sure, I guess. I've got the kerosene heater going in the other room. Come in."

They sat down at the *kotatsu*. Yoshiko sat on the opposite side of Harlan and pulled the *kotatsu* blanket up to her waist. "I have a favor to ask you."

"What is it?"

"I have to finish this translation by tomorrow. I've done all I can do and I was hoping you could check it for me."

"Let me see it."

Yoshiko handed him the papers and put her bottle and cigarettes on the *kotatsu*. Harlan glanced over the work she had done, looked up at her, and said, "This might take a little time."

"I can wait."

"Let me get you a glass and a clean ashtray."

Harlan took the ashtray off the *kotatsu* and went into the kitchen to empty it and bring back a glass. He then picked up a pencil and began making corrections and rewriting many sentences. He occasionally asked a few questions about context or word choice, but for the most part remained silent. He got up once to go to the toilet and get himself a beer from his refrigerator. It took about an hour to finish the proofreading.

Yoshiko felt her head spinning from the whiskey, but she also felt relaxed and relieved that he had not shown any anger and had proofread the paper. He was more like the old Harlan tonight. She poured him a drink.

"Here. You deserve this," she said and clinked his glass with hers. "I really appreciate it. I don't know what I would have done without your help. Thank you so much. I can pay you some money later."

"I don't need your money. It was nothing. So what have you been up to these last few months?"

Yoshiko found herself answering his questions with an honesty of which she had not thought herself capable. She talked about the three men she was seeing, about playing golf with the Cocos Island owner, tennis with the married man from her school days, and the ski trip with the university student and his friends. She said she was not serious about any of them because there were no obligations. She might think about getting married when she was close to 30, but for now she was interested in just making some money teaching English to children, playing golf and tennis, occasionally skiing, and not thinking about anything too seriously.

"Why are you so nice to me?" she asked suddenly, then stared at her glass for a moment, took another drink, and laughed nervously. "I'm just a bad girl. I want to be a good girl, but every time I get drunk I can't say no to men. I'll probably go to Hell. I hate sex, but I want to make the man feel good. I have to stop drinking."

Harlan was silent. Yoshiko seemed to be feeling guilty. He wanted to hear her confession. She said nothing about his letters. After a pause she continued.

"You're the only one who ever called me a bitch. I don't want to hear you call me a bitch. You scare me... all I do is hurt you and you're still nice to me. I'm not good enough for you...people who are abused when they're children are different, you know...you really think I'm a whore, don't you? You must hate me."

Yoshiko's words were becoming slurred. Her head nodded forward. She rubbed her eyes, then looked back at Harlan. "What do you want from me?" she asked.

"Honesty. What do you want from me?"

"Nothing." She poured herself the last of the whiskey. "How can you love me when I've been so cruel to you?"

"I can't judge you because I've done worse things to other people. Besides, love is accepting people as they are and not trying to change them." Harlan paused a second, then added, "That's what Jesus did."

Yoshiko moved on her hands and knees around the *kotatsu*, embraced Harlan tightly, picked up the rewritten paper, then stumbled out the door.

TORAWARE

*   *   *

Yoshiko did not come back again after the night Harlan proofread her translation. All the self-torture of his jealousy was rekindled. In the evenings after returning from work and going to the *sento*, he often bought a beer from Morita's vending machine and went to the park near Yoshiko's place. For several nights in a row the same car was parked in back of her place. He would wait for about an hour to see if a new boyfriend would emerge from the apartment. He would begin to shiver from the cold, get up stiffly, and return home a defeated man.

After two weeks of the same routine, a man finally came out of Yoshiko's apartment and got in the car. It was her father. Harlan felt a fool in suspecting Yoshiko of things she had not done, in believing she had done the worst. He asked himself: *Can I really be patient enough to wait for her? Do I really love her this much to spy on her night after night?* His questions seemed as ridiculous as his accusations and suspicions.

March 1st was her birthday. Harlan could not continue to wait for her to come to him. He decided to use her birthday as a pretext for seeing her again. She had mentioned the last time that she had started to enjoy playing golf. He bought her a new putter and some balls so she could practice putting at home. After teaching a company class in Osaka, he hurried back to Itami.

It was nearly ten o'clock when he arrived at Yoshiko's. The kitchen light was on. He went through the garden path that led to the back door. He knocked, opened the door, and stuck his head inside. Both Yoshiko and her mother were at the kitchen table. Harlan felt a tension in the room as they both stared back at him.

"Uh...I...uh...know it's your birthday today, so I brought you a little present."

Yoshiko rose from the table to come to the door. Harlan handed her the putter and balls. She looked at him with astonishment.

"You said last time that you were getting into golf. I thought you could use these to practice at home," he said.

He looked over at Yoshiko's mother and smiled at her. She did not reciprocate the smile, but said a curt "*Doomo*" and went back to her knitting.

Yoshiko held the putter and balls up and said, "This is too much. It's really too much. I can't accept these."

"Sure you can. I guess I'd better go. See you later. Happy birthday."

Harlan closed the door and made a quick exit. He

248

cursed his luck. He should have known her mother or father or both would be there to share her birthday. The strange thing was there had not seemed to be any celebratory atmosphere. He wondered if Yoshiko and her mother had been fighting.

*   *   *

That following weekend the softball season started. There was a cold wind and the field, particularly the left field area where Harlan was playing, was slick and muddy from the rain of the night before. The Sasa Club team played a doubleheader, winning the first game and playing to a tie in the second game. Harlan had two hits, a walk, two stolen bases, and scored three runs in the two games. With Sasa Club leading 5-3 with two outs and the bases loaded for the opposition in the fifth inning of the second game, the batter lofted a wind-blown fly ball toward Harlan. His feet slipped on the mud and he got a late start on the ball. He had been playing too deep. He raced toward the ball at full speed, stretched out his glove, and tried to make a shoestring catch. The ball hit the tip of the glove fingers and bounced away from him. By the time he retrieved the ball and threw it back to the infield, the batter was standing on third base and all three runners had scored. The other team was laughing, pointing at him, waving their caps, and yelling, *"Gaijin-san, ookini!"*

The next two weeks were cold and rainy with grey skies every day. It was the time of year when people were at their most irritable. Once again Harlan took to walking the streets late at night and pausing by Yoshiko's at the end of the walks. One night when no one was at her home he sat down in the park to drink a beer and lose himself in his thoughts. About ten minutes had passed when he saw a car approach slowly and park next to her place. Harlan bent down in the shadows to watch. Yoshiko and a man got out of the car and went inside the apartment. The kitchen light was turned on for a short while. Then it was switched off and a moment later the light in Yoshiko's bedroom went on.

A panic swept through him. All his worst fears came to his mind. His hands trembled. He felt if he did not act, he would regret it forever. He even had the thought that he had to stop Yoshiko because she was incapable of controlling herself. The irony of his thought process was not lost on him as he realized in a flash that his entire conception of morality was based on his early Catholic upbringing even though his intellectual mind could not accept those so-called truths. It was only emotionally that he reacted in a Christian manner to Yoshiko's behavior. He had always equated adultery by a woman as a sin nearly equal to murder. He had to save her from herself.

He raced to the pay phone in the park, shoved some ¥10 coins in the slot, and dialed her number.

"*Nakashima de gozaimasu.*"

"Yoshiko. This is Harlan."

"What are you calling for?"

"I know you're there with your married boyfriend and you can't do it."

"Can't do what?" Yoshiko said, anger rising in her throat.

"You can't sleep with him because you'll be committing adultery. You'll be committing a sin. Can't you understand what you're doing? You're the Christian. You should know better. It's not right. Please, don't sleep with him!" Harlan's plea was so naked it was sad.

"You're pushing me," Yoshiko said harshly. "I'll decide if I want to sleep with him or not. Leave me alone."

The phone went dead. Harlan stood a moment, stunned and staring at the receiver in his hand. He replaced it in the hook and ran back to his hiding place in time to see the light in her bedroom go off. He was incensed. He did not know what to do. He walked to Morita's, bought several more beers, returned to the park, and, in the silence and darkness, drank and brooded.

Harlan worked up the courage to confront the man
when he left in the morning. He practiced over and over
in his mind what he would say in Japanese, knowing he
would trip over his tongue and mispronounce the most
important words or become mired in a difficult verb
conjugation and lose the impact of what he wanted to
say, but he would still have the element of surprise in
his favor. He waited. The dawn sky turned different
shades of blue, then grey. A few birds chirped and
fluttered from telephone wire to telephone wire. Several
people began to appear on the streets. It was seven
o'clock and still the man had not emerged. Harlan was
exhausted. His eyelids were heavy and his brain sodden
with alcohol. He gave up and plodded home.

It continued to rain through the rest of March.
Sugiyama spent one weekend at the end of the month
working on some new paintings. Sugiyama often saw
Yoshiko because both she and her mother had accounts
at his bank. He had recently had a cup of coffee with
Yoshiko at one of the neighborhood coffee shops and
they had talked a lot about Harlan. Harlan spent much of
that Sunday morning badgering Sugiyama with questions about Yoshiko.

"What do you think I should do about her?" Harlan
asked.

"For one thing, I think whenever you see her you

should talk about normal things like the weather or how her job is going instead of always harping about morals and values and what's right and wrong. I think she's really afraid of you. She can't understand how you could go for such a long time showing no feelings and then suddenly start scolding her and getting overly emotional about her trying to find a new lover. She's confused by you. You're not the person she thought you were before."

"I don't know if I can talk about 'normal' things when I see her."

"Why not?"

"With Yoshiko there can be no middle ground for me. I can't be just a friend to her. I have to make her either love me again or totally hate me. If she hates me, I can use the hate to create a novel and gain something meaningful. If she loves me, I can live in a meaningful way by loving her like I've never loved anyone. If I stick to the middle ground, all I'll have is a life filled with painful memories of what might have been."

Sugiyama stopped his painting for a moment and considered what Harlan had said. "I suppose that makes sense. What is it that attracts you to Yoshiko so much anyway?"

"I think she understands suffering more than anyone I've ever met."

Three days later it was raining heavily again. Harlan decided to take the train to Mukonoso rather than ride his bicycle. As he stepped off the train at Tsukaguchi to change trains to Mukonoso, he saw someone who looked like Yoshiko. He approached the woman. It was Yoshiko. She was wearing a dress and some make-up. He could not recall having seen her dressed this way before. She was waiting for a train to Osaka. He remembered Sugiyama's advice.

"Hello, Yoshiko. What are you doing here?"

She looked at him indifferently. "I have a class in Osaka."

"How's your teaching going?"

"OK."

"You look nice in a dress. I think today's the first time I've ever seen you wear one."

"Thank you." There was no enthusiasm in her voice.

The train to Osaka screeched into the station. Yoshiko waited patiently for the passengers inside to get off the train. She then stepped inside, shifted her bag to her left shoulder, and reached up to grip one of the straps used by the standing passengers to keep their balance.

"I hope your class goes well today." Harlan attempted a smile.

"Good-bye," Yoshiko said.

The door closed and the train left the station. Harlan

stared after it for a minute, then trudged toward the
underpass that led to the platform on the other side of
the tracks.

22

I t was another grey, overcast day that threatened rain. It had rained throughout much of March and April. The blooming of the cherry blossoms had seemed briefer than usual this year. Yoshiko had not even had a chance to join in a blossom-viewing party because of the weather. May had been balmy and sunny and she had played tennis several times. Now the oppressive rainy season had started. Yoshiko was anxious for the next six weeks to pass so she could finally see Julie again. She had already reserved an airplane ticket to Toronto for July 30th.

She would not allow the weather to affect her excitement and anticipation. She was again experiencing the beauty and wonder of all of nature and life. She was learning to relax with her often complicated and confusing relationships with her family and her friends. She was determined not to create any more problems or complications with anyone. That included Harlan.

He had angered her greatly with his phone call the night her married friend stayed over. Who was Harlan to tell her what to do or not to do? She had always resented

anyone who presumed to wield authority over her. She
felt she was at fault for having brought out the monster
in Harlan, but she could not put her finger on what
exactly she had done to make him act in such a bizarre
and vindictive manner. The anger she had felt was
nearly gone. Her faith told her it was her duty to forgive
and forget. She could forgive, but she found it difficult
to forget the fear and indignation he had raised in her.

She had run into him three times in the last two
months. Each time he had seemed more like his old
self: tentative, laconic, amiable. Perhaps the distance she
had kept from him was working. Perhaps he was
beginning to accept their separation. Perhaps they could
be friends in the long run. She knew the odds against
that happening were not favorable, but she hoped for it
anyway. She did not want to feel that the time they had
spent together was wasted. She had shared so much with
him, given so much of herself to him, and invested so
much of herself in him, that the thought of achieving no
reconciliation was almost unthinkable. It was possible
the affliction of the rottenness inside her was at the heart
of the problem. She could only pray for some kind of
redemption.

In the past two months she had been reading the
English Bible Harlan had given her for Christmas a year
and a half ago. She had never taken much notice of the

Book of Ecclesiastes in the past, but recently she had turned to that section and her eyes had fixated on the passage about there being a time for every purpose under Heaven. The words "a time for love, a time for hate" and "a time to hold, a time to refrain from holding" had practically jumped out of the page at her as if they had been spoken to her directly by God. She took it to be a sign, perhaps even an order, to forgive Harlan and give him another chance to be her friend.

It seemed no coincidence that she had run into him at Hankyu Itami Station the very next day. She could tell he was intensely pleased to see her. Almost as if another person had taken control of her body and mind, she dropped the cold exterior she had put between them, greeted him warmly, laughed with him, and without knowing why, asked him if he would be interested in giving her two conversation lessons a week in order to help her prepare for going to Canada. The look of shock and disbelief that came over his face was still fresh in her mind. She had almost burst into a fit of laughter.

"Uh...well...sure, I'd...I'd be more than happy to," he had stammered.

He came over the next morning. She immediately set down the rules for their new relationship. She said, "We're starting from zero. Please don't be foolish. Don't call me at night. Don't ask me about my relationships with other men. And don't lecture me about my behavior. Can you agree to that?"

"Yes, I think so." He looked like a little boy when he nodded his agreement.

Everything had gone well up to now. He had prepared some interesting and useful lessons. They concentrated on her study. He did not mention anything about her affairs and, other than small talk, they exchanged little conversation beyond the content of the lessons. At the end of the last lesson, however, he invited her out for a drink. She was taking a risk by agreeing to go out with him tonight, their first actual date in almost a year, but it was also a challenge to see how he would act and speak at night and in a place other than the "classroom atmosphere" of her kitchen in the morning when he still had classes to teach later in the day. It was a test for him. She hoped he would pass.

There was another part of her that was anxious about tonight. What would she do if, under the influence of alcohol, he reverted back to the jealous and paranoid stranger who scared her so much? Or, worse still, what if she got drunk and submitted to his amorous pleadings? She had made that mistake with too many men before, but Harlan was the only one who had made her pay for it. This date was a test for herself, too. She felt the need for a drink, but thought better of it. If she started drinking now, it would surely lead to trouble later.

It was now 5:30 in the afternoon. They were to meet at 8:30 at her new hangout in the southern part of Mukonoso, the *okonomiyaki* shop where her university friends often gathered. It was a safe place. If Harlan got too carried away, there would be other friends there who could join them and distract him from becoming too probing or private in his conversation. She would try to limit herself to only two or three drinks. It was time to get up and move. The desire to drink was becoming stronger. She would go to the Cocos Island coffee shop first for some coffee and, if she felt the need, advice.

*   *   *

Harlan finished his last class at Rick's school promptly at eight o'clock and hurried to the scheduled meeting place. He arrived 15 minutes early. There were four other customers, all in their early twenties, seated at the far end of the counter. He ordered a draft beer and studied the menu. The place had most of the same items cooked on an open griddle as other *okonomiyaki* restaurants, but there were also many specialties of the house that seemed to be the owner's own recipes. He would wait until Yoshiko showed up before ordering anything to eat. He lit a cigarette. The owner brought him the beer. He downed half the mug in two swallows.

He felt as if he were inside a movie where the two main characters were the same people throughout the story, but kept changing personalities so often that they were, in essence, doomed continually to have to deal with each other as strangers. As soon as one thought he or she had an inkling of who the other person was and how to talk to that person, act around that person, adjust to that person's moods, accept that person, and finally love that person, a new personality would enter that person's body and the process would start over again.

It was frustrating. Harlan did not understand the person he himself had become. He did not understand the new stranger called Yoshiko. He understood only that the feelings he had realized too late and existed for the Yoshiko who had abandoned him last summer were now focused on the entirely different woman he was to meet tonight. If he tried to show his feelings, they would surely be misdirected and slammed back into his face.

After the last few months of misery and self-commiseration — even insanity if he were to be honest with himself — during Yoshiko's absence, Harlan's reaction to the sudden thaw in their relationship was one of bewilderment. He had almost come to accept that he had mutilated any possibility of ever entering into Yoshiko's life again, but then she had mysteriously tossed him the tiniest of straws to clutch at and he had foolishly and willingly grasped it like a drowning man who has no other chance for survival. He was without question under her control now. His life was hers to do with what she would. He yearned for nothing other than the charade of the twice-a-week, hour-long lessons they were acting out together. Nothing else seemed to matter, even if she did terminate the lessons and send him packing at precisely the minute they ended.

The words she had spoken that first lesson — "We're starting from zero" — rang in his head. Indeed, his life had been reduced to a zero. The question now was: Would he be able to repress his overwhelming urge to embrace her and unleash all the terrible words that would destroy this love he could not understand? How long could he realistically play this game of engaging in "normal" conversation?

He ordered another beer and looked at the clock on the wall. It was 8:45. She was late. Was this, too, part of the game? Was she playing with him? Telling him something? Had she forgotten about the date? He stamped out his cigarette, his third since he had arrived, went over to the pay phone, and called Yoshiko's number. No one answered. He hung up the phone. He heard the door open, looked in that direction, and there was Yoshiko entering. His heart jumped.

"Yoshiko, I was just calling your place. I thought you might have forgotten about tonight."

"I'm sorry I'm late."

She greeted the owner and other customers warmly. She and Harlan sat down and ordered two more beers. Yoshiko introduced Harlan to everyone and they asked several questions about him, made a few jokes about how they could not speak English, raised their glasses in a toast, then returned to their own conversation.

Yoshiko and Harlan ordered some fried noodles and gratin dishes. After the next beer they switched to whiskey. Yoshiko had her own bottle, which the owner brought out with some ice and water. They poured their own drinks, talked about Yoshiko's upcoming trip to Canada, and laughed several times. Two hours passed quickly.

"When I come back from Canada, I want to pay you for your lessons," Yoshiko said with a sudden seriousness. "I want to keep this a business relation-ship."

"I can't take money from you, Yoshiko. You know that. My teaching you is something I want to do for you from my heart. It's just a favor between what I hope are two people who are trying to get close again. It's no different from my asking you to wash a shirt for me or look after my apartment if I take off for a few days.

You'd do those things for me if I asked, wouldn't you?"

"Yes, probably."

"Besides, I don't want to have a mercenary relationship with you. I still want to be your number one lover."

Yoshiko stiffened noticeably, then said, "Well, let me pay my half tonight. It's time to go home."

She said little on the train back to Itami and nothing during the walk from the station to her apartment. Two times Harlan unintentionally bumped into her while they walked and she immediately moved to the side to put some space between them. When they reached the entrance to her backyard, Yoshiko said an abrupt "Good night" and hurried inside, leaving Harlan to stare after her.

He stood for a few seconds, admonished himself for saying what he had not intended to say, and headed home with a sinking feeling that this had probably been the last date he would ever have with her.

23

Harlan woke to the sound of rain outside. Grey morning light entered the six-mat room through the large window and penetrated his eyes. Thick phlegm stuck to the roof of his mouth. In the pit of his stomach and deep inside his head, his hangover unleashed its poison.

He lay on his futon unable to move and feeling sorry for himself. Scraps from scenes in the nightmare he had woken from came back: he the stalker being stalked by Vietnamese, Hindu Indians, Danny, others from the past; the scenery shifting from desert to jungle to the Gulf of Mexico to the small shrines in his Itami neighborhood; the panic of knowing he would be caught before catching his prey; Yoshiko in the distance having animal sex with two men, one young and one old; skeletal hands wrapping themselves around his neck, ankles, torso.

It was the same nightmare he had been having for a week. Slowly, he came to life, opened his eyes fully, and looked around the cluttered room. Clothes and books were everywhere. Scores of black ants were crawling in and out of the empty coffee and beer cans that had been on the *kotatsu* for days. The ants formed a long line that ran to the far wall, where a tiny hole disappeared into the broken plaster.

He looked at the clock on the *kotatsu*. It was 5:30 — two and a half hours since he had stumbled home, passing by Yoshiko's apartment and seeing she was not home. A momentary wave of helpless urgency passed through him as he rose to go to the kitchen and douse his head with cold water. Imprisoned as he was in his wretched condition, he knew he had to go through with it again. He had to continue his spying, to see if she had returned and with whom.

He was in the grip of something so powerful it had taken him over completely. It was something far worse than jealousy or vindictiveness. It was more like a summons to his own private purgatory.

He was into the fourth day of the binge. How had it started? Bits and pieces started coming back. Yoshiko had terminated the lessons the day after their last date. He had broken his promise and asked her again about her lovers. Her eyes had narrowed and voice sharpened. Her answer: She had phoned the one married man and cut off that relationship. She was still seeing the Cocos Island owner. His friendship was special, but she had stopped sleeping with him. She was sleeping only with the university student.

Then this:

Harlan: "Are you still afraid of me?"

Yoshiko: "Yes."

Harlan: "Why?"

Yoshiko: "Because I think one day you'll kill me."

A long silence. Then:

Yoshiko: "Please go, Harlan. And don't come back."

Harlan: "I only want to ask you one thing before I go."

Yoshiko: "What?"

Harlan: "Please, don't ever lie to your young boyfriend."

He swallowed two aspirins and shook his head, trying to clear the cobwebs. She had to know about his nightly spying. Why else would she have said she was afraid he would kill her? Was it the night about a week before when he had brazenly entered the unlocked back door late at night, entered her empty house (he had been polite enough to take his shoes off at the back entrance), gone up to her bedroom, found her diaries, tried to read them but the scrawled *kanji* lettering had been too difficult to read, panicked when he heard a noise outside, and left the apartment? That must have been the night. The sound he heard must have been

Yoshiko returning and discovering the kitchen light on. If it was Yoshiko, she had done nothing to show she knew he had been there.

He got dressed and walked outside. The rain had stopped. The streets were empty. He was thankful for that. He would not have to exchange with any of his neighbors the cheery, ritual greetings that he was beginning to despise. He passed by the park and concrete apartment buildings near Yoshiko's place. The sky was a leaden grey. Water was still dripping from the foliage on the trees that lined the streets. Parked under one tree near Yoshiko's backyard was a car Harlan had not seen before, a small, red Toyota. He knew immediately it belonged to the university student. He felt a sudden, vast fatigue. He was like someone stunned by a heavy blow, someone whose sense of direction has left him.

He proceeded around the building to the front, where he had done his most brazen and close-up spying. The front walkway was guarded by shrubbery and a large tree. No one could see him once he was inside the walkway. The front door was always locked as Yoshiko used the back entrance most of the time, but he could push the mail slot open far enough to hear much of what went on inside the apartment. He squatted and pressed his ear to the slot. He had an erection.

Yoshiko and the university student were upstairs in her bedroom. There were some muffled sounds in Japanese that Harlan could not understand. Then he heard Yoshiko giggle. She was drunk again. There was a moment of silence, then another Yoshiko giggle. He heard her say in Japanese, "OK, roll over on the count of three. One, two, three." More laughter followed the sound of bodies rolling on the floor.

He had expected something like this. He stayed in his squatting position, utterly at a loss what to do. An empty chagrin gave way to resignation. In a daze, Harlan realized Yoshiko was dead to him. He closed the mail slot quietly, crept out of the shrubbery, and returned home with an oppressive sense of doom building inside him.

Back at his apartment, Harlan lit a cigarette and noticed he had finished three packs since last night. He tried to focus his thinking, but lurking at the back of his brain like some unshakable grief was the knowledge he had lost control of logic. He could not stop the madness of his thoughts. He put out his cigarette, thought of the image of Yoshiko rolling and giggling on the floor, and masturbated furiously until it hurt. He went to the kitchen, grabbed another beer, and guzzled it down. He lay back down on the futon.

He had become a shameless rogue. He was so sick

that now the physical feeling of excitement that stemmed from his addiction to jealousy was giving him sexual satisfaction. He wondered if he had gone mad. He felt bruised and broken. Was it his fate to spend the entirety of his life fleeing from one desolation to another in search of an elusive anodyne? He closed his eyes and felt himself drifting.

* * *

He was back in Vietnam on an ambush run in the jungle, about a kilometer away from the main support base Alpha Company had hacked and cleared two weeks before. The base itself was a circle of high ground that had been stripped down to the red dirt itself. Bunkers had been dug and sandbagged. Coils of concertina wire had been strung around the perimeter. Another area beyond the perimeter had been cleared with explosives to remove trees and humps of earth the North Vietnamese could use for cover when they moved in for an attack.

All during the time they had set up the support base the soldiers of Alpha Company had been able to feel the enemy watching them in the daytime and hear supply trucks rumbling in the night. For a week the enemy had harassed them with a few mortar rounds every night, seemingly just to ruin their sleep and make them jumpy.

The daily patrols into the bush and the nightly mortar attacks had left the men haggard and sleepless. Many were coming down with something like malaria. Harlan, too, was running a high fever.

It was around midnight. The leader of Harlan's team suddenly heard the sound of enemy soldiers moving and whispering in the foliage just beyond them. He motioned Harlan and the five other members of the team into a stand of bamboo that had been blasted by mortars a few days before. There was a crater large enough for them to crawl into for cover.

They saw what looked like hundreds of the enemy marching past them in the darkness. Harlan was terrified and could hardly keep still. His heart was pounding in his ears. Then the explosions began and mortars were dropping on all sides. One round landed close to the crater, showering them with shrapnel. Harlan looked up and at the soldier next to him. The man was gasping and groaning. His guts were spilling out. He screamed, shuddered from head to foot, then fell silent.

An enemy soldier suddenly appeared above them chattering away in Vietnamese. The team leader fired four rounds from his .45 automatic into the soldier, but as the man fell he pulled the pin out of a grenade and threw it into the crater. It rolled to their feet. For one frozen moment everyone was paralyzed. Harlan instinctively buried himself under the body of his dead companion. The grenade exploded. Pieces of flesh, body parts, intestines, and bone fragments flew in all directions. Harlan lay under the dead body for a long time, whimpering and trembling and trying to catch his breath. The sticky scent of blood rose around him. Above the crater more troops kept moving through the dark. Mortar and rocket rounds cascaded down for an eternity. Tracer bullets streaked red and white across the sky.

A second enemy soldier jumped into the crater. The soldier could not see Harlan under the dead body. Stealthily, Harlan reached for his knife, found it, and gripped it tightly. Then the enemy was perched over him, reaching down toward the corpse. Harlan drove his knife upward into the man's abdomen. With surprising strength he flung his dead companion aside and jumped on the stunned soldier, slashing him repeatedly until his strength left him. He looked down at the butchered remains of what used to be a human torso. He looked at the face. It was that of a boy no older than 13. Harlan had killed a mere boy. He retched all over the boy's face, gasped, choked on his own vomit, finally got his breath back, then retched again. Tears came to his eyes, slowly at first, but faster and faster until he was pounding the ground with his fists and screaming at the top of his lungs.

Morning came and with it an eerie silence. Harlan crawled out of the crater. Scattered all around were dead bodies, already festering in the piercing heat. Then the bodies were suddenly slithering on the ground, maggots and worms feasting on the rotting insides, holding out their stumps of arms and legs, begging for money or food. He was back in India. The bodies were speaking in Japanese. He approached a group of huddled beggars. They lifted their faces. One was Yoshiko. Another was Danny. They were copulating. Two others were his parents.

Yoshiko said, "I know you're spying on me. Go away!"

Danny said, "You never tried to find me."

The others formed a ring around him and began closing in. He tried to escape. Someone grabbed him from behind, led him back to the crater, and shoved his head down close to the dead 13-year-old Vietnamese, whose mouth had formed the shape of a madman's grin and had blood flowing from it.

"You killed him! You killed him! You killed him!" the crowd chanted.

*　　*　　*

Harlan woke. His futon was soaked with sweat. He crawled to the toilet, tried to vomit, but could not. He poured a glass of water and gulped it down. He needed some food and coffee in his belly. He washed his face and put his head under the kitchen tap. He took a quick glance in the small mirror he kept above the sink. His reflection told the whole miserable story of his life. He trudged out the door and headed to the nearest coffee shop.

Two hours later his head had cleared and he felt a little better. He had to snap out of it, stop the binge right here. He knew himself too well. On several occasions in the past he had fallen into this state and ended up in a strange place with no money, no job, and no recall of what had taken place in the previous few days. His only course of action, the only way he could save himself, lay in exorcising his demons on paper.

An idea flashed in his head: a murder. He would end his novel with a murder. The story would take place during the three days of this binge and would include all the flashbacks and details he could garner from his many notebooks. He and Yoshiko would be the two main characters and the story would be a psychological investigation that probed into both of their deepest and most horrible neuroses and would conclude with his spying on and stalking her and the final murder. He would have his main character murder the woman in bed with another man.

He found a notebook among the mess of papers scattered throughout his room and began writing. He wrote in the notebook for three hours. He filled page after page with outlines for chapters, character descriptions, and how the tension between the two characters would build slowly until exploding like a volcano at the end.

He set his pen on the *kotatsu*, wiped the sweat from his brow with the sleeve of his shirt, and thought about how the murder should take place. He could not think of anything specific. Then an idea came for what should happen after the murder. He would have the main character return to his apartment to wait for the police.

A few minutes later the last line of the book came: *I hear them climbing the steps.*

24

Yoshiko was in the stage halfway between dream and consciousness that precedes full wakefulness. Her conscious mind told her she was dreaming, but her senses told her she was alive in the real world. She could feel the pulse of her heartbeat. She could feel the physical urge to urinate. She could taste the arid dryness in her mouth as she tried to swallow.

She opened her eyes. Her body was stiff and sore. She had been sleeping in an upright position. A terrific pain pulsated suddenly from her neck down her spine. She winced and tears formed in her eyes. A panic shot through her. She must be paralyzed. She tried to wiggle her toes. They responded. She tried to lift her arms off the bed. They obeyed. She held her hands in front of her eyes and examined them closely. Nothing was wrong. She moved her right hand to her face to wipe the sleep from her eyes. It banged against something metallic. There was a metal band surrounding her head and seemingly attached to her skull. There were four bars, two in the back and two in the front, that were also attached to the band and rested on her shoulders. The

whole apparatus formed a kind of neck brace. She tried
to turn to look to her side, but the neck stayed stationary.
Another piercing pain ran up and down her spine. She
could only stare straight ahead.

She wanted to go to the toilet, but could not lift
herself out of bed. Where was this bed? Where was
she? A nurse appeared in the room. She was smiling.

"How are you feeling this morning? I imagine rather
stiff. Here, let me help you get more comfortable," the
nurse said.

Everything started to come back. Yoshiko remembered now. She was in Canada, a Canadian hospital to
be exact, and she was here because of the accident
yesterday, the accident at the swimming pool. There she
was: laughing with Julie and some of Julie's friends as
each took turns trying to outdo the others for who could
do the craziest dive off the diving board. Some were
doing belly flops, some cannon balls, some half-twists
and full-flips, all enjoying themselves in the summer
sun. There was Yoshiko now taking her turn, deciding
to do a running backward dive off the board and
halfway into it slipping and falling sideways, and here
the memory slowing down, remembering laughing as
she screamed "Ooooohhhhh" while feeling herself
plunging headfirst toward the pool, waiting for the water
to envelop her, anticipating the cheers and whoops and

hollers of Julie and her friends when Yoshiko surfaced, grinning and knowing hers would have to be the craziest dive of all, then the sudden awareness that the water was not rushing up to greet her, seeing the side of the pool instead, the instant thought of "Oh God!" and the thud of neck meeting concrete, and...

"Do you have to go to the toilet?" the nurse asked.

Yoshiko tried to nod, but her head would not move up and down. In a weak voice she said, "Yes."

The nurse helped Yoshiko raise her body enough to slide a bed pan underneath. "It may seem awkward at first, but you'll get used to it."

When Yoshiko had finished, she felt an immense relief, as if a portion of her body weight had also poured into the pan and she was light enough to find a sitting position not as painful as the one in which she had woken. A doctor entered the room.

"You seem to have come through the operation in good shape," he said as he checked Yoshiko's neck area and the metal band around her head. "Do you remember anything about yesterday?"

"A little."

"You took a nasty fall off a diving board, cracked your neck against the side of the pool, and very nearly killed yourself. You're lucky you didn't. Your friends pulled you out of the water. You're also lucky one of your friends has had training in nursing. She recognized you had broken your neck and managed to keep it in a stable position until the ambulance arrived. If not for her, you might be paralyzed.

"Paralyzed?"

"Yes. You wouldn't be able to move your body. As it is, you have a crack in your neck that could worsen if we're not careful. It could still cause partial paralysis. That's why we've got this thing around your head and neck. We have to keep you stabilized until the bone is fused again."

"How long will that take?"

"Oh, I'd say about three months, but you could possibly be out of the hospital in about a month if you're a good girl. You seem strong to me. You're young and should heal quickly. The important thing for you is not to move around. I'll be checking in on you daily, checking your progress and making sure the screws are tight enough."

"The screws?"

The doctor laughed and patted Yoshiko's hand. "Don't you worry. We've got four tiny screws inserted in your skull. If they're loosened at all by a lot of movement on your part, the band becomes destabilized and then there's a possibility the crack in your neck could widen. We have to keep the screws tight to hold the band in place. You can't feel them and once they're removed there'll be just very small scars that can hardly be seen. I'm prescribing some pain pills to get you through the first few days. After that, I think the most difficult thing for you to deal with is the stiffness from being upright. We'll fix you up soon enough so you can lie down more comfortably. If you need anything, just press this buzzer next to your bed and a nurse will come. I want you to rest now."

"When can I see Julie and her family?"

"They were here for most of last night. I sent them all home. The most important thing for you, young lady, is to get some rest. Your friends can start visiting tomorrow. OK?"

"OK. Thank you, Doctor."

The pain pills took effect within minutes. The sharp pain turned to a dull throb, then faded to a remote distance inside her body. She wondered if this were a miracle or a kind of punishment. She had arrived in Canada only a week ago and the ecstatic joy of seeing Julie again after a two-year absence had been almost too much to bear. They had cried and cried as they hugged and kissed each other repeatedly at the airport. At last she had freed herself from the prison of her life in Japan, from all the entanglements and confusion and grief of her relationships, her thoughts, her worries, and her

TORAWARE

fears. All of it had disappeared the moment she felt Julie's arms around her. Yoshiko could not remember the last time she had felt such pure love that was absolutely free of any kind of complication.

Now she was in the hospital and facing another confinement with this metal band wrapped around her head. She had a period of trial ahead that would test her strength, but at the same time she was thankful to Julie and God for having saved her life.

Everything about her life in Japan seemed remote. She wondered if Julie had called her parents. Julie's Japanese was not good enough to explain everything in detail. Yoshiko's family would be worried sick. Yoshiko would have to call as soon as possible. Even here, halfway around the world in Toronto, she could not escape her family. It seemed that all her life she had been a source of trouble to them.

Who else back home would be worried about her? The men with whom she had been involved? She had sought to suppress those relationships, put some distance between them and her, and find a new direction, but now they would find out somehow — her mother could not keep this kind of news quiet and Itami was after all like any other small town — and she would eventually have to suffer their pity, too. The Cocos Island owner would be especially concerned. The university student would probably shrug his shoulders, say he was sorry, give her some words of sympathy, and move on to another more lively relationship, taking all his friends with him. So much the better.

Then there was Harlan. It was hard to guess what kind of reaction he would have to her accident. She hoped he would not follow her here, but that was something not beyond the realm of possibility. He had frightened her terribly the month before she left Japan. It had gotten to the point where she felt unsafe in her own home. He had entered her house that one time when she was not home. She had seen his shoes at the back entrance and fled, fearing he was inside waiting for her. About a week before her departure she had been in the room next to her bedroom, the room where she kept her letters and books, and looked out the window to see him down in the street among the shadows. She had looked directly into his eyes before shutting the curtains. She had felt his presence everywhere she had gone the last few weeks. No one had ever scared her like that. He was a problem she did not want to consider in her current condition.

Her eyelids grew heavy. She wished she could lie down like a normal person or just let her chin rest on her chest. But the pills were working and the pain was far away and she was tired. All she wanted was to sleep.

TORAWARE

*   *   *

She was prancing through a Canadian forest in her elementary school uniform and holding Obaa-chan's hand. In the dream Obaa-chan was lively and able to kick her feet up in the air the same as Yoshiko. They were giggling. Then Yoshiko challenged Obaa-chan to a race and began running. She was free and everything was deep green. She stopped to wait for Obaa-chan, but Obaa-chan was gone. Yoshiko yelled out a few times, but no answer came back. The forest grew dark and threatening. Yoshiko became afraid. She was lost.

She thought Joe's shack must be somewhere near. She started walking. There was an evil presence in the forest. She could feel its eyes. She began to run and heard insane laughter behind her. There was a shack up ahead. She reached it, rushed inside, and locked the door behind her. It was Joe's shack, but he was not there. There were voices outside calling to her. She crawled under the bed.

Something was looking in the window. It had a baby's face, but there was hatred written all over it. It had come for her. She recognized it as her own baby. She tried to cry out that she was sorry, but she was trembling so much that she could not make a sound. Then someone lifted the baby from behind and carried it away. The door opened and there was Julie saying, "It's OK, Yoshiko. Don't worry. I'm here."

Julie moved forward, but now Julie was Yoshiko's mother. Yoshiko ran to her and wrapped her arms around her, apologizing frantically for everything she had ever done and promising to change, to be a good girl, to stop drinking, to do anything to keep the demons and babies away. Her mother led her out of the shack and now they were in Yoshiko's apartment drinking coffee together. Her mother was knitting and Yoshiko was preparing the bath.

There was a shadow outside the bathroom window. The window opened suddenly and Harlan started to crawl through. He was crying and pleading with her, "I want to be your number one lover. Please come back to me."

Yoshiko slammed the window on his head and he shouted at her, "You whore! You bitch!"

She was running again. There was a cliff up ahead. She kept running and jumped over the edge and now she was flying over Itami. Two birds were flying alongside her. She tried to turn to look at them, but her neck would not move and she could see only clouds ahead of her. One of the birds flew ahead. It stopped in mid-air and turned around to face her. Its head was a human skull. It was laughing. It reached out a skeletal claw and grabbed her hand.

* * *

Yoshiko's eyes opened. The nurse was holding her down.

"You've been having a dream, dear. Here, have some water."

Yoshiko took the glass and drank. The nurse mopped Yoshiko's forehead with a damp cloth.

"There, that's better. You have a visitor outside. Shall I call her in?"

"Please," Yoshiko said.

A moment later Julie entered the hospital room. She walked to the side of the bed, held Yoshiko's hands in her own, smiled at Yoshiko for a second, then wrapped her arms around Yoshiko the best she could and burst into tears.

"Oh, Yoshiko, you're alive! You're alive! Thank God!"

25

The summer heat sapped Harlan's energy. Away from work all he did was drink, smoke, and sleep. He had stopped running altogether. His life was marked by a growing isolation from everything and everyone around him. The strength it took to deal with the hordes of people every day was tremendous. Life seemed to be a whirlwind of people and events spinning so fast it made him dizzy.

Over the last few months the whole of Japan had become distasteful, burdensome, and wearisome. It was not just the relationship with Yoshiko. It was everything about the country and having to deal with so many people and not understanding three-quarters of what was going on. When he went out in the daytime, he avoided the main streets. The children's cries, which he had once thought charming, now seemed derogatory and taunting. The local residents' stares, which had once seemed friendly and inviting, now pestered him like flies.

Even the nights were debilitating. The screams of wild cats fighting kept him awake and restless. When the heat drove him out into the dark streets, there were many bats dive-bombing around the few weakly-lit street lamps on the street leading to Koya Park. One night he returned home late and found a bat banging against the walls inside the six-mat room. He slammed the sliding door shut, wadded up a newspaper, waited a minute until the noise died down, and peeked inside the room. The bat had found a spot on one wall to clutch with its talons and was hanging upside down. Harlan tip-toed into the room and swatted it with his best home-run swing. It dropped to the floor, stunned. Harlan quickly picked it up by one wing and tossed it out the open window. He slammed the window shut and slumped to the floor, his heart racing.

He was burned out. He, like Yoshiko, had to get out of the country to gain strength and a different perspective. He had saved some money and could afford a round-trip plane ticket to the States. He wanted to visit his family's graves. Rick agreed to give him some time off in October.

August brought with it the old horrors of death-imagery. The nation was absorbed in the 40th anniversary of the victims of the atomic bombs dropped on Hiroshima and Nagasaki. On August 10th Harlan received a call at the school from Yoshiko's mother. He could not understand everything she said, but the gist of her message was that Yoshiko was in the hospital with a broken neck suffered in a swimming accident and had to stay in Canada for another few months. Harlan wept throughout that night, feeling helpless. On August 12th a Japan Airlines jumbo jet crashed into a mountainside west of Tokyo, killing 520 people and becoming the worst disaster in airline history. Miraculously, four people survived, but the mood of the nation was dark and somber. The *Obon* holiday, usually a colorful and festive time of year, seemed morose and dispirited. Everywhere Harlan went he saw downcast faces. His own nightmares continued to plague him.

Harlan saw little of anyone outside work. The Sasa Club members would not gather again until the autumn league started. Sugiyama had been dating a new girlfriend steadily for the last few months and rarely spent weekends at Harlan's place anymore. Inoue had dropped out of Rick's school. He was researching a book to be written about the history of a company in Kyushu and was away from the Kansai area a lot. When he was not drinking and brooding, Harlan tried to spend his free time studying Japanese.

One day late in September Rick called a teachers' meeting and had Harlan give a presentation on a new teaching technique using some props and indirect correction of students' mistakes. Harlan had not prepared adequately and lacked confidence during the presentation. It was as if he were outside his body observing the ridiculousness of it all — himself stuttering and stammering, the blank, uncomprehending faces of the other teachers, his own thoughts drifting and disconnected. Later he overheard one of the other teachers making a joke about Harlan's inarticulateness and inability to speak convincingly to a group of native speakers of English.

He was determined to find a correspondence course, graduate, and move on to a new job. He hoped the trip back to the States would ease his mind and provide a direction out of his waywardness. He had hit bottom many times in the past, but always there had been a reserve of strength hidden in the resilience of youth. The question in his mind now was whether there was any of that resilience left. He was, at 35, feeling old and broken.

Finally, the day for his return came. He paid off his rent for the next two months, received a reentry permit from immigration, and boarded a Korean Airlines plane bound for San Francisco.

* * *

Harlan stood in front of the graves of his mother, father, and brother. He had been there for over an hour. His beliefs were inconsistent with prayer, but he thought it would not hurt him to compromise and allow the possibility of its efficacy. His prayers were not Christian prayers. They were more like private conversations. He had always thought it a bit odd that Yoshiko, as a Christian, could still pray before a Shinto or Buddhist altar, but now he understood. Perhaps that part of Japan had rubbed off on him. He took solace in speaking directly to his dead family members.

He bent down to straighten the bouquets he had placed on the graves. He said good-bye, then turned around to walk to the church in front of the cemetery. The front door was open and he went inside. Not much had changed since he had attended church as a boy. There were still the grim rows of benches, the pulpit, the dark closet for confession, the organ his mother had played every Sunday, and the door leading to the classroom in the back where he and Danny had had to attend catechism lessons and he had begun asking the nuns all his precocious questions concerning the existence of God.

There were only dead memories in this place. He left the church, walked past the high school, relived a few minutes of high school basketball glory, then continued down the hill to the Arcata lowlands, where his father had operated a sawmill. The sawmill was still standing, now run by a large corporation, and the pungency of freshly-hewn timber brought back a rush of childhood memories. As a five- and six-year-old boy, Harlan had loved to climb the huge log decks, explore the workers' lunchroom with its pinup pictures of naked women, play among the piles of sawdust, and listen to the roaring machinery that lifted, sawed, carried, and stacked the logs and boards of his father's world of toil and sweat, all of this a few years before the logging accident.

He returned to Arcata Town Square and saw that most of the shops had changed. There were now mostly book stores and restaurants lining the four streets that surrounded the square instead of the bars and hardware stores and department stores he had known in the past. Two or three bars were the same, so he stopped in one to have a beer. There were no familiar faces, only college students who retained the same hippie uniform of the 1960s and 1970s: T-shirts, jeans, long hair, and beards.

He decided to have one last look at the old family house out in Jacoby Creek. He took a city bus to the bus stop at the end of Jacoby Creek Road. There were several more homes than he remembered from his childhood. The area had taken on the atmosphere of a middle-class suburb with large lawns and two- and three-storey houses. There were still extensive fields with sheep and horses and a few head of cattle grazing lazily in the October sun. He walked the three miles to his old home and was pleased to see it still standing. Much of the timber beyond the backyard had been felled and more homes had been built. The tree house and mini-baseball park with its backstop were gone. The trees that remained were much smaller than those he had conjured up from memory.

He walked back to the bus stop. The old elementary school was only a half mile farther on the road leading to Sunny Brae, so he decided to go have a look at it. Not much at the school had changed. Two new buildings had been added, but the old buildings still bore the signs of aging he remembered — paint peeling off the walls, pipes turning to rust, and a few broken windows that had been boarded up. He walked out on the field where he had played Little League baseball. Two memories came back to him: the no-hit game he had pitched and the time his father had been hitting fly balls for outfield practice and an errant throw came back in while his father was in the middle of a swing and struck him square in the groin. Even then, while flattened to the ground in what must have been excruciating pain, his father had exuded dignity. He had not uttered a sound. He had simply sat up quickly, arms folded around his legs, head hunched down and gritting his teeth for a moment while all the players rushed to gather around him. He had managed to lift his head, smile at everyone, rise stiffly to his feet, hand the bat to Harlan, and say, "Here, Harlan, you hit fungoes for a while. I'm going to take a break."

Harlan smiled to himself, thinking of the continents and time and distance he had covered since then. He realized nothing remained for him in his hometown but the dried fragments of distant memory. He had paid his respects. It was time once again to move.

By the time he returned to Japan, Harlan was ready for a fresh start. He now had a focus for his future. He would renew his efforts in his Japanese studies and pursue a degree in the teaching of English as a second or foreign language. The trip back to the States had cured his madness. He felt mentally stable again. He found an American college that had a branch school in Tokyo offering correspondence courses and credit toward a degree if one could document enough life experience. He set about preparing a portfolio to submit to the college.

* * *

Yoshiko was weeding in her garden. The afternoon May sun was warm on her neck. She stood up, stretched, and did a few neck rolls to loosen the muscles, feeling thankful she was fully healed and could perform this simple movement. She wiped the sweat off her brow with a towel and went back inside the apartment to make a cup of coffee and take a break.

She sat at the kitchen table and thought again about Canada. Her life had changed irrevocably both times she had gone there. Something close to a miracle had occurred this last time. It was as if God had planned for her to have the accident and be forced into a long period of near immobility and rehabilitation in order to reexamine her life and realize how lucky she was to be alive. All the things she had fretted over before the accident now seemed trivial. The long days of having to lie still in bed and rely entirely on Julie's family for help in carrying out all the mundane activities of day-to-day existence — from going to the toilet to feeding herself — had taught her to appreciate the simple things in life.

Above all, she had learned to appreciate her own family. The letters and phone calls from her parents and brother were as responsible as anything for her recovery. She had been overwhelmed by the open expression of love they had given her throughout the whole ordeal. There were times when she thought she would never see them again. When she returned to Japan shortly after Christmas, the reception they gave her at the airport had caused her to break down into such tears of happiness that she felt surely she had undergone a religious experience.

The accident had also brought her closer to Julie than she had ever imagined. Always in those moments when Yoshiko began to fall into a dark depression, Julie was there with her faith and humor to bring Yoshiko out of her self-commiseration and see the bright side of things. Julie passed up a job offer to spend her time nursing Yoshiko back to health. The two spent countless hours together baring their souls, reshaping their hopes and dreams, and loving each other so sincerely and honestly and deeply that no words would ever describe it.

With the help of Julie, Julie's family, and her own family, Yoshiko made a clean separation from her past. The Yoshiko from that past was a stranger anymore, as were all the pains and frustrations and misunderstandings connected with that person. She still loved the men from that time, but with the love of someone who has moved on to a different world. The love she had for the Cocos Island owner was that of a college girl who has outgrown her infatuation with a sympathetic professor. The reverse could be said for the university student. She had taught him what she could, but the time had come to set him free.

She was not sure about Harlan. When she first returned, they went out for coffee once, had a pleasant conversation about the changes of the last year, and agreed to let bygones be bygones. He had pestered her with a few phone calls, but she had listened to him patiently and explained that he no longer had a place in her life. She had not heard from him in three months. From what he had told her, she understood he was working hard on a college course and thinking seriously about quitting Rick's school if he could get another school or company to sponsor a work visa.

She no longer feared him. His own trip to the United States seemed to have provided tonic for calming the furies inside him. He had wanted to explain everything in detail, but she cut him short with a gentle yet firm insistence on her need for distance from him. He said he understood. He was like a scar on her skin.

She had a lot of scars. Each one told the story of a different chapter of her life. The scars on her wrists were constant reminders of the wild, selfish, and self-hating teenager who had caused grief to many people. But that same person was also the one who had fled to Canada looking for answers to unanswerable questions and had found in Julie the best friend of her life. The tiny scars in her skull, visible only when she pulled her hair back, told the latest story. They were the marks God had given her that gave proof of the possibility of miracles really happening. All she had to do was look in the mirror and the whole process of her transformation and perhaps even redemption was right there to reaffirm that it had happened and was not her imagination.

For the first time that she could remember, she was noticing the subtleties in the seasons, especially the flowers. Since returning to Japan, she had made several trips to Kyoto to visit the many shrines, temples, and gardens with numerous and varied flowers. She had recorded in her diary the date of each visit and the flowers seen.

During the winter she had seen the clusters of crimson nandina seeds at Shoorin Temple, the yellow tea blossoms at Kennin Shrine, and the brighter yellow silverleaf at Entoku Garden. In the spring she had gone for long walks to see the varieties of peach, plum, and cherry blossoms, as well as camellias, spirareas, and magnolias, but her favorite flower was the rape growing wild along river banks, turning the banks into a bright, gilded yellow as the sun reflected off them.

At each place she had picked one flower for Obaa-chan and one for Julie. She had placed the flowers at the base of the temple or shrine, tossed a ¥5 coin in the offertory box, and said a prayer for happiness in the afterlife for Obaa-chan and in this life for Julie. She had then prayed for her family.

She loved these long walks, both in Kyoto and here in Itami, when she was alone with her thoughts and absorbed in the moment. She had turned 26, but had only vague thoughts about the future. She was teaching twice a week at ECC again, but her interest in teaching was waning. She thought for a moment that she might like to try moving to Tokyo and working in a travel company. Her uncle had a connection there, but the thought of accepting help from someone who had once molested her did not sit well. She had forgiven him and her cousins for their crime, but there was no need to reestablish a bond.

The important thing was she felt peace within herself. She did not know how long it would last, but she would relish it for now. She had managed to stop drinking whiskey and the pains in her stomach had disappeared along with the darkness under her eyes. Her skin was becoming smoother.

She got up to retrieve her tools from the garden. She had promised to prepare dinner for her mother, who was stopping by almost every evening. Yoshiko looked forward to their nightly visits. They laughed a lot together now. Her mother had lost the energy and will to resist Masanori, who had refused to bow to the family and was planning to get married at the end of June. Their father had fallen sick in February, spending two weeks in the hospital, and Masanori had taken over for him at the office and proved himself capable. There was no one else the family could count on and, married or

not, Masanori would be the man of the family from now
on. Yoshiko's mother had come to accept the situation.
Yoshiko liked to tease her about it, much as her mother
liked to tease Yoshiko about her own past failures and
misadventures.

Her mother had begun to tell stories from her own
youth. Yoshiko would listen intently to the difficulties
her mother endured during the postwar years of taking
care of Yoshiko's father after the operations on his leg
and of having to scrounge for food and work before they
started his business and had Masanori and her. In years
past there had been a note of bitterness connected with
stories about those days, but now Yoshiko's mother was
recalling them with nostalgia and humor.

Yoshiko washed her hands and face, turned on the
rice cooker, and began making a sauce for curried rice.
While the sauce simmered, she prepared a large salad.
She placed a bottle of red wine in the refrigerator to
cool. They usually had one glass of wine together with
their meals. Toasting each other after a prayer together
gave an air of ritual to their evenings.

Yoshiko sat down to have a cigarette. Her mother
disapproved, so Yoshiko did not smoke in her presence.
She took a long puff and watched the smoke curl up and
evaporate as she exhaled.

The sound of a car parking outside interrupted her

thoughts. She snuffed out the cigarette, got up and stirred the sauce, and went to the back door to greet her mother.

"Have you been smoking?" her mother said with a mock look of disapproval.

"Who me?"

They laughed, hugged each other, and began setting the table.

26

Harlan was working on a paper for his correspondence course. He was seated opposite Satomi at the large table placed in the middle room of her apartment. They were practically living together now and almost every night would sit at the table for two or three hours immersing themselves in books, tapes, and written reports. Satomi was as disciplined and hardworking a student as Harlan had ever known. Her goal was to become a simultaneous interpreter. She was attending interpreting classes two evenings a week.

They were both teacher and student to each other. In addition to his correspondence course, which was about half completed, Harlan was continuing to study Japanese. Satomi's explanations of difficult vocabulary, idioms, and grammar were helpful, and, in order to prod Harlan's memory, she always remembered to weave into their conversations, which were half in Japanese and half in English, expressions with which Harlan was having difficulty.

They had first met at Rick's school two years before when Satomi started taking conversation lessons. She had been a member of the most interesting class, which consisted of four young women and Shimada, a businessman in his forties who was a high-ranking manager in a large company. The class had been the last one on Saturday afternoons and for a year all the members and Harlan often gathered afterward for a party at a restaurant or at Rick's house. The four women, including Satomi, had since gone their own ways. Four new members had joined. Only Shimada remained from the original group.

One night shortly after returning from the States, Harlan and Shimada went out drinking and talked about what had become of the four original women. Shimada mentioned that Satomi was working for a foreign trading company and had recently done some translation work for him. Harlan said he would like to see her sometime. Shimada gave him Satomi's phone number.

Harlan had remembered Satomi as one of the most interesting and intelligent students he had taught. Her English was excellent. She had always impressed him with her uninhibited participation in class, her philosophical attitude toward life, her inquisitiveness, and her sense of humor. Embroiled as he had been in the vicissitudes of his affair with Yoshiko, he had not looked upon Satomi as anything more than a highly-motivated and articulate student. But talking with Shimada had made him think that Satomi might be the type of woman with whom he would like to spend time.

He called her the next night. They agreed to meet for a drink the following weekend. She lived in Nishinomiya, about a half hour by train from Itami, and they decided to meet at a *yakitori* shop near her apartment. It turned out to be an enjoyable time. They began seeing each other on weekends. During the week he often called her at night from a pay phone. Their relationship seemed almost to blossom overnight.

Harlan began spending Saturday nights at her place. Within a few weeks he had practically moved in. It was as if they both had waited a lifetime to find each other. Their conversations often lasted deep into the night. They confessed every detail of their life histories, love affairs, adventures, childhoods, friends, successes, failures, hopes, and dreams. Their conversations always seemed to start out seriously, then take multiple twists and turns, a single thought or word digressing into a flurry of related and unrelated stories until they would realize the original point they had wanted to make was lost and irretrievable and their only recourse was to summarize the entire evening with a drink and a fart and an explosion of laughter that left them with their sides aching.

Spring had come and with it the need in Harlan to

make a change. He had spent nearly three years working at Rick's school and it was time to move on. He found a vocational language school in Ashiya that had an opening for a part-time teacher. The Seinan Language Institute had an organized curriculum, published its own materials, had connections with several private schools, and had a good reputation. At about the same time, Satomi heard through a friend about an employment agency that was looking for a native speaker of English to work two days a week as a proofreader for a chemical company in Kobe. Harlan was given an interview. The employment agency agreed to sponsor his work visa. He started the proofreading job in mid-April.

He had kept his Itami apartment, but now spent much of his time at Satomi's. It was closer to Seinan and the chemical company. He was still playing softball with Sasa Club on weekends and jogging around Koya Pond two or three times a week. Sugiyama was still occasionally using the Itami apartment as his atelier.

Harlan enjoyed listening to Satomi's stories about her family. Her father was from a small fishing village in Wakayama Prefecture. Her mother came from a farming family in another Wakayama village. Theirs had been an arranged marriage. Satomi's father had spent part of his youth in Korea. Many Japanese families had migrated to Korea, Taiwan, and Manchuria during Japan's occupation of those countries in the 1930s and during the war. After the war, her father had returned to his hometown and worked a variety of jobs: fishmonger, clerk, security guard, and supervisor of prisoners making gloves at a prison for women.

Satomi said her father was a dreamer-philosopher with grand ambitions and little common sense, a stubborn, loquacious man who loved to expound on his theories of history, science, philosophy, and politics to anyone with a sympathetic ear. He loved to drink. When Satomi was a child, he had often come home stinking of sake and covered with mud and blood from a fight with someone who either had not agreed with his theories or had simply gotten tired of listening to them. He was an inventor with a hundred ideas, but without the wherewithal to carry them through to realization.

One of his schemes had come near the end of the 1960s. He had wanted to become an international businessman. He decided to try to make use of his contacts in Korea. He set up a business importing fish from Korea. Things went smoothly until the oil shock of 1970 and the normalization of bilateral relations between China and Japan combined to destroy the business. Since Japan at the time no longer recognized Taiwan, trade between the two countries deteriorated. All the large Japanese trading companies in Taiwan had moved their operations to Korea. Small companies like Satomi's father's could not compete. By the time he decided to give up, he had been saddled with a ¥10 million debt.

It had almost destroyed the family. Satomi remembered a depressing home atmosphere all throughout her junior high and high school days. Her brother and father had fought. Her mother and father had fought. She and her brother had fought. In the midst of all the feuding, her mother remained the rock of stability. She had worked all day long in the small stationary and book store that she still ran. She had taken on side jobs knitting and delivering magazines and newspapers to the train station. She had also worked as a runner for the local pachinko parlor, returning the goods exchanged for cash at a nearby pawn shop every night to the pachinko parlor, where they would again be given to customers as prizes to be exchanged for cash at the pawn shop. For the next 15 years Satomi's mother did not miss a single day of work. Due mainly to her efforts, the family, with Satomi's father working salaried jobs and Satomi and her brother working part-time jobs after school, had managed to pay off the enormous debt.

After graduating from high school, Satomi moved to Kobe to attend a women's university. She supported herself for the next four years by working as a receptionist in an English conversation school, a hostess in a bar, a coffee shop waitress, and an assortment of other jobs before graduating with a degree in English. English had become an obsession. She did a three-month homestay in Britain and another one-month homestay in California. She took on other part-time jobs tutoring junior high school students privately and teaching adults in another conversation school. She never stopped studying. While attending Rick's school she passed Japan's top-rated English proficiency exam. She used her new qualification to land a job at a Danish-owned company that manufactured pumps. She was now working directly for the company president as a combination translator-interpreter and person in charge of inventory control.

Harlan respected Satomi as much as he loved her. Living with a woman, even on a part-time basis, was a new experience for him, but with Satomi it was easy. They had both been independent for so long that there was no need to worry about playing a particular role in the relationship. Doing laundry, shopping, cooking, cleaning, all the daily household chores had been part of their routines for years. Neither had to worry about keeping up with a fixed schedule to please the other. They were both accustomed to entertaining themselves, keeping themselves occupied. Often for long stretches of time in her apartment they could both be seen quietly absorbed in reading, taking notes, or writing, but when the mood hit them for conversation, they gave totally to each other. They never argued. Harlan had never felt as comfortable with any woman in his life.

* * *

One afternoon in October Harlan was on his way from Hankyu Itami Station to his apartment. A light rain was falling. He took the shortcut past Yoshiko's apartment. He had not seen or talked to her in several months. Her figure suddenly appeared before him. She was working in her garden. A young man was squatting next to the back door, watching her weed and trim. He seemed a shy and quiet man. At once an impression of Yoshiko's strength and domination over the men who loved her swept through Harlan's mind. She was more beautiful than ever. Harlan stopped to watch her for a moment. She looked up, saw him standing there, wiped her face with the side of her right arm, and smiled.

"This is a helluva day to be working outside," Harlan said.

Yoshiko laughed. "It's the best day for it. I don't need to take a shower. How are you?"

"Fine. I'm just heading home to take it easy. Maybe I'll go for a jog. I have an easy schedule today."

"Did you have a class already?"

"No, just one later tonight."

There was a pause. Many things were racing through his brain, but Harlan could not think of anything more to say. Yoshiko wiped her face on her arm again.

"Well, see you later. Good luck with your class," Yoshiko said, then returned to her gardening.

For the rest of the afternoon Harlan cursed himself for not taking advantage of the chance to lay everything to rest between them. There was much he wanted to explain about how he was getting along. There was much he wanted to ask her about how she was doing. There was the one final request he wanted to make. On his way back to the station he stopped at the pay phone in the park.

The tone of Yoshiko's voice on the phone did not hide her irritation. "Harlan, you're not going to start bothering me with phone calls again and telling me not to sleep with whoever I'm with, are you?"

"No, I'm not going to do that."

"You understand I'm not interested in you anymore, don't you?"

"I understand. I just have one thing to ask you."

"Only one? I find that hard to believe."

"Yes, only one."

"What is it?"

Robert W. Norris

"Do you still have all those letters I wrote you?"

"Yes, but I never read them."

"That's good. I want you to burn them. Will you do that for me?"

"Yes, I will."

"Do you promise?"

"Yes."

"Thank you, Yoshiko. Good-bye."

"Good-bye, Harlan."

Harlan hung up the phone and walked to the station. He had a class of 15 high school students to teach at six o'clock. There were a few new ideas he wanted to try tonight. As the train pulled out of the station, he opened his notebook and began reviewing his lesson plan.

Epilogue

San Francisco: Tuesday, January 17, 1995

Sachiko rose quietly from the bed in her stylish, two-bedroom apartment. Pablo, her lover of two years, was still sleeping soundly. Their love-making last night had exhausted them both. She watched him for a moment, smiled, then went into the kitchen to prepare coffee and breakfast.

Her life had changed immeasurably since coming to the United States. These last few years had passed quickly. She had completed her master's degree and shortly after graduating landed a job as an assistant secretary for the curator of the Oriental Museum of Art in San Francisco. The museum had sponsored her visa and now she had a green card. Within two years she had been promoted to personal secretary and was responsible for not only correspondence and other paperwork, but also interpreting and translating. Her language skills and knowledge of oriental art and art history made her invaluable to the museum. She could probably work there as long as she wanted.

She loved her work, but more than the work she

311

loved the time the curator allowed her for developing her own artistic career. She could take one or two extra days off whenever things were not busy and spend that time working on her own paintings. The curator had introduced Sachiko to some small gallery owners around the Bay Area and they had agreed to let her give occasional exhibitions of her work. She had sold several paintings.

Her love life was more than satisfactory. In her two years at graduate school she had found two men, one a Caucasian and the other a Spaniard, who helped her release all the pent-up passions and inhibitions that had imprisoned her for many years. The orgasms she had experienced with them had been, as Yumi once expressed, beyond imagination. They had both been gentle and taught her many things for which she was grateful. More then anything, they had taught her to love and respect herself and to be confident in the company of strangers. She had also learned to accept separation as the natural conclusion to human relationships. She had worried that the Spaniard, who had been bisexual, might have AIDS, but he had consented to a blood test and the results came back negative. She had also learned to make sure her men always used a condom.

Now there was Pablo. He was five years younger. She had met him at one of her exhibitions. He asked her out for a drink and they slept together the first night. He was Mexican and they had spoken only in Spanish for the two years they had been together. He was an artist, too, and they both used her other bedroom for their workshop. He had talent, but it was the raw talent of youth, unharnessed and filled with bold strokes and bright colors. She was trying to teach him restraint while retaining the passion that he poured onto his canvases. He was learning. She loved his charcoal portraits best.

She thought of her family. She still saw them once a year when she returned to Japan during the winter holidays. She was glad her father had sold his company and retired with her mother in Karuizawa. Their home was smaller now with Sachiko and her brother gone, but it had a subtle luxuriousness that fit her parents' personalities. Sachiko loved the walks she would take with them in the snow and woods surrounding the home. She loved the weekend shopping excursions in Tokyo with her mother, the evening discussions with her brother about their separate American lives. He was working as an engineer for a firm in Boston and also always came home for the holidays. She was happy her family was content and doing well.

She turned on the television to watch the news. Her coffee cup nearly fell out of her hands when the announcer said there had been a major earthquake in

Kobe, Japan. At first she could not believe what had been said about the location of the earthquake, not her beloved Kobe, but there on the screen were all the horrible images of buildings and sections of freeway toppled over, fires spreading through entire neighborhoods, streets warped and buckled, and ambulances and fire engines at a standstill with their lights flashing and sirens screaming. The announcer was saying that early reports had over 1,000 people dead and thousands more injured. It looked like a scene from a war zone.

A picture of the collapsed Hankyu Itami Station appeared on the screen. Sachiko's heart stopped and she heard herself cry, "No! Not Itami!" and for the first time in years she thought of Harlan and Yoshiko. A sense of panic gripped her tightly. Then some scenes of destruction in Ashiya appeared and Sachiko could no longer control herself. Her tears ran in torrents. Her sobs came from the deepest part of her bowels. She was pounding the table with her fists.

"What is it? What's the matter?" Pablo asked in Spanish and put his arms on her shoulders. She pointed at the television.

"Jesus Christ," he said.

When Sachiko finally collected her emotions later in the day, she was left with a feeling of shock and helplessness. She had tried throughout the day to call her parents, but all the lines to Japan were tied up. She was thankful her parents no longer lived in Ashiya, but there were scores of friends and acquaintances still in Ashiya and there was no way of finding out what had happened to them. She knew her family was feeling the same shock and helplessness. There was only one thing to do. She had to go to her family, if only to grieve with them. She called the curator, explained the situation, and received his permission to take two weeks off. Then she called a travel agency. There might be some difficulty, but the agency said they could get her on a plane to Tokyo by the end of the week.

At two o'clock in the morning Sachiko finally got a phone call through to her mother and father. She had seen them just over two weeks ago, but hearing her mother's voice on the phone brought on the tears again. Her mother was crying, too. When they were able to speak, her mother said some of their friends had been able to call and, as far as she knew, everyone was safe. There had been extensive damage to houses, most were without gas and water, but those friends who had called were alive and that was the important thing. The worst damage seemed to be from the fires that were raging through the poorer sections in western Kobe, where there were many small wooden homes that had gone up in flames like tinder boxes. There was still fear of a large aftershock, but for the time being many of their friends were accounted for and all the family could do was pray.

Five days later Sachiko boarded a plane bound for Tokyo.

Fukuoka, Kyushu: Saturday, January 28, 1995

The past two weeks had been a nerve-wracking time for Harlan. It had been worse for Satomi. She had never experienced a disaster of this scale before. They were fortunate in having moved to Kyushu a few years before when Harlan found a better job, but as they watched the news updates day after day Satomi was forced to watch the near complete destruction of the city where she had spent the best years of her life. The frustration of making dozens of calls every day and not getting through and not knowing what had become of their many friends was unendurable.

Over the last few days, however, the phone lines had started to open up and to their astonishment all of the friends they had gotten in contact with were all right. Some had been evacuated, some were staying in school grounds set up as temporary shelters, some were still in their homes without gas and water, but all were uninjured. Harlan was amazed at everyone's strength and sense of humor in coping with having to start from scratch in putting the pieces of their lives back together.

He thought back to the first day. Satomi had received a call from her mother at 7:30 in the morning. A large earthquake had jarred the family house in Wakayama Prefecture. The television on top of the kitchen cabinet had toppled and crashed on the table. Some glass cases in the second-storey clothing shop had fallen over and glass had scattered all over. No one was hurt, but it was the worst quake they had felt in a long time. The quake was supposedly centered in Kobe and the family was watching the news on the upstairs television.

Satomi switched on the television and woke Harlan. At first there were only pictures from a helicopter trying to assess the damage. The city had seemingly not yet come to life. Reports were broadcast telling commuters in Kobe and Nishinomiya to stay home as some of the main lines were closed. Most of the Osaka subway lines, train lines, and highways were still open. Commuters there were told to stay tuned. There was a section of Hanshin Expressway that had collapsed, but there had been only a few cars on it. Harlan remarked it was lucky the earthquake had struck so early. If it had happened two hours later, there would have been hundreds of cars on the roads and trains on the tracks.

The aerial views showed a few plumes of smoke rising here and there, but the overall mood was not one of panic. It was more of a wait-and-see attitude that seemed to convey a sense that the damage was limited. There were a few confirmed reports of deaths and injuries piling up, but the numbers were not staggering. As the day progressed, however, it became evident that this was no ordinary earthquake. More helicopters were sent out by the major television stations and the images began to grow horrifying.

Trains had flipped on their sides, many sections of track had snapped in two or torn loose, cars had been catapulted off the toppled sections of elevated express-way, commercial buildings in downtown Sannomiya had suffered pancake collapses, water and gas mains had ruptured and entire neighborhoods were being engulfed in flames, and the numbers of dead, missing, and injured began to rise into the hundreds. It was Harlan's day off and he and Satomi sat riveted to the television.

Harlan finally tore himself away about one in the morning. He was tired and had to work the next day. He woke at five to the sound of Satomi's sobs. She had stayed up all night, watching the inferno engulf Nagata-ku, the area where she had lived for four years as a university student and two more years after gradu-ating. Many of her old friends were still living there and may have been trapped in the blazes and the rubble.

Over the next few days Satomi's shock turned first to frustration and then to anger. Why had the government not responded more quickly? Why had the National Guard not been called out in the first hours? Why had the government initially refused help from outside the country? Why had the Japanese people been lulled into a false sense of security?

Later in the week the news reports began to show signs of reborn hope. Blankets, portable toilets, clothes, food, water, and medicine began pouring from all over the nation into the evacuation camps. Interviews in the streets showed a stoicism, determination, and emotional strength that seemed unbelievable to Harlan. Children's smiles began to dot the screen among the many ruins and smoldering ashes. Here and there makeshift shops cropped up to dispense hot meals for little or no money. There was little looting and even the infamous Yamaguchi yakuza group pitched in during the worst days in the beginning, directing traffic and passing out food and blankets, first to the elderly, the sick, and the pregnant, then to the healthy and the young.

By the tenth day, Satomi and Harlan had finally gotten in contact with most of their friends. Everyone, it seemed, had survived: Inoue, Shimada, Nishimoto, Rick and his wife, Sugiyama, who was now married with two children and living near his hometown in northern

Hyogo Prefecture, all the Sasa Club members and people from his old neighborhood in Itami, and Yoshiko's mother.

Harlan had just finished talking with her. He had learned that Yoshiko's father died three years earlier and that Yoshiko's mother was living with Masanori and his wife and two children. Yoshiko had gotten married shortly after her father died, now had a two-year-old child, and was living in Yokohama. Yoshiko's mother had said Yoshiko would probably like to hear from Harlan and had given him Yoshiko's telephone number.

Harlan felt nervous as he picked up the receiver and began dialing the number. What would he say after all these years? Would she be happy to hear from him? Would his call trigger all the bitterness he had once caused in her? Would it bring back all those ghosts from the past? When he heard her voice, would his own repressed and forgotten feelings come flooding to the surface? He dialed. Yoshiko's husband answered the phone.

"Is Yoshiko home?" Harlan asked in Japanese.

"No, she's out at the moment. She should be back soon. May I ask who is calling?"

"This is Harlan Cooper, an old friend from Itami. I was just calling to tell her that I've been able to talk to her mother and some of our friends and that all of them are OK, but many have had a lot of damage to their homes."

"Oh, yes, Mr. Cooper. Yoshiko has often mentioned your name. Would you like me to have her call you back?"

"I would appreciate it." He gave his telephone number and thanked Yoshiko's husband.

Fifteen minutes later the telephone rang. Harlan answered it on the second ring.

"Harlan, I can't believe it's you. How are you?" Yoshiko sounded sincerely happy to be talking to him. Harlan felt an enormous surge of relief.

"I'm great, just great. How about you?"

"Me too. You sound great."

"I called your mother today and she and your brother and his wife and kids are doing fine. Not much damage to their place. And I got hold of Sugiyama. He's not in Itami anymore, but he's got a family, too, and is doing well. I also got in touch with all my friends from the softball team and everyone is fine other than the damage to their homes. I thought you might want to find out about everyone in case you haven't been able to get through."

"That's nice of you to think of me. Actually, I couldn't reach anyone for a couple days after the earthquake, but I tried calling from a pay phone on the fourth

day and was able to reach my mother. I plan to visit
them sometime in February when things settle down a
little. Did you call Sachiko?"

"No. I lost her phone number years ago, but I think
most of the people in her part of Ashiya escaped."

"I hope so," Yoshiko said.

"Anyway, when you visit Itami please give everyone
my best. So how is married life? I hear you have a
child."

"It's the most wonderful thing in the world. I'm
very happy. My son is healthy and my husband has a
good job in a big company. I miss Itami, though. Tokyo
and Yokohama are just too big. How do you like
Fukuoka?"

"Things couldn't be better. A lot of changes since the
last time I saw you. I finally finished my degree, took a
master's course and finished that, and now I've got a job
teaching at a women's junior college. My wife and I
don't have any children, but we're very happy together.
She's doing a lot of work translating and interpreting.
We're both doing what we want. I guess we're very
lucky."

"I'm happy to hear that."

"And guess what? I've got a novel coming out. I
found a small publisher in England that's willing to take
a gamble on it. And a Tokyo publisher is going to

publish my first textbook."

"That's wonderful. I really admire you, Harlan. I admire your guts and determination. You've worked very hard in Japan and deserve all the success you can have. Your Japanese has improved, too. My husband said he thought he was talking to a Japanese with a foreign name."

Harlan laughed. "I speak a lot better when I'm drinking."

"I still like my cup or two of sake in the evening, too. Are you still playing any sports?"

"No, I'm getting too old. I'm 45 now and my ankles are shot. All the sprains over the years turned into arthritis, but I swim three or four times a week to keep the beer belly at bay."

"Don't feel bad. I'm 34 myself and even though I still weigh the same as ten years ago, the weight has all shifted downward."

"I don't believe it. I'll bet you're still as beautiful as ever. Listen, I better go. I just wanted to make sure you were OK and let you know what I found out about everyone in Itami."

"Thank you for calling. If you ever come to Yokohama or Tokyo, please give me a call. I'd like to introduce you to my son. Take care of yourself, Harlan, and be good to your wife."

"Good-bye."

Harlan hung up the phone. He sat for a long time staring into the distance and allowing himself to indulge in memories from the past. He was happy. The one great weight he had carried over the years had disappeared. It seemed almost impossible, but he could now say it truthfully, confidently, and out loud: He and Yoshiko were no longer strangers. They were friends.

* * *

After the phone call, Yoshiko went into her son's bedroom. He was sleeping soundly. She looked at him for a long time. She loved him more than anything in the world. She bent down, pulled the covers tighter around him, and kissed him gently on the forehead.

She turned off the bedroom light, lingered for a moment, turned around for one more look at the child, and whispered, "You know, son, under different circumstances that man I just spoke to on the phone might have become your father."

Conqueris au demon

About the Author

Robert W. Norris is the author of *Looking for the Summer*, a novel about a former Vietnam War conscientious objector's search for identity on the road from Paris to Calcutta in 1977, and *The Many Roads to Japan*, a novella used as a textbook-reader in Japanese universities. He has also written several articles on teaching English as a Foreign Language. He and his wife live near Fukuoka, Kyushu, where he is an associate professor at Fukuoka International University.